The Photographer's Lens

Bryce Sterling

Published by Flashbulb Fiction, 2023.

Table of Contents

FLASHBULB FICTION

Published by Flashbulb Fiction

First Edition

ISBN: 978-0-6458847-8-4

Cover design by Bryce Sterling

Book design by Bryce Sterling

For more information about the author and upcoming works, visit https://www.brycesterlingauthor.com/

Prologue:

Australia. A land of rough beauty, where the harsh sun paints dramatic shadows across the Outback, and the persistent crash of waves against the coast whispers of relentless determination and quiet resilience. It's a place where each person carries their own story, as unique and textured as the landscape itself.

Emma's story begins in a small, nondescript flat in Melbourne, a city where modernity and tradition blend in a unique tapestry of life. The room is filled with the scent of day-old fast food and stale beer, the remnants of Emma's attempts to drown her confusion in the forgetfulness that comes with solitude.

But within these walls, a revelation awaits. It's hidden within a camera, an object seemingly ordinary yet soon to become the catalyst for an extraordinary transformation. It's a journey of self-discovery that will bring to light truths about Emma she's spent a lifetime ignoring, truths that will challenge her, scare her, and ultimately, liberate her.

Emma's journey is not a straightforward one; it never is when it comes to matters of identity and self-acceptance. There will be twists and turns, moments of fear, and overwhelming uncertainty. But with every snapshot, she takes a step closer to understanding who she is and, more importantly, who she wants to be.

"The Photographer's Lens" is more than just Emma's story. It's a testament to everyone who has ever felt lost within themselves, to those who are brave enough to question, to search, and to accept who they truly are.

Welcome to Emma's world, a world that, much like ours, is filled with doubts, fears, but also hope. A hope that one day, we'll be able to look at our reflection without fear or judgment, but with love and acceptance.

Join Emma as she embarks on this profound journey, navigating the turbulent waters of self-discovery, one photograph at a time. Witness the evolution of a woman learning to accept herself, in all her flawed, human beauty. And perhaps, along the way, you'll find a bit of your own story in hers.

Shutterbug

Emma was marooned in the bottom of a dive bar, swathed in shrouds of squalor and second-hand smoke. Shadows of regular patrons lurked in dim corners; their broken dreams woven into the fabric of the worn-out stools. The air was dense with failure and cheap perfume, the stench of rotting ambitions seeping from the woodwork. This was a place the sun had long forgotten, a place you ended up when the world had discarded you.

In her hand, a glass of poor-man's whisky was her partner in crime, a co-conspirator in her self-loathing party. Each gulp a testament to her crumbling dreams, each tasteless burn furthering her descent into creative purgatory. The ambience in the bar, the cheap booze, her quiet desperation; it all had a spectral harmony, as if the universe conspired to mirror her internal chaos.

Across the stained counter, bottles of all sizes and shapes stood like defeated soldiers, their hollow insides reflecting her own emptiness. The amber liquid within promised to drown her disillusionment, to suffocate the beast of artistic frustration gnawing at her soul.

Her fingers traced the rough edges of her camera lying next to the glass. Once a beacon of her dreams, it was now nothing more than a cruel reminder of her broken aspirations. Each weathered groove, each chipped corner was a scar, a tangible mark of her capitulation to the world's cynical demands.

The shutter, the lens, the viewfinder – they were shackles that bound her, reducing her vibrant imagination to a monotone greyness. Her art was now a business, the soul sold for the currency of societal approval. The sound of the shutter closing was a haunting echo, a death knell for the raw, the real, the spontaneous she once sought to capture.

As the night crawled forward, Emma drowned deeper into the whisky-soaked abyss, a lighthouse lost amidst the fog of lost artistry. She wasn't sure if the path ahead led to salvation or deeper into damnation, but for the moment, the whisky provided a blissful, if temporary, oblivion.

The bar, a ship adrift on the sea of societal rejects, carried an unruly crew of misfits and wayward souls. Emma observed them through the hazy smoke - each face a canvas of tragic poetry. There was an ironic beauty in their despair, a raw, undiluted humanity that she yearned to capture.

Slouched over the bar, a washed-up boxer nursed his drink, his battered face a landscape of lost bouts and broken dreams. His bloodshot eyes stared into the void, perhaps replaying his fall from grace. Every line on his face, a blow life had dealt, a fight he had lost.

In a corner, an ageing prostitute, the remnants of her beauty painfully clinging to her weathered features, painted her lips a vibrant red. Each stroke, a desperate attempt to cover the cracks, to mask the reality of her existence. Her practiced smile never reached her eyes, those tired, hollow mirrors that reflected a life traded in shadows.

Across from her, a musician strummed his guitar, fingers dancing on the strings, creating melodies that were half lament, half defiance. His music was his resistance, his protest against a world that had relegated him to its fringes. Each note, a cry for recognition, for validation, echoed in the bar, swallowed by the indifference of its patrons.

Emma, she sat there, soaking up the faces around her like a sponge. Each one of 'em with a yarn to tell, a life lived in stark contrast to the painted smiles she'd been peddling. This was the world that was unfiltered, raw and real. It was the kind of honest reality she had dreamed of capturing. A punch in the guts reminder of what she'd lost in her art - the humanity, the truth.

Sat in that boozer, listening to the cacophony of heartache and laughter, she was struck by a powerful yearning. She longed to take her camera, to immortalise these stories, these bloody life spectacles in all their rough, untamed glory. But tonight, she was just another drinker, just another battler knocking back the grog in tune with their collective disillusionment.

The day's work rolled over her like a ripper of a wave, with the morning's wedding gig looming like some kind of garish ghoul, all done up in pretence. A posh wedding it was, full of sheilas and blokes draped in over-the-top clobber, grinning like Cheshire cats, but their eyes - as vacant as a paddock after shearing season.

The bride, tarted up to the nines, face layered with slap, couldn't hide the panic under the surface. Each chuckle, each smile was as calculated as a footy play, a well-rehearsed act for the photo-hounds. Emma's lens caught the fake fun, the whole bloody charade.

The groom, he looked as lost as a roo in the middle of the city, questioning his own spot in this big bloody circus. The smile was plastered on his face, a reluctant peace treaty with the life he was stepping into. The snap of Emma's camera seemed to amplify his doubts, chronicling the uneasy joining of two strangers shackled by societal expectations.

Guests were buzzing about, chatting empty words, their laughter as hollow as a didgeridoo. It was a mob of pretend partygoers, a parade of shallow grandeur. Through her camera's eye, Emma watched the routine of joy, the orchestrated jollity. Each shot, a monument to the fabricated bliss that was a world away from the genuine emotions she was aching to capture.

The wedding party kept up the show, every one of 'em playing their parts in the drama. The supposedly happy couple, the chuffed parents, the ecstatic relos - all put together like a carefully staged scene of matrimonial ecstasy, just right for the social pages.

Emma, she'd done her bit too, snapping every phoney grin, every pretentious laugh. But behind that camera, she was an observer, a silent critic of the mockery unfolding in front of her lens. She saw the painted joy, the made-up merriment that was the backbone of the wedding.

Sitting in the dingy pub, the day's images flickered in her mind, like a surreal flick of pretend joy. She could still feel the chill of the camera in her hands, a stark reminder of her artistic sell-out. The day's events, the laughter, the joy, all faked, trapped in digital limbo on her memory card.

With a glass of cut-price whiskey in her mitt, she raised a toast to the harsh realities of her craft, to the joke her art had become. The pictures she'd taken weren't reflections of life, but carefully spun illusions, choreographed snapshots that stabbed in the back the very essence of the moments they were supposed to immortalise. The weight of this realisation was heavier than the cheap grog scorching a trail down her gullet.

The whiskey, all amber and harsh lessons, caught the dim light of the pub, throwing shadows that danced a macabre waltz with her gloomy thoughts. Emma found herself tumbling into the abyss of her profession's fakery - a never-ending performance of light and angles, a staged show that hid the truth and pandered to vanity.

Emma, she sat there, right in the thick of the bar's grime and music, soaked up all the bloody faces around her. They weren't your everyday pretty pictures, nah mate, they were the real bloody deal - harsh, raw, honest. Far cry from all the polished rubbish she'd been selling off in the name of art. Each look, each tale, was a bloody slap in the face, a grim reminder of what her snaps used to capture - the raw truth, humanity in all its unvarnished glory.

Lost in the symphony of this seedy bar, a nagging itch sparked in her - to train her lens onto this spectacle of life, strip it bare and showcase it to the world. But for tonight, she was just another punter, just another lost sheep drowning in the sea of shared disillusionment.

The happenings of the day washed over her like a bloody rogue wave, that morning's wedding gig was a looming spectre, a gaudy mockery of reality. An ostentatious shindig filled to the brim with posers, all decked out in their gaudy glad rags, flashing hollow smiles for the camera, their peepers empty of any real joy.

The sheila, looking more like a bloody barbie doll than a bride, was a picture of hidden nerves beneath layers of spackle. Every giggle, every grin, was a calculated act, a performance for the photo-hungry crowd. Emma's camera zoomed in, capturing this sham for all its worth.

The bloke, he stood there, looking as lost as a roo in the big smoke, grappling with his place in this circus of life. His forced grin, a clear sign of the bloody compromise he was making. Emma's camera seemed to mirror his doubts, freezing in time the uneasy alliance of two strangers shoved together by social expectations.

The guests, all flitting about exchanging sweet nothings, their laughter as hollow as the words they spewed. It was all a bloody circus, a show of superficiality, devoid of any authenticity. Through her lens, Emma recorded this spectacle, this well-rehearsed charade that passed for joy. Every frame screamed of the manufactured happiness, a stark contrast to the raw emotions she sought to capture.

The wedding mob, each playing their part in this grand drama, the beaming couple, the chuffed parents, the overjoyed relatives – all fit together in a perfectly arranged tableau of matrimonial bliss, a picture-perfect snapshot for the society pages.

Emma, she did her part too, the professional snapper, freezing each fake smile, each empty display of cheer. But behind the lens, she was a silent observer, a critic of the sham unfolding before her. She could see right through the cheery veneer, the contrived joy that was the true face of this celebration.

There in the bar, the day's happenings replayed in her mind, a surreal flick of fake smiles and pretend joy. She could still feel the chill of the camera in her hands, a sharp reminder of the creative compromise she'd made. The day's events, the faces, the hollow laughter, the pretentious joy, all captured on her memory card, entrapped in a digital hell.

With a glass of plonk in her hand, she drank to the harsh truth of her craft, to the farcical nature of her art. The images she'd captured weren't bloody reflections of life, but cleverly crafted illusions, stage-managed snapshots that betrayed the essence of the moments they were supposed to represent. The reality of this was a far weightier burden than the sting of the cheap booze burning a path down her throat.

Her whiskey, a liquid sermon on the harsh truths, caught the dim light of the bar, casting blurry shadows that danced with her heavy thoughts. Emma felt herself getting sucked into the vortex of her profession's deceit - a never-ending ballet of light and angles, a meticulously orchestrated performance that masked reality and fed vanity.

Her trusted old shooter, once her digger in the battle for veracity, had done the Harold Holt. Turned rotten as a dingo's dinner, it had chucked a sickie in the pantomime, its lens bending the truth like a boomerang bending to the taste of those who fancied a pretty picture, its clicker as compliant as a 'roo caught in the headlights.

She remembered the countless times she'd dicked around with the sunbeams, called the shots on the shadows, fiddled with her angles - all to get a shot that'd please the old peepers, something easy for the punters to swallow. Every snap taken was a flaming testament to her getting good at the trickery. A still life as lively as a dead dingo's donger. A portrait without a ghost of spirit. A landscape as wild as a caged kookaburra.

Photography, she pondered, was no longer about nabbing a moment, it was about whittling one up. The raw cut of life was too much of a bitter pill for the mob to swallow. So, she sweetened it up, coated it in porky pies, served it up on a digital dish. The photos weren't echoes of life but just mirrors to people's big heads, feeding their ballooning egos and their relentless hankering for flawlessness.

Her camera had morphed into a wizard's toy, cooking up mirages from the everyday. The lens was a seeing stone that couldn't see the bloody obvious but just what the punters wanted to see. She wasn't a snapper but a bloody con artist, selling dreams to the gullible mob. She was a master of trickery, her charades praised as masterpieces, her fibs toasted as strokes of genius.

And as she sat there, the cheap grog burning a track down her throat, she couldn't help but see the irony of it all. A trade that was supposed to bottle up the guts of life had turned into a monger of lies. The weight of this truth was a far bitterer drink to stomach.

Swishing the amber liquid in her glass, Emma spun around to the rugged mug behind the bar - old George, a mate of sorts and the unwilling audience to her boozy rants. With peepers wise beyond his years and ears used to the yarns of the lost, George was her reluctant sage, her uninvited shrink.

"The bloody frauds, George," she slurred, her words doing a freestyle in the sea of cheap grog. "These new-age snappers, they wouldn't know the real deal if it bit 'em on the bum."

George just gave a shrug, swabbing down the bar with a worn rag. He'd heard this tune before, banged out on the same battered instrument. "It's a racket, Em. People pay for dreams, not the drab."

She slammed her glass on the counter, the clink like a nasty full stop to her growing frustration. "And what use are those dreams, George? Made up, doctored fantasies flogged off as the truth. What use are they?"

Her words were red hot, tossed around the dimly lit room, looking for a mark in the thick soup of smoke and despair. The old barman just sighed, pouring her another shot. He'd seen enough of the world to know that truth and honesty rarely got a gig in it, especially in a world as subjective as art.

"Can't argue with what sells, Emma," George replied, his words ringing with resigned pragmatism.

She knocked back her drink, the fiery liquid a sour reminder of her sentiments. "That's where we've fucked it up, George. Arts now bloody sold to the one with the deepest pockets. Photography, it's not just point and shoot. It's about capturing the spirit, the guts. It's about the truth."

George met her fiery gaze with tired eyes. "That may be so, Emma, but at the end of the day, folks want pretty snaps. Can't blame them, life's ugly enough as is."

They fell into a silence, each nursing their own glass of disillusionment. The bar seemed to shrink around them, a world on the brink of an uncomfortable truth.

The clock cracked two, its grating chime a prickly reminder of the relentless march of time. The sorrowful notes of the last call washed over the dimly lit bar, sounding the end of another day's cycle of dreams and despair. Emma looked around at the thinning crowd, the lingering shadows of the night's patrons like spectres in the smoke-filled room.

Wishing George a slurred hooroo, she stumbled towards the exit, her feet tripping over the uneven floorboards, her thoughts teetering on the brink of her growing frustration. The door moaned as she shoved it open, the rusty hinges groaning under the burden of the relentless passage of time.

The night air was a slap in the face, the darkness a sudden blanket over her drunken senses. She found herself walking towards nowhere, her feet tracing a familiar path in the unforgiving

pavement. The city seemed to hold its breath as she staggered
through the gloom, the rustling leaves and distant howls the only
signs of life.

Emma found herself standing in front of an antique store, a relic
of an age lost in time. The dusty windowpanes were a canvas of dust,
the blurry shapes behind them like ghosts of the past. She pressed
her face against the cool glass, peering into the murky depths of
forgotten history.

A lonesome object caught her eye - an old film camera, its faded
leather body and clouded lens a silent echo of countless moments it
had captured, countless lives it had seen. It was a relic from an era
when every click was a commitment, every frame a deliberate choice,
every roll of film a meticulous narrative of captured time.

The sight of the ancient device sent a jolt through her, the
familiar silhouette a haunting memory of the origins of her love for
photography. The old camera was a testament to an age when every
snap was a tribute to the truth, every picture an honest portrayal of
life.

There it sat, an old player in a forgotten game, its worn body an
echo of her own weary soul. Emma found herself drawn to it, a pull
as deep as the unending ocean, as profound as the silent abyss of the
cosmos. The camera seemed to whisper to her, its faded leather body
echoing the silent isolation she felt within the ruthless grind of her
trade. The dust-laden camera was a lighthouse in the foggy haze of
her disillusionment, a tangible embodiment of the authenticity she
craved.

Her eyes, heavy and bleary, stared at the old device through the
dust-covered glass, a silent dialogue unfolding between them. The
camera, with its tarnished brass and cracked leather, was far from the
sleek aesthetic of her modern equipment. And yet, it resonated with
her on a level that her sophisticated gear never could.

With her palm against the cold glass of the shop window, she found herself being pulled towards the weathered camera, its silent beckoning like a lifeline in the choppy sea of her thoughts. The cheap grog hadn't completely washed away her sense of reasoning. She peered into the worn-out pocket of her jeans, her fingers brushing against the rough edges of crumpled dollar bills. They were as dishevelled as her current state of mind, as messy as her thoughts, as worthless as her trade.

The crumpled notes felt heavy in her hand, each crease a testament to her battered hopes. The grog in her veins, the desperate desire in her heart, and the raw pull of the old camera merged into an irrational resolve. She could just afford the camera, with not much left for anything else. But what was the worth of a few meals when compared to a shot at redemption?

As the first rays of dawn kissed the horizon, a new determination kindled in Emma's heart. The camera wasn't just an old piece of technology; it was a beacon, a lighthouse in the choppy sea of her disillusionment, promising a path to an unfamiliar shore.

Emma stumbled away from the store, her steps uneven but her resolve firm. She could feel the dawn creeping up, the darkness surrendering to the stubborn light, an echo of her own struggle. Her path, though uncertain, seemed a little brighter in the soft glow of dawn. Her camera, her newfound hope, was waiting for her, waiting to unlock its secrets, waiting to guide her back to her lost passion.

As the day broke, Emma walked away, leaving behind the store and the camera, but carrying with her a renewed sense of purpose, a spark that hadn't been there when she stumbled into the old bar. The shadows of the night were lifting, and with them, the weight of her disillusionment. Emma was on her way back, one step at a time.

Old Relics

T he city was a bloody shambles, as hammered as Emma's noggin after a rough night. The concrete monsters, half-fallen and coated with a century's muck, mirrored the woman's spirit - knocked about but bloody unbreakable. Another arvo hotter than a sheila's phone number, and her wanderin' feet take her through the jagged jaws of the old city. A place where time moves as slow as a dingo with a belly full of roo, a ghost town of dreams gone bust.

She stumbles onto this beaten-up antique shop, a place more worn out than an old roo's pouch. The display window, a stained mural of discarded treasures and oddities. Each piece a reminder that human cravings are as temporary as a drop bear's sobriety. But amongst the abandoned, a vintage camera sparkles like a gold nugget in a dry creek bed.

It's not a flashy gadget, but it's aged with a dignity that makes it stand out. It's old, but it ain't useless; it's seen better days but it's still fighting. It speaks of a time where a photo was more than just a click, it was a moment frozen in truth, away from the modern world's hogwash. The camera seemed familiar to her, like a story she's yet to hear, yet already part of.

The camera, not a spectacle or a shiny bauble, but it draws Emma in like a thirsty bloke to a cold tinny. It feels like a hero from a forgotten yarn, refusing to go gentle into that good night. The vintage camera was a silent bard; its lens had seen it all - the good, the bad, the ugly, the beautiful. It's different from the other junk because it feels real, a quality her own snaps are missing.

Glancing at the camera, she feels this invisible bond between them, two warriors weathered by time, but still not ready to chuck in the towel. It feels like the camera is beckoning her, whispering of the past and promising a road back to her lost love for photography.

It's a batty feeling, a bizarre connection, but it's strong as a croc's bite, offering a journey back to her craft's roots.

The city, with all its racket and filth, falls into the background as Emma's gaze zeroes in on the camera, like a blowie drawn to an old light. It ain't just a tool, not for her. It's a time capsule, a piece of the past when photography was more than just a hobby, it was a calling. The body's worn, paint flaked and peeled in places, like the scars of a forgotten battle. The leather case has faded, the colour bleached by time, holding the echo of hands now dust.

The camera's a puzzle wrapped in a mystery, an old soul catching forty winks in the musty corner of an abandoned antique shop. It carries its age with grace, a digger standing tall in the debris. Its dignity, despite the wear and tear, is a nod to its resilience, its refusal to be labelled as just another relic. Emma feels herself being drawn to it, hooked line and sinker, curiosity spiked by its silent determination.

Each dent, each flake of paint, seems to invite her, whispering stories of a time long past, asking her to unravel its mystery. She feels a strange kinship with it, an unexplainable pull towards its quiet enigma. The old camera's more than an object; it's a piece of history waiting to be explored, a tale begging to be told. And Emma, the artist who's lost her mojo, feels a spark within her, an excitement she hasn't felt in yonks. This ain't just an old camera; it's a test, a riddle, a walkabout. The more she looks at it, the more she sees a chance for redemption, a way back to her lost love. She feels this urge to unlock its past, to dive into its history, and maybe, just maybe, in doing so, find a way to breathe life into her future. It ain't just about the camera; it's about her, about her lost art, her lost self. It's about taking back what's been lost and finding a path forward.

The city outside the dust-caked window is a mad orchestra of sirens and honking, vendors spruiking, the relentless hum of life, but in the presence of the vintage camera, Emma finds a quiet corner, a calm in the storm. It's there in the cluttered window, an old-timer surrounded by a jumble of past decades. The camera's been through the wringer, battered by time, the paint chipped and peeled, and the leather case bleached. It's a relic from a forgotten time, a whisper of an era where things were built to last, not to be tossed aside.

A tingle of curiosity tiptoes up Emma's spine as she peers closer, her eyes following the lines of the camera. The scratches and scrapes aren't flaws, they're medals of honour, each a chapter in the camera's tale. The old camera promises untold stories, moments captured and frozen in time, waiting to be freed. It's allure ain't in its looks but in the depth of its silent narrative. It's seen a life before her, through lenses that have focused on faces and places she can only dream about.

Emma feels this pull, a force that settles in her chest, weaving around her heart. It's like the camera's calling her, reaching out through the years, tugging at her curiosity, nudging it awake. The camera is a bridge to the past, a link to an era where capturing a moment was more about the art than the gear used.

She's spent her career sugar-coating reality, but here in the old camera is history, raw and unedited. The idea of breathing life back into this old beauty, of giving it another shot at capturing the world in all its rough and tumble, lights a fire in Emma. A need, a primal yearning to revive its story, to let it see the dawn of another day. The thought is heady, as strong as the grog she'd drowned her worries in the night before. The vintage camera ain't just a gadget; it's a forgotten verse in the ballad of photography, and Emma finds herself itching to let it sing again.

The bell over the door jangles a sad tune as Emma pushes into the dim shop, a relic housing relics. It's a time capsule, a mirror to a past long kicked into the curb, its air heavy with the scent of decaying wood and the sweet sorrow of bygone years. The smell of old leather, dust, and neglect hangs in the air, not unpleasant, but oddly comforting, like an old, well-read book or the scent of a long-gone lover.

An old bloke, as weathered as the antiques he sells, peeks over the newspaper he's been reading. The spark in his eyes matches Emma's fascination as she threads her way through the labyrinth of lost times and forgotten tales. She moves past worn-out chairs, chipped tea sets, and washed-out paintings, her ticker pounding like a kangaroo in a stampede, giddy with the anticipation of a long-anticipated rendezvous.

There it was, this old clicker, feeling more real in her mitts than it had sat behind that grubby glass. Her fingers tracing its worn shape like it was something sacred, every nick and scrape spinning yarns of days gone by. The old cobber running the shop watched her, those knowing eyes had seen that look before, that strange bond between a person and a relic from a forgotten era.

The haggling dance followed. Offers and counteroffers tossed back and forth, every price knockdown a small win, getting her closer to claiming the camera. When the shopkeeper finally gave the nod, it was like she'd struck gold. Satisfaction surged through her, a real fair dinkum triumph.

She handed over the agreed quid, her fingers lingering on the old camera as if it was an old mate. The exchange felt like some kind of ritual, like she was being let into some secret mob, a pact sealed with a bit of dosh and a silent understanding. As she stepped out of the shop, the old clicker secure under her arm, she wasn't just a snapper anymore. She was a keeper of history, a carrier of tales waiting to be spun again. And within her, something stirred, ready to spark into a blaze of creation. The real journey was just kicking off.

Back in her quiet flat, a single lamp throwing long shadows around the room, Emma sat on her worn rug. The Argus C3 in her lap, a blast from the past, a testament to the ingenuity of yesteryears.

The city outside was buzzing with life, the ceaseless hum a faint echo in her tucked-away sanctuary.

Her fingers, grimy from the city and stinking of cheap grog, danced over the camera, feeling the cold brass, the chipped paint, the leather skin worn with time. Each detail was like a secret shared, a whispered tale from the past. Her eyes drank in the worn letters on the metal: Argus C3. There was a rugged beauty to it, a resilience born from time and use.

Picking it up, her palms fitted to the contours of the camera. It felt comforting, not sleek like the digital gizmos she was used to. The mechanical bits - the manual focus, the wind-up shutter, the separate rangefinder and viewfinder - all called for her touch, her involvement. A far cry from the touchscreen and autofocus stuff she was accustomed to.

Her heart pounded a wild rhythm, matching her growing anticipation. The Argus C3 wasn't just a tool to capture images. It was an instrument demanding her engagement, her passion. Each photo would be a trophy, a prize earned, not some easy digital snap. It felt real, tangible, mirroring the raw authenticity she craved.

This wasn't just a camera. It was a promise of a raw, unfiltered vision of the world, of tales etched in wrinkles and battle scars, of lives lived on the fringes, of beauty found in the rough and uncouth. It was a symbol of her newfound rebellion against the sanitised, prettified world she used to peddle. The worn-out rug, the woman with her dreams of capturing the raw truth - everything seemed to hum with purpose. A purpose as old and as tangible as the Argus C3 in her hands. Emma, with the camera as her compass, was ready to chart her own course into the heart of life.

It was funny about the Argus C3. Not its age, or its weathered look, or the history it whispered of - it was the strange sense of belonging Emma felt when she held it. Like this camera, this piece of another era, had been waiting in the dingy corners of that forgotten antique store just for her - Emma, the disenchanted snapper seeking the rough edges of life.

Cradling the camera, its weight was like a comforting presence, like the rough hand of an old mate. It was a tangible reminder of time's relentless march. Yet, within its archaic form, it held a power that the sleek digital tools of her trade lacked. It held honesty. It held grit. It held a promise of a vision untouched by the icy precision of technology.

Every groove, every dent told a story. Stories of joys and sorrows immortalised in grains of silver salts. And Emma, her soul yearning to capture similar stories, to etch them in film and ink, felt an indescribable connection. The camera, with its old-world charm and unyielding resilience, mirrored her journey.

Her mind was filled with images of the unseen - the tired waitress pulling a late shift, the homeless bloke with his dog for warmth, the woman whose smile never reached her eyes. These were the stories she wanted to tell. These were the stories the Argus C3 was built to capture.

The camera was more than a tool; it was a part of her. It was her eye, her voice, reaching out to those who existed in society's shadows. It was an extension of her newfound vision, a symbol of her determination to reveal the world in its raw, unvarnished glory.

The Argus C3, in all its imperfections, was a reflection of Emma's own journey, her evolution. Just as she sought to uncover the hidden stories around her, the camera too had its story dug up, brought back into the light from a dusty antique store window. They were two old souls, discovering the unseen, echoing each other's path, tied together by the invisible thread of destiny.

Emma's nerves were jangling, a cobber in a boxing ring, as she geared up for the next photo session. The Argus C3, this ratty relic that had become more than just a piece of gear, was her mate for this dance. It was a leap into the unknown, a dinky-di gamble, far from the cushy tech of her modern gear. But Emma wasn't one to shy from a stoush - she thrived in the thick of it.

There was a rawness to the old clicker, a brutal honesty that was as daunting as it was freeing. The Argus C3 didn't come with any digital trickery, no airbrushing or polishing of real life to fit into a picture-perfect frame. It got down to the knitty-gritty, capturing life in its rugged, unapologetic glory.

Operating the camera was a grind. Every tweak to the aperture, focus, shutter speed had to be done by hand. It was a world away from the convenience of her Nikon D850. It felt like a dance, a rhythm she had to find and sync with. It was a hard yakka, slow and painstaking, but that's where its charm was. The fight for the perfect shot was a testament to her grit, part of the journey.

As she squinted through the viewfinder, the world seemed different. It wasn't just about nailing the perfect shot, but about understanding the yarn within that frame. The Argus C3, with its limited controls and unforgiving lens, forced her to think deeper, to ask questions, to dive into the moment she was capturing.

She fumbled, she squinted, she almost threw in the towel. But with every press of the shutter, every roll of film she burned through, Emma felt a sense of satisfaction, a joy that had been missing. The camera wasn't just snapping photos, it was mapping her journey, her evolution from a snapper to a storyteller. The Argus C3 wasn't just an old bit of kit anymore, but a beacon guiding her towards her destiny.

The Argus C3, loaded and ready to fire, was aimed at her own reflection in a dusty, cobweb-covered mirror. She held her breath, then clicked the shutter, the sound echoing in the stillness of her flat. No screen to preview the shot, no button to erase the blemishes. Just a thrilling wait.

The picture had to be developed in her makeshift darkroom, the eerie red light throwing odd shadows as she worked. The smell of the chemicals, harsh and pungent, hung in the air as she transferred the negative onto the photo paper.

Slowly, her reflection appeared on the paper, captured in greyscale. The shabby mirror had distorted her image, the dust and imperfections creating a play of shadow and light on her face. It was her, yet it wasn't. The camera seemed to have captured not just her physical form but a part of her soul, a raw vulnerability she hadn't seen in a while.

She looked at the grainy image, at the depth and contrast the monochrome film had brought out. It was unlike any of her past work. It lacked the crispness, the sharpness, the sleek look of her digital photos. But that's what made it beautiful. It was imperfect, just like her, just like the world. The camera hadn't masked those flaws, but accentuated them, celebrated them.

It was a picture that scoffed at beauty standards, at correctness. It was a picture that dared to be flawed, dared to be real. Emma held the photo, her fingers tracing the contours of her reflection. There was a sense of triumph, a sense of freedom. This, she realized, was the beauty she sought to capture, the truth she yearned to tell. The Argus C3 hadn't just taken a photo, it had made a stand - a bold claim of authenticity that echoed in her flat.

As Emma looked at the picture, a realization washed over her like a sudden wind from an open window, stirring up the stale air in a room. This old, beat-up camera wasn't just a tool to snap photos, it was a comrade, a fellow wanderer in her new journey.

The camera's scratches and worn-out leather case were like her own scars, her own imperfections. They were the marks of time and experience, of a life lived. The chipped paint, the faded exterior, the rusty bits - they weren't defects but badges of honour, worn with pride. They told a story of time passed, of moments seized and frozen in time, of a purpose fulfilled.

The camera's lens, devoid of digital touch-ups and enhancements, captured the world in its raw, untempered glory. It didn't fiddle, it didn't make things prettier, it simply observed and recorded. It held a mirror to life, reflecting it in all its unpolished honesty.

The Argus C3 didn't just capture images, it captured truth. It peeled back the layers of pretence and lies, revealing the essence. It was an ally in her battle against the shallow, the fake. It was her weapon of choice in her quest for the authentic, the real.

Emma held the camera, the metal warming up in her hands. It was a feeling of camaraderie, of shared vision, of understanding. This camera, in its silent, unassuming way, resonated with her newfound vision. It amplified her voice, it echoed her views, it shared her passion.

She was more than a photographer now. She was an artist, a storyteller, a truth seeker. The camera was more than a tool. It was an extension of her, an echo of her soul, a reflection of her vision. Together, they were embarking on a journey, a quest to capture the world, not as it's supposed to be, but as it is. The revelation was clear, powerful, and irreversible - Emma and the camera, they were one.

Emma cradled the Argus C3, heavier than the intangible world of digital pixels she was used to. It felt solid, a relic from an era when things were built to last, a silent testament to the enduring power of moments once they were immortalized on film. There was a finality to it, a lack of any easy way out that a digital delete button couldn't offer. There was something comforting about it.

She'd been wrestling with the superficiality of her profession, the fake smiles, the artificial light, the manipulation of reality to fit an aesthetic. But this old clicker, it didn't cater to vanity. It didn't gloss over reality or hide the flaws. It was brutally honest, with an integrity that she found herself drawn to.

With a nod, she made the decision. This was it. The Argus C3 would be her tool, her weapon, her partner in crime. She was done with the frills and the phoniness. It was time to expose reality, to strip it bare, to reveal its naked truth. She was starting a revolution, a revolt against the synthetic beauty and pretensions. And she was going to do it with the camera that shared her vision, echoed her spirit.

There was a fire in her belly now, a kind of buzz that hadn't set her veins alight in yonks. She had a path, clear as day. Her project, her unadorned snapshot project, was no longer just a fair dinkum try. It was her track, her journey. It was her stoush, and the Argus C3 was her tight-lipped mate, her co-conspirator.

As the town lights threw whopping great shadows on her tiny shack, Emma felt a new sense of resolve surging within. The future was as clear as mud, the road unmarked, but she felt ready to face the music. She was up for the adventure, ready to give the world a red-hot go, one raw, naked snap at a time.

Emma's world was now a quiet as a church mouse, with only the drone of the vintage fridge providing a bit of background noise to her musings. There she sat, the Argus C3 close by on the weather-beaten kitchen table, its chilly, metal body catching the feeble shine of a single, swaying light bulb.

She felt a sort of kinship with the camera. Like her, it was thrown aside, a keepsake from an era when things seemed easier, more dinky-di. It had seen its fair share, watched a ton of yarns play out before its lens, stories now lost, much like the city she was keen to catch in its raw form.

Her fingers ran over the rough and worn-out surface, a surface that had watched the world shift while it remained unchanged. It was more than just a tool to freeze images, it was a mate, a co-worker in her mission to find and document the straight-up, barefaced truth.

Her thoughts drifted to the city, a backdrop of unscripted yarns etched on disregarded faces and overlooked corners, yarns that remained silent, swallowed by the constant drone of the modern world. She thought of the camera, discarded in a dingy corner of an antique shop, its story obscured under layers of dust and indifference.

The silence of her flat mirrored the peace within her, the calm before the creative storm that was yet to break. A promise hung thick in the air, a crackling energy that chimed with her plan. This camera was going to be her mate, her confidante. They were two outcasts, brimming with untapped potential, ready to stir up a storm.

As she gave the camera another Squizzy, she knew. Knew she was on a journey that would lead her somewhere unpredictable, somewhere real. It wasn't the camera that was an old relic; it was the world around her. And together, they'd frame it, one shot at a time.

The sun slipped through the cracks in the cheap blinds like a burglar, throwing hard, unforgiving shadows across the floor of Emma's flat. Her head was a cyclone, the leftovers of cheap grog turned poisonous in her gut. A taste, bitter and unrelenting, lingered in her mouth. It was a hangover from hell, the kind that made itself at home in your bones and echoed in your noggin.

Blinking against the harsh daylight, Emma rolled over in her messed-up sheets, her hand coming to rest on something solid and alien. Reality's intrusion into her world of headache and regret was unwelcome, a stern reminder of her night-time slip-ups.

She was the picture of defeat, a woman lost at sea anchored in the harbour of self-pity. But the day had no mercy for the remorseful, gave no quarter to the hungover. The morning pressed on, cold and relentless, offering no relief to those ensnared in the grip of regret.

Dragging herself into a sitting position, she caught sight of the object. Amid the regular mess of her flat – takeaway boxes, clothes scattered – sat the vintage Argus C3. It stuck out like a sore thumb, a dirty memento that was now hers. The sight of it sparked something in her, a glimmer that fought against the hangover. The Argus was her ticket out of her creative slump, her weapon against the dreariness of her life.

With the new day, amidst the wreckage of the night before, Emma remembered that she was more than just another washed-up artist drowning her sorrows at the bottom of a whiskey bottle. She was a woman with a purpose, a woman with a camera that promised mystery and a whiff of magic. And no hangover was going to stop her from discovering what it had in store.

First Shot

Rubbing her eyes against the daylight's harsh glare, Emma tossed about in her tousled sheets, her hand landing on something solid and strange. The bastard reality cutting into her personal headspace of pounding headaches and remorse was an unwelcome guest, a bloody hard reminder of her midnight sins.

She looked like a right shambles, a wreck of a sheila stuck in a harbour of self-loathing. But the day had no sympathy for those drowning in regret, didn't give a rat's arse about the hungover. The morning trudged on, cold and ruthless, giving no quarter to those wrapped in regret's tight grip.

Hauling herself to a sit, she spotted the object. Amidst her flat's usual anarchy - the takeaway boxes, clothes scattered about - there sat the vintage Argus C3. It stood out like a roo in a shopping centre, a grubby relic now in her possession. The sight of it sparked something in her, a glimmer that countered the hangover's gut punch. The Argus was her ticket out of this creative dry spell, her weapon against the humdrum of her life.

As a new day dawned, amid the wreckage of last night's party, Emma was reminded she was more than just another washed-up artist necking whiskey to forget. She was a sheila on a mission, a woman with a camera promising intrigue and a dash of magic. No bloody hangover was going to stop her from exploring its potential.

The Argus C3 perched on her bedside table, an old digger amongst green recruits. It seemed as out of place as a dugong on a dancefloor, this old-timer amidst her digital doodads and modern mess. The camera bore the marks of time and memory, a tough old relic with scars whispering tales of a bygone era.

Sitting upright, she carefully took hold of the vintage camera, her fingers running over its cold metal and worn leather. The camera was weighty, a comforting heft that gave a sense of solidity in her hands. It was a jarring contrast to her usual digital, a foreign object in her world of pixels and autofocus.

A bloody-minded urge bubbled within her as she handled the device, temporarily ignoring her thumping headache. A challenge had been thrown down, the call of unknown waters echoed in her ears. It was an invitation, a whispered dare she was too stubborn to refuse.

In a world of perfect grins and sanitised poses, the Argus was a battle-hardened beast of truth, a silent observer that could slice through the fakery. It was her weapon of choice in her newfound rebellion against her profession's false pretties.

Fuelled by fresh resolve, she decided to take the camera for a spin, to savour the city air and to catch the raw, unfiltered essence of the city. The pounding headache, once a grim spectre, now seemed just a pesky annoyance, a small toll to pay on her quest for the real deal.

Un-showered and with yesterday's makeup smeared under her eyes, Emma plunged into the city with the Argus C3, her hangover a badge of honour, her camera the instrument of her uprising. The day was still a bub, and the city called out to her, an unwritten canvas awaiting her truths.

Melbourne welcomed Emma with a brisk morning, the city rousing to a racket of sounds and sights that seemed harsher than usual, echoing the beat of her whiskey-induced hangover. The Argus C3 was a clumsy weight around her neck, a lump of metal and glass that felt as alien as she did.

The camera hung heavy against her chest, a jarring stranger amidst the slick DSLRs and flashy smartphones that populated the city. It was an ugly duckling, a weathered relic carrying an old-world charm, a reminder of a time when photography demanded grit and perseverance.

She roamed the streets without aim, the city's hustle barely touching her solitary focus. She was a wraith lost in a sea of faces, the lens of the Argus her only link to the world. Her trusted digital camera seemed a faraway memory, a child lost in the wilderness of her new reality.

With each step, the reality of her decision hit home. Her usual point-shoot-move-on routine replaced with the demanding task of adjusting manual settings, waiting for the perfect shot. This was more than photography; it was a dance with time and light, a pas de deux demanding her full focus.

Feeling more like a stranger than the camera, Emma pushed on, tackling the city's chaos with a dogged defiance. The city was her canvas, the Argus her paintbrush. She was ready to etch her vision, one frame at a time.

Emma's roaming gaze found a gnarly old gum tree, twisted and weathered by time. Standing defiantly amidst the concrete jungle, its branches reaching out like desperate hands in search of comfort. The rough bark told stories of countless seasons, the deep grooves a testament to its survival. It felt familiar, like her own reflection, old and overlooked, yet doggedly holding on.

Something about the tree struck a chord with her. She felt a strange bond with it, as if it too was a silent witness to the world. She decided to make it her first subject, a fitting start to her journey with the Argus C3.

Raising the camera to her eye, she squinted through the dusty viewfinder, framing the tree in the small square. The world looked different through the Argus lens; it was bare and unfiltered, stripped of digital gimmicks and enhancements. This was the world in its raw form, its beauty in its stark simplicity.

The camera felt mechanical and alive in her hands. She fiddled with the focus, her fingers caressing the cold metal dials, adjusting the aperture, letting the morning light filter into the camera's belly.

It was a dance of patience and precision, an intimate connection between observer and observed.

Holding her breath in anticipation, she pressed the shutter button. The sound was a mechanical orchestra, a click resonating in her ears, pulsating with her heartbeat. Emma, standing in the frosty Melbourne morning with a vintage camera in her hands, had taken her first shot. A shot that felt more real than any she'd taken before.

Back in her flat, Emma set about developing the film. It was a process almost forgotten in the digital age. The darkroom, bathed in its dim red glow, smelled of chemicals and unseen images awaiting birth.

She carefully unspooled the strip of negatives from the Argus C3, her fingers running over the frames she'd captured. As each image came into view, she felt the thrill of discovery, the excitement of unveiling what was caught in those small squares.

But when she reached the frame with the gnarled gum tree, something caught her attention. She held up the negative to the dim light, studying the image. It wasn't the tree that held her gaze, nor was it the composition. Instead, it was a figure, a shadowy silhouette in the background, which she didn't recall being there when she took the shot.

The bloke, blurred but deadset human, loomed a bit from the tree. Foggy, a ghostlike vibe that seemed out of place in the otherwise everyday scenery. Gave her the willies, her noggin filled with what-ifs. Had there been someone when she clicked the shutter? Was it a fluke of the sunlight, a weird shadow dance?

Felt odd, like a puzzle piece on the wrong side of the map. She eyeballed the figure, a shadowy existence reaching out from the photo, a mute wraith stuck forever in film. She couldn't dodge the weirdness wrapping the photo, a vibe that had the cogs in her brain spinning.

In her pocket-sized flat, under the old smell of chemicals and drying film, Emma felt goosebumps rising. The bloke in the photo was a riddle, a question scribbled in the grainy black and white. Holding the photo, her eyes strained to make out the ghostly shape, her mind swinging between curiosity and disbelief.

"Light playing tricks," she grumbled, writing off the figure as a glitch, a bug of the ancient camera. But the weird feeling kept gnawing at her, the strange hunch that someone had been there, hidden, spying on her.

She walked about the room, the worn carpet rough under her foot. The world outside, brimming with life, seemed oddly distant, muted by her bewilderment. She eyed the photo again, the silhouette seeming to take the piss. A chill rushed through her, making her skull down the last of her cold coffee. It tasted sour, much like the unease in her gut.

"But it's just a bloody photo," she sneered, trying to laugh off the unease. She knew her mind was playing up, making ghosts out of nothing. She was an artist, after all, her creativity was both a blessing and a curse.

As the day went on, Emma forced her focus on other stuff. She shoved away the photo, stuffing it in a drawer, burying the phantom with it. Yet, the image stayed, like a fog stuck to her thoughts, a chilling whisper refusing to bugger off. This was just the beginning of the puzzle that was about to unfold, a taste of the unusual journey she was unknowingly stepping into.

Emma aimed to catch the soul of her city. She wandered the streets and lanes, following the graffiti lines, catching the quick shadows of passing strangers. Each shot felt like a secret, each click of the shutter a soft whisper. But the more she shot, the more she felt something off.

As she developed the photos, the darkroom around her buzzed with the night's pulse. In the red glow, faces and forms popped up on the photo paper. A thrill tingled her fingers as she washed the images, unmasking their secrets. But alongside the excitement was a pinch of unease.

There, hiding in the shadows, within the dance of light and dark, were the figures. Warped, barely visible, yet undeniably there. Their vague existence seemed to take the mickey out of reality, quietly growing in the corners of each photo, a spectral mark that couldn't be shaken off.

They were bloody everywhere - in the snaps of the twisted gum trees, in the graffiti-filled back alleys, in the forsaken lanes where moggies stalked. They hung about in the shadows, a shapeless mob growing with each developed photo. What were these ghostly intrusions, these unclear whispers of existence? A blunder, a flaw, or something more?

Emma stared at the photos, her ticker thumping in her chest. The figures were off-putting, messing up the balance of her works, marking her art with a creepy presence. She shivered, caught in the thick of a mystery that was deepening with each shot, each development, each shadowy figure growing in the backdrop of her work.

Emma sat among the scattered photos, her mind wrestling with the absurd. The figures in the photos weren't just random shadows, they started to form patterns. Subtle at first, but unmistakable as she combed through photo after photo. They seemed to tell a tale, convey a story that was as slippery as it was intriguing.

The patterns weren't consistent, they shifted with each photo's subject. In some, they seemed like old carvings, cryptic and uncrackable. In others, they looked like the wild movements of a lunatic maestro, fierce and frantic. Each photo was a piece of a puzzle she was desperately trying to solve, a cryptic message whispered in the language of shadows.

With every passing hour, the figures seemed more alive, their vague bodies almost shaking with a purpose that was both disturbing and captivating. As if they were begging to be seen, understood, their story brought to light from the shadows they lived in. Emma found herself pulled into their mysterious tale, unable to shake the urge to decipher their cryptic language.

A strange fear started to crawl in her, sneaking into her bones. It was a weird feeling, as if she was staring into a void, and the void was staring back. Yet, she felt driven to understand, to decode the creepy spectacle that the camera was showing.

Emma held the old Argus C3, its cold metal a comforting presence against the growing discomfort. She felt a sense of determination steeling within her. She would reveal the story hidden in the shadows. She had become an unwilling soothsayer, pulled into a story spun in the ghostly half-light of the spectral figures. And she was prepared to delve deeper, to understand what the camera was trying to show.

The room squeezed at her like a python's coil, a claustrophobic stew of old air and creeping shadows stretching from the lone and dim goanna lamp on the table. Emma, hunkered down in her beat-up old armchair, was nursing a flat tinny, her fingers ghosting over the beads of cool sweat on the bottle. But her brain was wandering far off, adrift in a shadowy maze of thoughts, standing in stark contrast to the stale reality of her lounge room.

She necked the dregs of her beer, the sharp bitterness a mirror to her internal jumble. Just what kind of a bingle was she getting herself tangled in? Was she toying with danger, or was this just a silent bell from the depths of her noggin, craving a break from the dull and dreary, yearning for a bite of the extraordinary? Buggered if she knew. But one thing was as certain as the sun coming up in the morn, she was teetering on the edge of something, something that made her feel as small as a roo in the outback, something as wild and unfettered as a bushfire ripping through the gum trees.

She blew out a heavy sigh, squashing the empty beer can. To hell with fear. Emma wasn't the type to duck out of a scrap. She picked up the Argus C3, its cold, solid touch grounding her. Come the morn, she'd be out again, toting her camera, tearing away at the layers of this bloomin' puzzle. But tonight, she'd sink her worries in the familiar embrace of another beer, her dreams a dance with the unknown.

Final Decision: It's the end of the day, and the world outside her window is settling into dusk. She's alone in her flat, surrounded by the random spread of prints she's made. The shadows in the photos seem to move, to shift in the fading light, whispering tales from a bygone era.

She's sitting on the worn-out rug, photos tossed around her like puzzle pieces, her heart pounding with a mix of fear and excitement. Her fingers trace the figures in the photos - the unseen spectators of her new, bizarre reality. She thinks of the bottle of grog on her shelf, contemplating drowning her fears, but then decides against it. This isn't something she can run away from, not this time.

She knows she's walking a thin line, a path filled with uncertainties and possible perils. But Emma's never been one to step back from a challenge. With the camera by her side, her fears take a backseat to her curiosity. The mystery of the camera, the shadows, the silent whispers - they're a puzzle she's been unwillingly thrown into, and she's deadset on solving it.

As the city's noises fade into the quiet hum of the night, she makes her decision. The camera, the shadows, the story they hold - she's in it for the whole bloody thing. As the chapter closes, Emma is no longer just a jaded photographer - she's turned into an explorer, ready to dive into the heart of this mystery.

With the Argus C3 in her hand, a symbol of her new purpose, she steps into the mysterious maze waiting for her. The sheila who walked into the antique shop has vanished. In her place stands a woman on the brink of an extraordinary adventure, ready to take on whatever comes her way.

Soulful Portraits

There's a low rattle as Emma chucks her latest batch of prints across the battered and scarred table that consumes her poky Aussie flat. Each snap a black and white testament, a bushfire of something more than just light and shadow. It's a grating hum that nibbles at her brain, each ringing a different tune she can't quite understand.

It's late, bloody late for the desk jockeys, but for Emma, time is some fairy dinkum nonsense from another bloke's world. The ghostly figures floating in her snaps, they should have been the big deal, the star attraction. But nah, they're only the back-up band, the bass player in the shadows while the lead guitarist goes off.

Instead, it's the depth she can't turn a blind eye to. The rawness, the intimacy that each shot seems to ooze. These are her mates, her cobbers. Blokes and sheilas she'd had a bevvy with, cracked jokes with, even had a blubber with. But these pics...they're bare as a joey, stripped down to their bones in a way that's more revealing than any nudity could ever be.

She traces her fingers over one of the prints, tracing the ghostly overlay on the familiar mug. She's on the hunt for something, a clue maybe, to decode this bloody mystery. Her head's a buzzing beehive, each thought a busy bee trying to make head or tail of this nectar of intrigue.

There's a strange beauty in this, in the unknown. It's alluring, a temptress in its silence. The half-drunk bottle of cheap vodka by her elbow is lost, its numbing comfort replaced by this far more thrilling enigma. Emma's hooked on a new poison, one that's as much a riddle as it is a revelation.

She grabs another print, holds it up to the gloomy light seeping through the filthy window. Her ticker's beating out a mad rhythm against her ribs. She's on the edge of something here, something big.

It's like peering into a bottomless pit that gazes back, whispering secrets you're not sure you're ready to hear. But Emma, she's always been more of a snooper than a scaredy-cat. And this, this intimacy she can't pin down...it's a puzzle that won't let go. And neither does Emma.

The next day, or is it still the same day? Emma doesn't give a toss about the sun's comings and goings. She decides to call over her ragtag band of misfits, those who floated in and out of her life, revolving planets each with their own mysteries, their own yarns to spin. The word goes out: "Drop by the flat, let me snap your mug." No reason, no explanation. But they show up anyway, because Emma is a puzzle, a magnet that draws them in, even when they can't work out why.

She sets up a makeshift studio in her tiny refuge, clearing out half-eaten pizza boxes and empty booze bottles that are as much a part of her decor as the beat-up couch and the peeling wallpaper. The harsh, naked bulb hanging from the ceiling won't do the trick, not this time. So, she gives it a burl. A lamp, a diffuser cobbled together from an old shirt, anything that could bend light. Every click of the camera a whispered secret, capturing fleeting moments and freezing them into solid form.

There's something holy about this process, the kind of divine that Bukowski himself would snort at, but would secretly tip his hat to. Each shot is a dance between what's seen and what's hidden, the solid and the spirit, the real and the spectral. It's a dance she's busting to learn, each step revealing a new side, a new layer of her clueless partners. And with each click, the camera seems to breathe, a living thing feasting on the raw, silent emotions of its subjects.

She clicks away, a puppet master pulling on strings made of light and shadow. A chuckle, a scowl, a sly glance, all freeze in a quiet stillness, locked within the cold frame of the camera. The air turns thick with a potency, a sensation so real it makes her head spin, yet she holds her ground. If anything, she dives deeper, surrendering to the intoxicating rhythm, the elusive charm that her camera seems to be pulling off.

The session stretches on for hours, or maybe it's just minutes. Time again, taking the mickey. The usual natter and banter are gone, replaced by a silent agreement that they're all part of something bigger, something that can't be put into words. It's a quiet symphony, the air humming with the unsaid feelings each click of the camera seems to immortalize. Emma is on a journey here, steering a ship through uncharted waters. And just like any old hand sailor, she knows better than to ignore the call of the sea, or in her case, the call of the lens.

She's up into the witching hours, or maybe it's the break of dawn. The sun again, with its game of hide and seek. Emma's got her fingers in chemicals, the smell strong and a bit sickening. But there's a certain joy in it, a rush that courses through her veins as the images start to take shape, coming alive from the blank canvas of the photo paper. They're not just snaps, they're revelations, raw and honest.

Her misfit mates, free of their masks and pretences, look back at her. But it's not their faces that she sees. It's their essence, their bare souls spilled across the photo paper. The ghostly figures that once ruled her work are now mere whispers in the backdrop, overshadowed by the roaring storm of emotions each portrait belts out. The sun was rising, casting the first faint hints of light into the room, diluting the red glow from the safe-light. Emma stood there, awestruck, surrounded by the black and white tales of her friends. Her heart pounded in her chest, her mind raced, but it was a beautiful kind of chaos. She felt a warmth spreading within her, an understanding, a realization. She had become a custodian of emotions, an archivist of the unseen, the unspoken. She had tapped into the realm of raw, undiluted emotion, an elusive, intoxicating world that threatened to consume her, and she was ready to surrender. The morning light spilt into the room, casting long shadows and adding a soft hue to the black and white photographs spread out on the table. Emma looked at the spectral figures in the photos, now benign bystanders to the emotional drama of her friends. She'd gone looking for the spectral, the unknown, but had stumbled upon the known, the familiar. She'd gone looking for ghosts but had found the living.

Each snap was a yarn being spun, a corker of a story unravelling, a perplexity decoded. She'd gone and got their essence, the guts of their existence, the tales tucked away behind their smiles. Those portraits weren't about their mugs but their inner song, the raw howl from their souls. They were chockers with the silent wails and muffled chortles. Each picture, a reflection not of their dials, but of their ticker, their core. Her camera, that spectral chaser, had morphed into a truth diviner, ripping the cover off the souls it captured, leaving no room for any furphies.

Through these snaps, Emma had dug up the unseen, the untouchable. She'd plunged into the soup of emotions, capturing what skulked beneath the façade. And in doing so, she'd unveiled a cosmos that lived beyond the touchable, a cosmos as mind-boggling as it was striking, and fair dinkum human.

Emma sat alone in the developing room, gazing at the stark contrasts of black and white, the sharp lines of the images she'd seized. She was ready for shadows and light, maybe the occasional grin or knitted brow. What she didn't see coming was the bucketload of raw, unpolished emotion every picture seemed to seep. It was like holding her mates' hearts in her hands, each beat narrating their yarns, their tussles, their triumphs.

She studied Mickey's snap again, his fool's crown swapped out for a prickly crown of gloom. That larrikin charm, that vibrant joy, all hiding a reservoir of sadness. Emma felt a bit crook. How many times had she, like others, hidden behind his laughter, used his cheer as a shield against their own hard yakka? Mickey was always the life of the do, but his own life seemed a do he couldn't stomach.

Then there was Mary, her steel-faced front hiding a blooming joy Emma had never noticed before. Could it be that behind Mary's frosty shell, there was a sheila bursting with untamed joy? It was a bonza and delightful discovery, like finding a secret garden behind a formidable wall.

This was unsettling. Emma was uncovering depths of people she thought she knew, depths she had no clue existed. Her camera wasn't just snapping images; it was peeling back layers, spilling the beans, telling yarns that her eyes and ears had overlooked.

Sitting there, the red glow of the darkroom throwing creepy shadows around her, Emma felt a peculiar blend of awe, unease, and thrill. It was as if she'd been handed a peculiar gift, the ability to see beyond the surface, to dive into the soul's deep. Her camera, once just a tool for capturing moments, had become a revealer of truths, a spiller of secrets. And she, Emma, was driving this journey, navigating through unfamiliar emotional waters. The weight of this revelation rested heavy in her chest; an insight that felt as terrifying as it was exhilarating.

As Emma peeled back her subjects' layers, she found herself sliding into her own emotions' rabbit hole. Each photograph was like a mirror, throwing back pieces of her own self, fragments of feelings she'd been careful to stash away. There was an unsettling kinship in Mickey's hidden gloom, a resonating echo in Mary's concealed joy.

The snaps were whispers of her own unexpressed feelings, a tangible embodiment of her inner storm she could no longer avoid. It was as if the spectral figures in her snaps had jumped off the frames and started haunting her, their presence, a constant reminder of the turmoil brewing within her.

A sensation buzzed at the base of her spine, crawling its way up to her neck, making her aware of a physicality she'd never felt before.

It was a raw, thumping energy, much like the spectral figures, living just under her skin, itching to break free. A primal urge stirred within her, a force demanding attention, recognition.

This awakening gave her the willies. Emma had always prided herself on keeping a lid on it, keeping her emotions under control. But now, she was standing at the precipice of a world that was all feelings and sensations, and a wild, reckless part of her wanted to leap headfirst into it.

She felt alive, aflame with a strange fire that both consumed and liberated her. It was a dance on the edge, a tango with the unknown, and for the first time in her life, Emma felt genuinely free. The shadows no longer spooked her, the light no longer blinded her. She welcomed them both, the light and the shadows, the joy and the sorrow, the fear and the desire.

And so, amid the red-tinted gloom of her developing room, Emma started to find herself, facing her fears, acknowledging her desires, giving in to the whirlwind of emotions that was becoming her new reality. It was frightening, sure, but it was also the most thrilling journey she'd ever taken. Emma wasn't just developing photographs; she was developing herself.

Emma's curiosity was a constant itch, and her camera was the only balm. She'd snapped countless faces, caught numerous souls, laid bare countless emotions but had never thought to turn the lens on herself. It was uncharted territory, scary yet thrilling, like standing on a cliff edge, feeling the call of the unknown. So, like any good explorer, she jumped right into the abyss.

Arranging the camera to focus on herself, Emma felt a peculiar rush. The lens stared back at her, cold and unblinking, a silent dare. It was spooky, like gazing into a void that mirrored her own soul. And she was about to plunge in, yield to its charm, expose herself to her own scrutiny.

She set up her stage, the familiar room suddenly alien under the harsh lights. The room, strewn with negatives and prints of other souls, was now a theatre for her own unmasking. It was intimate and scary, having the roles swapped, being the observed rather than the observer.

Click, whir, the camera seized her essence, the tale of the sheila behind the lens. It was a terrifying spectacle, every shutter release echoing her vulnerability. Each flash lit up the room like a lightning bolt, leaving ghostly traces of her in its wake.

As she moved, posed, and shifted, she was acutely aware of the intimacy of the moment. The camera was no longer just a tool; it was a confidant, a mirror, an entity that was just as much a part of her as she was of it.

The session was an exploration, an experiment, a raw, unfiltered journey into her soul. It was a quiet tete-a-tete between Emma and the camera, a mutual exchange of secrets and discoveries. The cold lens probed, and she answered, offering fragments of herself she never knew were there.

In the quiet of the room, stripped of her defences, Emma wasn't just a snapper anymore. She was a subject, a story, a mystery waiting to be revealed. And with every click, every flash, she peeled back another layer of her own mystery, the anticipation of the result matching the rhythm of her thumping heart. This was Emma, raw and uncut, exposing herself to her own lens, her own scrutiny. Emma was starting to But Emma was made of sterner stuff. She didn't shy away. Instead, she found herself standing tall, meeting the camera's icy stare with a brazen gaze of her own. Every click of the camera was a resounding affirmation of her existence, a pulsating beat in the symphony of her soul's awakening. Each frame, a testament to the raw, naked, unapologetic Emma. And as the lens captured her truth, it became clear that her camera was her true soulmate, her mirror, her confidant. Through its unblinking gaze, she had discovered a universe within her, a world teeming with a storm of emotions, a whirlwind of desires, a chaos of thoughts. Emma found herself on a journey of self-discovery, excavating her emotions, unearthing her desires, laying bare her fears, all through the unyielding lens of her camera. It was an adventure, a revelation, a dance of the soul. It was Emma, photographed in her purest form, exposed and unashamed. It wasn't the nakedness of her body that startled her when she developed the film, but the nakedness of her soul. The pictures laid bare her emotions, her fears, her desires, all stark and raw, in black and white. The mirror had been turned on her, the observer had become the observed. And it was a revelation, a raw and beautiful revelation, that sent a shiver down her spine. She was looking at her own self through the gaze of the camera, and it was liberating. The photographs were not just an external representation of herself, but a deep dive into her soul, revealing aspects of her being she had never acknowledged. The fear, the joy, the sorrow, the desire - they were all there, staring back at her. The realisation hit her like a bolt of lightning - the truth of her own emotions laid bare. She wasn't just a photographer, she was a story, a riddle, an enigma waiting to be unravelled. And in that moment, she knew - this was just the beginning. The journey into the depths of her soul had just begun.

The indifferent chill of the camera's metallic shell, untouched by her turmoil, meticulously etched every cringe, every rigid shoulder, every shy glance, in the harsh and unforgiving permanence of film. The images that began to emerge were more than mere physical likenesses; they were emotional landscapes, mapping the uncharted expanse within her. As she watched the ethereal traces of her figure surface from the developing bath, a subdued undercurrent of her own sexuality awoke.

In the rough and textured greys of the prints, she discerned more than just the physical contours and shades of her body. She saw the latent reverberations of a sexuality she'd been oblivious to. It wasn't about her external appearance but her internal sensations, her desires, and her cravings.

Each photograph unfolded as a revelation, a silent admission of a lust that had lain dormant, unnoticed within her. Every image seemed to magnify a mute yearning, an unfamiliar and burgeoning hunger that stirred, then pulsed with a life force of its own.

Her sexuality, once a quiet spectre, now thrashed within her like a beast unshackled. The societal norms that had constrained her, the layers of polite pretence she had donned, now lay shattered under the probing gaze of her own lens. Each raw, vulnerable self-portrait stood as a defiant testament to her awakening desires. She had been merely surviving in the shadows of her own existence, and now the stark light of her camera was revealing the hidden topography of her longing.

She felt the quakes of her own awakening, a silent eruption shaking her from within, a primal call impossible to ignore. Emma, the observer, was transitioning into Emma, the observed, and this transition was a tumultuous yet beautiful dance of self-discovery.

The session concluded, the camera fell silent from its relentless surveillance, but Emma was altered. The room, once a safe haven, had transformed into the stage for her awakening. She had confronted her anxieties, her desires, and found a strength and sexuality as terrifying as it was liberating. As the final image dried, Emma found herself spellbound by her own metamorphosis, the woman in the photograph a stranger, yet somehow more familiar than ever.

In the soft red light of her makeshift darkroom, Emma watched as the images she had captured gradually sprung to life. The paper steeped in chemical baths held the secrets she had only recently revealed to her camera. This was no mere display of naked flesh, but a procession of emotions unfolding, one after the other, like a dreamy, surreal reel of film.

Loneliness appeared first, an unexpected presence amidst her self-portraits. It stood there in stark contrast against her solitary figure, a cold echo of the emptiness she hadn't realised she carried. She'd always seen herself as alone, she'd thought, a lighthouse on the outskirts of a quiet town. But she was no longer a lighthouse; she had transformed into the storm-tossed sea herself, yearning for land.

Next, a smouldering desire for companionship began to creep into the images, twining its way around her solitary figure. A longing for another soul to comprehend her newly discovered depths, a yearning for someone to truly see her, as she now saw herself. It was a plea captured in silver halide, a silent cry to an unknown other, a wish cast out into the void.

And underneath it all was the sensuality. It wasn't merely a physical yearning, but a deep, soulful ache. A sensuality that craved not touch, but connection. A longing not just for another body, but for another soul to understand, share, bare themselves as she had. A sensuality that spoke of shared whispers, lingering glances, and understanding silences.

Examining these self-portraits, Emma felt a dissonance between the woman she believed herself to be and the woman revealed in the images. Yet, she couldn't deny the truth that gazed back at her from the glossy paper. Each picture was a mirror, reflecting not her physical form but her emotional canvas.

She was no longer just Emma, the photographer. She was Emma, the lonely; Emma, the yearning; Emma, the sensual. She was a woman who had learned to peel away the layers of societal expectations and delve into her own depths. And in doing so, she had unearthed a myriad of emotions she didn't know she harboured.

Each self-portrait was a revelation, a soulful image that encapsulated a fragment of her existence. It was her world in shades of grey, an intimate display of her solitude, her longing, and her burgeoning sensuality. Each photograph, a testament to the journey she had embarked on, the inward voyage. And she was only at the beginning.

Closing the door to her makeshift darkroom, Emma found herself steeped in the aftermath of this self-revelation, the ghostly scent of photographic chemicals clinging to her like a mysterious perfume. It was late; the city had descended into the silent tranquillity of the witching hour, leaving her alone with her thoughts and the striking starkness of her portraits. She had shed her old skin in that darkroom, and like a snake inspecting its discarded scales, she was left to contemplate the nature of her transformation.

A stirring sense of awakening seeped through her, a rustling of something foundational within. Something that recoiled from societal norms like a wild cat from a bustling street. The pillars of her existence seemed to be crumbling, dissolving under the potent river of her emerging awareness. The person she had been was no longer fitting, no longer appropriate. She was growing, her consciousness expanding, spilling over the edges of the box she had been neatly tucked into.

Images of her friends, captured in their emotional undress, adorned the walls of her mind, each narrating a story deeper than the last. They were no longer mere acquaintances; they were reflections, their revealed rawness mirroring her own concealed truths. Was it possible that she harboured within her the same spectrum of emotions? Could it be conceivable that she, Emma, the straight, predictable, uncomplicated Emma, was capable of such complexity?

Her eyes returned to the self-portraits, to the figure that was her yet seemed someone entirely different. The bisexuality she'd tentatively acknowledged, an incidental product of her exploration, now clamoured for attention from the glossy surfaces. She wasn't merely looking at a portrait. She was peering into a new reality, a new existence that promised discovery, a journey of intimate exploration. The mere thought of it made her feel like she was teetering on the edge of an unseen precipice, a sensation both exhilarating and terrifying.

Exhausted, Emma fell into bed, her mind abuzz with the day's revelations. The moonlight streamed through the window, casting a silver glow over her solitary figure. The room filled with an expectant silence, the air heavy with the promise of the unknown. Her gaze landed on her self-portrait, the spectral figure in the photo seeming to reciprocate her stare. The eyes, her eyes, seemed to harbour a cosmos of unspoken emotions and untapped potential.

And so, she fell asleep, the anticipation of the impending journey reflected in the depths of her closed eyes, her dreams painting vibrant scenes of the possibilities that lay ahead. The night was young, and her journey had just commenced. But she wasn't alone. She had herself, As she slipped into unconsciousness, she whispered to the darkness, "I am Emma, the photographer. I am Emma, the lonely. I am Emma, the desiring. I am Emma, the sensual. I am Emma, the bisexual. And I am ready."

Denial

The dawn is a bloody shocker. Emma's peepers snap open, harsh reality bulldozing the dreamscapes that linger. The foggy grogginess of slumber fades, and what she's left with is the raw bonza truth of the night before, the 'no punches pulled' revelation of her newly minted bisexuality. It's a bloody ripper, an unexpected uppercut that leaves her gulping air, flailing about in the sheets like a kangaroo in the headlights.

She chucks a u-ey, burying her dial in the pillow. How much simpler it'd be to believe she'd imagined the whole shebang. That the rush of emotions was just some buggered up trick of light in the darkroom, the result of too many ticks alone, stewing over reels of film. Maybe it's just her mind pulling a swifty, yearning for a bit of a thrill in a world of greys. The lie is a cushier fit in her head than the truth.

But lies are sticky buggers, and the truth, persistent as a possum in the bin. The stark evidence lies strewn about her flat - proof you can't argue with. Her self-portraits glare back at her from the walls, each a mirror casting back emotions she'd never reckoned she carried. It's not just the thick layer of desire, but also the loneliness skulking in the shadows, the corners of the photos.

She can't help but see the unvarnished, barefaced truth they dish up. Her denial, weak as a two-bob watch, buckles under the weight of her unyielding reality. The self-portraits are the stress fractures in the dam, and the truth crashes through, a king tide sweeping away the remains of her denial.

Each snap is a ghost of her own emotions - yearnings she'd never nodded to, feelings she'd buried in the red dirt. The images confront her, their expressions mirroring her own dread and wonder. No more could she skulk behind the facade of normalcy; her truth is out in the open, starkers and staring her down.

And as the first wave of shock recedes, the guts of her situation dig in. She's Emma, snapper, in the middle of a bloody cyclone of self-discovery, a tempestuous ocean of emotions she can't disregard or dismiss. It's a revelation that sends a tremor through her, shaking the roots of her world. Emma, the sheila who thought she knew her own song, now stands on the edge of the unknown, eyeballing the dark abyss of her own truth.

Emma's days start to feel like some strange new dance. Between the unnerving mystery of the camera and her own sapphic revelation, she finds herself drawn to an unexpected bolt-hole: a bloke she knows. A bit of a drongo who'd always been part of the scenery. He'd never really tickled her fancy before, just another average Joe Blow.

But now, it's a different ball game. His company becomes a handy diversion, a distraction from the harsh truths poking around her mind. She begins to weave fantasies around him, spinning yarns of carnal intimacy that, while thrilling, felt out of step with her. She was on the run, and he was her hidey-hole, a refuge of normalcy in her twirling world.

Yet, her dreams dob her in. When the black night stretches out and reality is as thin as a goanna's g-string, the genuine desires of her ticker come forward. A sheila, undefined yet familiar, invades her dreams. Her identity was as hard to pin down as the morning mist, but her allure was no furphy.

This femme fatale was a riddle, a tantalising jigsaw piece that fit snugly into the voids of her desires. There was a pull, a magnet drawing her in that niggled at the edges of her heart, a siren's call that left her feeling raw and stripped bare in her own swag.

So, here she was, caught between two worlds. By day, a bloke who offered a getaway from the disconcerting truths she was too bloody scared to face. And by night, a woman who embodied those very truths, a sharp reminder of the desires she tried to bury under layers of denial.

In this tussle between what's real and what she wants, between the bloke who provides shelter and the sheila who is her truth, Emma finds herself in a constant state of turmoil. The days blur into one another, a loop of denial and desire, a fair dinkum emotional whirlwind. As she keeps wrestling with these clashing feelings, Emma gets hurled deeper into the labyrinth of her own mind, on a track that leads to god-knows-where.

Now, Emma's no goody two-shoes. She's always been a lass who knows what she wants and how to snag it. But this, this was a new kind of rodeo. She was pulled by a yearning that felt alien, a stranger in the outback. A sheila yearning for another sheila, that wasn't on the cards. Yet, here she was, trapped in the clutches of a desire that threatened to drive her round the twist.

In a desperate crack at regaining control, she starts playing a risky game. She invites the bloke over to her beaten-up flat. It's just a chinwag, she tells herself, nothing out of the ordinary. But she knows, way down deep, it's anything but.

The bloke, the poor bugger, hasn't got a clue about the storm brewing inside her. He shoots her a curious look as he steps into her dimly lit flat, not knowing he's just a pawn in her self-deception game.

She hones all her pent-up sexual tension on him, hell-bent on snuffing out the flames of her desire for women. He is her lifeline, her shot at escaping from the mad chaos within her. She uses him like a schooner at the end of a hot day, hoping that the physical release will dull the sharp edges of her emotional turmoil.

Every touch, every pash is planned. She fancies he's the cure for her queer desires. His body is just a tool, a means to an end. But as she loses herself in the physicality of their encounter, the harsh reality of her situation becomes bloody obvious. This isn't a fix for her longing, it's just a band-aid solution.

The physical release does sweet F.A to tame the tempest within her. If anything, it only amps up her turmoil. Each stroke, each pash, each moment of physical closeness only turns up the dial on her desire for the sheila in her dreams. She is left feeling more lost and muddled than before, the gaping void within her expanding with every ticking second.

Emma gives him the boot as soon as she's done with him, not bothering to hide her lack of interest. He takes off, a puzzled look on his dial, while she's left alone in the silence of her flat, her desires still not satisfied, her noggin a whirlpool of clashing emotions.

The physical act has done bugger all to quench her desires. If anything, it has only deepened her yearning for the elusive sheila who haunts her dreams. Emma It was a bitterly hollow victory. Even as the man left, his face flushed with the afterglow of their encounter, Emma was left with an unsettling emptiness. His touch had done nothing to quench her thirst. It was a thirst that could only be satisfied by the tender touch of the woman she desired, the woman who seemed just out of her reach. In her quiet flat, Emma was left to confront the harsh truth. She couldn't run away from her desires. She couldn't ignore the whispers of her heart. Her attraction to women was a reality that she could no longer deny. The truth was harsh and unforgiving, but it was hers. She was a woman in love with women. It was a realization that filled her with dread, but also with a sense of relief. She was finally able to acknowledge the truth, to accept herself for who she truly was. Her journey was just beginning.

She shut her peepers, lettin' the daydreams take over. She wasn't ridin' him, but the sheila of her dreams. She got stuck into the imagined softness, the tenderness, the gentleness that she connected with the woman. Each sigh, each quiver was for her, the ghost of a woman becoming more real with each tick of the clock. It was a no-holds-barred dance of want and refusal, a buggered up shot at wrangling the wild beast within her.

By the time the throwdown ended, Emma was more of a shambles than ever. Her body was chockers, but her noggin was a cyclone. She had a nibble of the forbidden fruit, and now there was no pulling a U-ey. The bloke, none the wiser to the storm brewing within her, left with a chuffed grin. Emma, on the flip side, was left with a worrying hollowness, a gnawing feeling of not quite being done. She was losing herself in the maze of her own yearnings, and the exit was nowhere in sight.

The ghost of their romp was thick in the room, a bitter reminder of what she'd hoped for and how far off the mark she'd been. The bloke lay spread out across the rumpled sheets, a self-satisfied smirk across his mug. But Emma was already a million miles away, her brain a whirling dervish of thoughts refusing to chill.

With a wave of her hand, she gave him the bum's rush off her bed. "You should nick off," she said, her voice colder than the cheap bottle of grog on the kitchen counter. There was no warmth in her words, no afterglow of shared intimacy. It was a deal, and the deal was done.

He got up, his face a picture of confusion, his pride knocked by her sudden chill. But she didn't give a toss. He was an afterthought now, just a bit player in her stormy journey of self-discovery. He was the drink that failed to drown her woes, the sideshow that only turned up the volume on her muddle.

The door clicked shut behind him, leaving her alone with her raging thoughts. The silence was deafening, the emptiness of her flat a mirror of the hollow satisfaction gnawing at her. She sank onto the floor, her back against the chilly wall, her ticker pounding away.

Her head was a war zone of emotions. The bloke's touch still clung to her skin, but it was the ghost woman's stroke that sent shivers down her spine. The harsh reality of her physical fling was overshadowed by the siren call of her head fantasies.

The quiet of her flat echoed with questions too scary to face. The fling hadn't given her any answers, and if anything, had only muddied the waters. As she sat in the middle of the chaos, one thing was becoming painfully clear: Emma was on a walkabout, and the destination was a bloody long way off. The track was rough, the view cloaked in mist, but one thing was clear as day - there was no turning back. The sun was up on her realization, and the night of denial was quickly fading.

On her tod in her castle of solitude, the reality of her life and the lies she'd been spinning were staring back at her, clear as day in her newly developed snaps. The bloody camera sat there, practically smirking at her from its perch on the desk. It was an extension of her, a piece of her soul trapped in plastic and metal, its lens holding a mirror to the dark parts of her psyche.

She'd tried to ignore it, to bury it under the pile of everyday grind, but it was like turning a blind eye to a ticking bomb. It was there, always there, gnawing at the edges of her consciousness, whispering to her in her dreams. The ghostly figures that haunted her snaps were physical manifestations of her secret yearnings, pieces of her subconscious given form.

Emma sighed, her breath catching in the silence of her flat. She sat on the cold, hardwood floor, her gaze fixed on the camera. Her fingers ached to hold it, to feel the familiar heft. But she fought it, a hopeless attempt to deny the undeniable.

The camera wasn't the enemy, it wasn't the agent of chaos she'd made it out to be. It was her truth-teller, a channel for the raw, uncut truths she'd been too scared to face. It was the shrink she'd never had, the mate she'd always needed, a silent listener to her secret yearnings.

In the brutal silence of her flat, she finally owned it. The camera wasn't pulling a swifty, it wasn't a cursed piece of kit warping reality. Nah, it was a tool, a medium, shining a light on the truths she'd been trying to outrun.

Her ticker thudded in her chest, the weight of her confession pressing on her. Her secrets weren't safe anymore, tucked away in the maze of her mind. They were there, in black and white, staring back at her from her snaps, demanding to be recognized. It was a hard pill to swallow, but the taste of truth was strangely freeing. As the chains of denial fell away, Emma found herself standing on the edge of acceptance, the first step on her journey of self-discovery.

Emma flopped on the beat-up sofa, her legs tucked under her, an untouched bottle of cheap whiskey in front of her on the coffee table. The air was thick with the silence after a storm, filled with her wild thoughts running loose like rogue kangaroos in her brain.

She thought about the bloke, how she'd used him like a throwaway toy, a means to an end. She'd ridden him hard, using him to quench the raging bushfire of her lust. She'd tossed him aside after, like a used durry, flicked into the gutter, its use spent. There was no tenderness, no love, just raw, primal need. It left a sour taste in her mouth, a twisted satisfaction that made her guts churn. She felt grubby, marked by regret and guilt.

Then there was the sheila, the ghost woman from her dreams, her fantasies. The woman who held more sway over her than any real person ever could. The softness of her skin, the heat of her touch, the intoxicating scent of her hung in Emma's mind, a haunting shadow of her hidden desires. She longed for the woman, her heart crying out with a need she'd never felt before. She wanted to taste her, to roam the contours of her body, to get lost in the depths of her eyes.

Emma's head was pounding with confusion. She couldn't make heads or tails of these clashing feelings, these desires she'd always kept buried deep. She'd always thought she was straight, had dated blokes, had fallen for blokes. But this pull towards women, this powerful tug she felt for the fairer sex, it was undeniable, as real as the blood in her veins.

She felt lost, bobbing in a sea of self-doubt and fear, waves of shame washing over her. She'd always thought she knew who she was, but now, she wasn't so sure. It was a terrifying prospect to face, an unravelling of her self-identity that left her feeling like a stranger in her own skin.

But in the quiet stillness of her flat, in the aftermath of her self-realisation, Emma's heart began to beat with a new rhythm, a rhythm that sounded a lot like hope. Despite the storm of confusion swirling within her, she felt a strange calmness, a glimmer of clarity in the chaos. It wasn't much, but it was a start, a point of light in her darkness.

She wasn't sure where this road would take her, but one thing was for certain: She was no longer willing to live a lie, to bury her truth. As scary as it was to embark on this journey of self-discovery, she realized that it was even scarier to deny who she truly was. And with that, her heart pounded with a newfound resolve, a resolve to face whatever lay ahead, a resolve to embrace her true self, no matter where this path led her.

Emma found herself parked on her tod in her little flat, the only company being the carcasses of tucker wrappers and spent stubbies littering about. She was like a roo caught in the high beams, rooted in place and not knowing which way to go. Life had become like a bludger, and she'd been playing a one-sided game of cricket with no runs scored.

Her telephone would ring, echoing in the stillness of the flat, reminding her of a world she felt disconnected from. She ignored the blower, her mates' pleas fading into the background. They wouldn't get it, she reckoned. They'd see her as a curiosity, their gazes holding either sympathy or revulsion. The thought was harder to swallow than a bad batch of prawns.

So, she chose to be a lone dingo, preferring her own noggin to the shallow comforts of the herd. The sun would rise and fall, days blurring into nights and nights into days, each marked by a struggle to keep her head above water in her own sea of turmoil. Her flat had turned into a hidey-hole, a retreat from the storm outside and inside her mind. It was like being wrapped in a prickly blanket – uncomfortable, yet familiar.

Amid the stillness, she spelunked into her mind's caverns, seeking understanding in the whirlpool of her feelings. It was like wading through a billabong at midnight, teeming with unseen dangers and surprises, but also speckled with moments of pure, bright moonlight.

She grappled with her desires, her fascination for blokes and sheilas alike, piecing together the mosaic of her identity. Her bisexuality wasn't a boogie man under the bed, it was a part of who she was, something she needed to bring into the daylight. It was like wrestling a croc, this journey of discovery, but she was starting to get a grip.

While the city around her hummed and hawed, Emma sat alone in her den, a solitary figure among the whirlwind of life outside, slowly stitching together the fabric of her being. She was a lone ranger, but she wasn't lonesome. She was getting to know herself, truly and authentically, and that was an adventure in itself.

Our girl Emma was holed up like a bilby in a burrow, mucking about with that camera again. She'd tried to give it the flick, to set it aside like a worn-out pair of thongs, but it was like trying to resist a frothy on a scorching arvo. The camera was an unspoken challenge she just couldn't say no to.

Click. Flash. Each shot was a wake-up call, a confronting glance in a mirror. Her eyes held a dingo's wild fear and curiosity, her lips hinting at the larrikin spirit hidden beneath. That little black box didn't sugarcoat a thing, it showed Emma, raw and unplugged, a bonza mess unravelling the mysteries of her own feelings. It was scarier than finding a spider in your daks but also gave a rush of adrenaline like streaking through the surf under a full moon.

There she was, in all her raw glory, reflected in the snapshots. A sheila trying to make sense of her desires, a drongo stepping into unknown territory, armed with nothing but her camera and a dash of hope. The destination was anyone's guess, but she was hell-bent on enjoying the ride.

Emma was standing on the edge of a cracking epiphany. All those misgivings, all those cheeky dreams about blokes and sheilas – it was all clicking into place. Looking at those images, those frozen echoes of her own bewilderment and desire, the truth hit her like a freight train. Crikey, Emma, she thought, you're as queer as a footy match with no footy.

And you know what? It wasn't half as bad as she'd thought. It was like finally slapping that mosquito that's been giving you the shits. She'd been doing her head in, trying to fit herself into some neat little box, but now, there it was, out in the open like a budgie smuggling an extra banana. Emma liked blokes. Emma liked sheilas. And that was just how she rolled.

She was done with playing silly buggers, done trying to make herself fit into a mould she wasn't meant for. If anyone had a problem with it, they could bugger off. Emma was as queer as they come and wouldn't have it any other way.

That camera had been a true mate, showing her the unvarnished truth. That black box was more than just a gadget with a lens, it was her compass, her confidante, her reality check.

A grin broke across her face. She could almost hear herself saying, Struth, Emma, this is just the start. A whole world was out there waiting to be explored, a world where she could love and lust freely, a world where she could be her true self. It was daunting as a shark-infested rip, but it sent a thrilling shiver up her spine, a feeling that made her feel more alive than ever before.

Emma, armed with her camera and newfound self-acceptance, was ready to leap into the fray, to dive headfirst into the tumultuous waters of love and lust. It was a new dawn, a new day, a new Emma, and she was ready to set the world alight. Let the bloody games begin.

Proof

E mma sat, her fingers gliding over the rough edges of her camera. Her mind churned like a tempest at sea, her thoughts mirroring the chaotic whirl of emotions within her. She'd tangoed with her bisexuality, acknowledging it with the grace of a seasoned dancer, and accepted the uncanny power of her camera with a touch of terrified awe. But even as she tried to stitch her new reality together, doubts gnawed at the corners of her mind like a starved rat.

Was she really seeing the world as it was, or was she simply spiralling down a labyrinth of her own illusions? Was the camera truly a gateway to the soul, or was she just losing her marbles, seeing things that weren't really there? It was a possibility that lurked in the shadows of her mind, a dark spectre that made her question her sanity.

It wasn't enough to just sit there, staring blankly at the camera as if it would sprout a mouth and answer all her questions. She had to know. She decided to put her treasured device to test, to strip it down to its very essence. She would use it on a mate, someone she reckoned she knew as well as she knew the camera she now doubted. Her goal was as clear as the Sydney Harbour on a sunny day. If her camera could unearth her friend's secret emotions as it had done hers, then she'd have her proof. If not, she'd know that she was chasing her own tail, lost in the labyrinths of her mind.

With a deep breath, she picked up her phone, dialled her friend's number, and waited, her heart pounding in her chest like a runaway jackhammer. She was on the brink of a precipice, ready to leap into an abyss of knowledge or madness. Either way, she'd know the truth, and that was enough for her.

Doubts be damned, she thought, her fingers clutching the camera tighter. She was ready for whatever truth the lens would reveal, ready to confront her realities, be they ugly or beautiful. There was no room for denial, no place for pretences. Her journey of self-discovery had led her here, to this moment of truth, and she was prepared to see it through to the end. No more hiding, no more running. It was time for proof.

Her choice was an easy one to make. The guinea pig for her little experiment would be her mate, a Sheila she'd known since her days of pigtails and scraped knees. They'd grown together, two seeds nourished by the shared experiences of life, drawing from the same soil of joy, heartache, and growth. This friend, this sister of her soul, was a lighthouse of optimism amidst life's murky waters, her cheeriness a beacon that refused to be extinguished even in the face of life's relentless waves.

Her friend, she thought with a chuckle, was like a kangaroo on a sugar rush – perpetually bouncing with an energy that seemed almost unnatural. No matter what life threw at her, she shrugged it off with an ease that left Emma in awe. And now, she'd be the subject of Emma's camera's scrutiny.

She concocted a plan, a ruse to get her friend to drop by her flat. She spun a tale of a fun, casual photoshoot, promised her friend a handful of Insta-worthy photos that would garner hundreds of likes on social media. It was bait her friend couldn't resist. A date was set, and plans were laid down.

She waited for the day with bated breath, her anticipation a tight knot in her stomach. The doubts lingered, whispering sinisterly in the back of her mind, but she brushed them off with a scoff. She'd come too far to back out now. She had questions that needed answers, secrets that demanded to be unearthed. And come hell or high water, she would uncover them.

She busied herself with the preparations, setting up the perfect lighting, positioning the camera at just the right angle. The mundane tasks were a welcome distraction from the tornado of thoughts within her. As she adjusted the lens and fiddled with the settings, she couldn't help but marvel at the irony of it all. She, who had always been the one to capture emotions, would now be the one to expose them.

A part of her quivered with excitement, a tiny voice in her heart whispering of the possibility that she was on the brink of a discovery that could change everything. Another part of her recoiled in trepidation, afraid of what she might uncover. But as she looked at the empty space before her camera, all doubts and fears seemed to dissolve. She was ready for the truth, however bitter it might be.

The photoshoot unfurled, a dance between the photographer and the subject. Emma orchestrated it all, the maestro of this strange symphony. She called the shots, guiding her mate through a labyrinth of poses, coaxing emotions onto her face with the skill of a seasoned puppeteer. But even as her friend smiled and pouted and looked wistfully into the distance, Emma couldn't shake off the growing unease that gnawed at her insides.

Guilt seeped into her like a persistent drizzle, dampening her spirits, blurring her focus. She felt like a rat, a sneaky bugger using her friend as a test subject in her unholy experiment. The thought made her feel as grubby as a bloke who'd just rolled around in the outback dust.

She wrestled with her conscience, a bare-knuckled brawl inside her head. It was for the greater good, she told herself, attempting to justify her actions. Yet, the guilt clung to her like a stubborn gum stain on the pavement, refusing to be scrubbed away.

As the camera clicked and whirred, as the flash illuminated her friend's face, something shifted. Each flash was like a lightning bolt, casting her friend's features in stark relief, unmasking the facade of familiarity. In those moments, her friend seemed like a stranger, a puzzle whose pieces didn't quite fit together.

She peered through the viewfinder, her eyes scanning the stranger before her. It was as though the lens had ripped away the veneer of familiarity, exposing a layer of her friend she'd never seen before. Each snapshot was a revelation, an unspoken confession laid bare in the artificial glow of the camera flash.

And with each click of the shutter, the unease within Emma grew. She was peeling away the layers of her friend's life like an onion, each layer revealing a deeper truth, each truth a sharp pang that added to her growing turmoil. But she couldn't stop now, not when she was so close to unearthing the truth. So, she pressed on, the weight of guilt a leaden anchor tethering her to this reckless pursuit of knowledge.

The camera whirred and clicked, the sound echoing in the silent room, a ticking time bomb counting down to an inevitable explosion.

Back in her fortress of solitude, her darkroom, Emma's hands trembled. She felt the anticipation swell inside her, a seething cauldron of nerves. It was the suspense of waiting for a pot to boil, the thrill of the unknown that came before the unveiling of a mystery. She was an archaeologist on the cusp of a significant discovery, her heart thrumming a wild rhythm in her chest.

Her breath hitched as she submerged the photographic paper into the developing solution, the chemical fumes filling her nostrils with a scent that was equal parts familiar and comforting. It was the smell of progress, of revelation, and today, it reeked of the dread of impending doom.

She watched as the images emerged like shy apparitions, hesitant at first, and then bolder, as they revealed themselves under the dim red light of the darkroom. She squinted at them, her mind teetering between denial and acceptance, a tightrope walker precariously balanced on the cusp of a fall.

Her mate's face materialized on the photographic paper, a phantom etched in grayscale. But something was amiss. Emma's heart lurched. There, in her friend's eyes, where joy and laughter usually resided, was a void. It was a chasm of sorrow, so profound and stark, it caught Emma by surprise.

She stared at the images, her mind racing to comprehend what she was seeing. This wasn't the vivacious woman she'd known since childhood, the eternal optimist who greeted every day with a smile as broad as the Sydney Harbour. This was a stranger cloaked in a familiar face, her eyes a window into a world of pain that Emma had never glimpsed.

She felt a cold rush of disbelief, a gut punch that left her winded. This couldn't be right. It had to be a mistake, some fault with the camera, or the chemicals, or the lighting. But the image was relentless, an immutable reality staring back at her from the photographic paper.

Emma's hands shook as she held the photographs up, the reality of her friend's hidden sorrow slicing through her like a raw, unfiltered truth. It was a revelation that sent her spiralling down a rabbit hole of disbelief and shock, a storm of emotions that left her feeling as battered as a dinghy in a cyclone.

But there it was, printed in stark black and white, an undeniable testament to her friend's secret sorrow. The photographs held up a mirror to the reality that Emma had overlooked, a reality that now sent a ripple of shock through her. Her friend's sorrow stared back at her, an unspoken plea from the photographic paper. It was proof, irrefutable and heart-wrenching, and it shook Emma to her core.

Emma sat alone in the dim glow of her darkroom, the processed photographs spread out before her like an accusatory testament. The truth they harboured was a paradox, both a victory and a defeat. She had won her war with reality; the camera did not lie. Yet, the victory tasted as bitter as swilling a pint of cheap beer that had turned.

She ran her fingers over the images, the figures frozen in monochrome that revealed a truth harsher than the Aussie sun in mid-summer. The camera, she realized, was no traitor. It was a soothsayer, a teller of harsh truths. And the truth was a pill more challenging to swallow than a handful of cockleburs.

Her friend, her mate, was hurting. It was a revelation that felt like a slap in the face, a wake-up call that left her feeling as naked and vulnerable as a joe without his pouch. She had been blind, ignorant of the grief that had been gnawing at her friend's insides, like a termite silently hollowing out a eucalyptus.

She felt a pang of guilt that was more potent than a sting from a box jellyfish. She had been there, right by her friend's side, yet so distant, so lost in her own world that she had failed to see the pain lurking in the shadows of her friend's eyes. The photographs taunted her with this truth, each snapshot a cruel reminder of her obliviousness.

Her friend's secret sorrow stared back at her from the stark black and white images, a silent accusation that was impossible to refute. She felt a rush of devastation, the crushing weight of her newfound knowledge sitting heavy in her gut like a leaden anchor. Yet, there was also a strange sense of triumph. Her camera, her confidante, had proved its power. It was no longer a suspect but a mirror, reflecting the truth in all its harsh, merciless glory.

Emma held the photographs close, the hard truth they harboured seeping into her skin, a stark reality she could no longer deny. As the dim red light cast eerie shadows around the darkroom, she was left with the reality of her friend's concealed pain, and the acknowledgment of her own obliviousness. The photographs were her proof, an undeniable testament that brought with it a rush of pain and acceptance. The truth was harsh, but it was there, laid bare in black and white, impossible to ignore.

A storm brewed inside Emma, a tempest of uncertainty and courage that left her as shaky as a kangaroo on a pogo stick. She had to confront her friend, had to bridge the gulf of unspoken sorrow that the photos had starkly revealed. The snaps lay before her, a silent testament to her friend's hidden agony, a truth that neither could run from any longer.

She took the plunge, her voice wavering like a gum leaf in a dust storm as she revealed the photos to her mate. Initially, her friend responded with dismissive laughter, waving it off like a pesky blowfly, blaming the gloom in her eyes on dodgy lighting or a poorly timed blink.

But Emma knew better, knew the truth was buried under layers of laughter and deflections, and she pushed on, as relentless as an Aussie summer. She turned the images towards her friend again, her voice firmer this time, demanding her attention, forcing her to face the truth that was as plain as the nose on her face.

Her friend's facade started to crumble, the seemingly impervious shell cracking under the weight of unshed tears and concealed torment. She broke down, her tears staining the black and white photographs, as though adding colour to the monochrome reality. She confessed, her voice barely a whisper, carrying the weight of the world in its soft timbre.

Personal struggles, private battles that she had fought alone in the shadows, came tumbling out in a torrent of words, each syllable heavy with the strain of unvoiced suffering. Emma listened, her heart aching, her hands clutching the tear-stained photographs, the proof of her friend's struggle etched in every line and curve.

The laughter was gone, replaced with raw, unfiltered truth, the kind that cut deep and left scars. But as her friend's confession hung in the air between them, a strange sense of relief washed over Emma. It wasn't a victory, nor a defeat, but a step towards understanding, towards bridging the distance that had unknowingly crept between them.

As they sat together in the aftermath of the confession, silence enveloping them like a comforting blanket, Emma realized something. The camera didn't just capture images; it captured truths, secrets, and emotions, rendering them visible to the naked eye. It was a tool of revelation, of connection, and, in its own strange way, of healing.

Emma sat still as a statue, her insides churning like the sea during a storm, as her friend spilled out her feelings like an overflowing beer. The unshed tears finally found their way out, carving tracks of loneliness and sadness on her friend's once cheerful face. Her words were raw and unfiltered, like an aged whiskey, hitting hard and leaving a lasting impact.

Emma kept her trap shut, letting her mate do the talking. Her own turmoil seemed small compared to the mountain her friend was climbing. The realities of loneliness and sadness, subjects they'd often sidestepped, now lay bare between them, as tangible as the chilled stubbies in their hands.

Emma, the listener for a change, felt a strange sense of gratitude wash over her. Despite the ugly reality, the bare-faced honesty and vulnerability brought them closer. Their friendship was no longer a shallow river but a deep, flowing stream, enriched by the knowledge of each other's hidden pains.

They found solace in each other, two misfit souls bound by shared secrets and newly discovered depths. Their battles, different yet so similar, became the foundation of a bond stronger than the hardest of metals. They were two women fighting their own wars, bearing their own crosses. But they were no longer alone, their struggles were shared, and in sharing, the burden seemed lighter, the path less treacherous.

Emma's mind wandered back to the camera, the catalyst of this raw and profound revelation. She couldn't help but marvel at the peculiar power it held, the ability to uncover concealed truths, peeling back layers of facade like an onion. It captured more than images; it captured souls, laying them bare in the harshest and most beautiful of lights.

The evening wore on, their beers turning warm, but the chill of solitude slowly dissipated in their shared companionship. A new understanding was forged in the crucible of shared pain, creating a bond that was unbreakable, undeniable. They were fighters, survivors, and together, they were invincible.

Emma felt a sense of calm settle over her. She had proof now, proof of her camera's powers, proof of her own strengths, and proof that even in the darkest corners, there was a glimmer of light, a spark of connection. The camera had done more than just capture images; it had captured the essence of their lives, raw and unfiltered. And in doing so, it had created a bond that was as profound as it was unexpected.

Emma sat alone in her room, a bottle of cheap wine her only company. She stared at the camera, its mocking gleam seeming to laugh at her newfound predicament. She held in her hands a device more powerful than she'd ever imagined. It was no mere camera, but a window into the soul, a trespasser into the private sanctums of human emotion.

She took a swig of her wine, the bitter taste a match for her current state of mind. The laughter and smiles from the day's shoot felt like distant memories, lost in the sombre quiet of her darkroom. Her mind circled around her friend's tear-streaked face, the raw hurt that had been hidden behind her vivacious charm. It was a sharp reminder that beneath the surface, everyone carried their own private hell.

As the silence of the room pressed in on her, Emma knew she was playing with fire. This camera, this damned thing, it could unravel lives, expose truths best left in the shadows. She couldn't just wield it recklessly, snapping away without a thought for the consequences. It demanded respect, a caution in its use, because in her hands she held not just a camera, but the power to expose a person's most intimate vulnerabilities.

Sitting back in her chair, Emma let out a long, shuddering breath. This was not a game. This was not a novelty. She was dancing on the edge of a precipice, and one wrong step could send her tumbling down. She finished off the wine, the burn of the alcohol a temporary distraction from the weight of her thoughts. As she placed the empty bottle on the table, she knew one thing for sure: things were never going to be the same again.

Emma sat in her cluttered flat, the old camera sitting ominously on her rickety table. It felt heavier now, burdened with the secrets it held. It wasn't just a camera anymore, it was a bearer of truths, a revealer of the hidden and the lost. And it was hers to wield, hers to control.

She let her gaze settle on the instrument, a newfound respect sparking within her. The thing had power, real power, and it was up to her to harness it right, to do justice to the voices it unearthed. She was no saviour, no white knight, but she had a tool that could make a difference, and she was damn well going to use it.

Her thoughts trailed back to her friend, her usually vibrant eyes now echoing with a silent sorrow. Emma had been oblivious, but she was aware now. She wouldn't turn a blind eye anymore. She couldn't. She owed her friend that much, owed it to her to be there, to listen when she was ready to talk. Her own troubles felt insignificant compared to the raw, unvoiced pain her friend carried.

She grabbed a pen and a scrap of paper, jotting down a promise to herself - to use the camera responsibly, to be there for her friend. The words were a contract, a commitment she was making to herself and the world. The weight of it settled in her gut, a rock of resolve anchoring her down. She was stepping into uncharted territories, a brave new world that she was ill-equipped to navigate. But she'd learned one thing, if nothing else - she was tougher than she gave herself credit for. She'd stumble, she'd falter, but she wouldn't break.

Finishing off the remnants of her cheap wine, she stood up, the room spinning a little from the alcohol. But amidst the blur and the confusion, one thing was clear - Emma was ready. Ready to step into the fray, to embrace her new reality. Because if there was one thing life had taught her, it was that it had a habit of throwing curveballs. And she was getting bloody good at catching them.

Emma was an island now, isolated by a sea of truth she hadn't asked for but had to swim in nonetheless. But islands didn't sink, and neither would she. Not now, not when she was finally making sense of the tidal waves crashing over her. She was wiser now, hardened by the trials of the past and armed with a camera that exposed more than just pretty faces.

She took a moment to reflect, her gaze roaming around her flat, lingering on the photos scattered around, the stories they whispered. Stories of loss, of pain, of secrets well-guarded behind carefully painted smiles. She thought of her friend, her sorrow revealed through the unforgiving lens of the camera, her own unsuspecting oblivion, her newly embraced sexuality. She'd been on a roller coaster, and she was just catching her breath.

The camera lay on the table, quiet, unassuming, belying the power it held within. It wasn't just a camera anymore. It was a weapon of truth, a bearer of raw reality. It didn't judge, didn't embellish, it just showed you as you were. And that was its magic and its curse.

Looking forward, Emma knew she had a path to tread. She had seen what the camera could reveal, and she was now bracing herself for the journey that awaited her. There was a lot she didn't know, about herself, about those around her. But she was willing to find out, willing to weather the storm. The camera was her compass, guiding her through the murky waters of hidden truths, leading her to stories untold.

She was eager, thirsty to dive deeper, to unearth more, to help where she could. She had been given a unique gift, one that could bring about change, understanding, maybe even healing. She held the power to shine a light into the darkest corners, to expose the truths that lie buried beneath facades. And she was ready. Ready to take up the mantle, to carry the responsibility that came with it.

The camera was her tool, her guide. It was a part of her now, as much as she was a part of it. She was ready to embrace it, to leverage its power for good. It was no longer a simple device, but a conduit for truth, for transformation. And Emma was the woman to wield it. The woman who would step into the chaos, undeterred, unapologetic, driven by a desire to understand and to help.

With a sigh, she picked up the camera, feeling its weight, its promise, its potential. She had a long road ahead, but she was ready. Ready to face the world, one secret at a time.

Acceptance

Emma sat in the guts of her flat, her eyes raking over the chaos that yesterday's shoot had left behind. Her trusted camera, a weather-beaten Argus C3, was sprawled on the table, its glass eye indifferent to the turmoil it had sparked. Fair dinkum, that bloody thing had a knack for stirring the pot, revealing the raw, hidden sorrows of her mate.

The harsh truth was still a slap in the face, a kick in the guts. Emma clung to her cup of coffee, the warmth bleeding into her palms, a poor antidote to the cold dread snaking its way up her spine. She felt like a bushwalker who'd unwittingly stumbled upon a tiger snake, deadly and fascinating all at once.

She rested her head on her hands, raking her fingers through her mousy brown hair. Her pulse banged away in her ears like a bloke gone troppo on the drums. The weight of the responsibility was a yoke, as real as the setting Aussie sun casting long shadows in her room.

Her gaze fell back on the Argus C3. It was more than just a clicker of pretty pictures now; it was a key to Pandora's box, a revealer of deep, dark secrets. The realization gave her a sinking feeling, like stepping into a billabong, expecting to feel the squish of mud, and finding a bottomless pit instead. The aftershocks of this knowledge clung to her, like sticky beer residue on a pub table.

The Argus C3, as always, stared back, its one-eyed gaze impenetrable. The power at her fingertips, the responsibility, was no laughing matter. It was as serious as a snakebite, as delicate as holding a redback spider. The fear of what lay ahead nibbled at her insides, like a possum at a backyard veggie patch.

She was at a crossroads. One path led to her stashing the Argus C3 away, letting dust claim it, and the other path held the promise of diving into the unknown, challenging the shackles of convention.

It was like being asked to choose between a rough as guts swag in the bush or a cushy bed in the city. She knew she had a ripper of a decision to make. The question was, was she game enough to face the bushfire her choice might ignite?

In the grungy haven of her flat, Emma studied the Argus C3 sprawled across her messy table. She had to squint through the smoke of her cigarette, its pungent aroma mingling with the stale air of her dingy digs. Her heart swam in a cocktail of awe, fear, and determination; it was like staring down a salty croc in the billabong.

The camera, with its uncanny knack for uncovering truth, had a presence now. It was as real as a surfer wrestling a gnarly wave, as potent as a hard-earned thirst quenched by a cold one at sundown. Her fingers twitched with an odd yearning to caress the worn leather of the Argus, to wrap around the chilly metal of its body. Fear gnawed at the edges of her courage, sharp as a shark's tooth and as nagging as a blowfly in the outback.

"Strewth," she muttered, staring into the camera's unblinking eye. It held a world of secrets, more potent than a witch's brew. The knowledge it possessed could shake the foundations of any bloke or sheila's existence. It was enough to send shivers down a brumby's spine. And she, Emma, was its reluctant custodian.

Her mind buzzed, like a mob of roos bounding through her thoughts. She was a simple photographer, not a bloody oracle. But she knew deep in her gut that ditching the camera was as foolish as telling a boxing kangaroo to play nice. This was her rodeo now.

A sigh wriggled past her lips as she nodded, a silent conversation with the Argus. "Alright, ya old drongo," she whispered, a smirk tugging at her mouth. "You and me, we're in this together."

Emma would keep the camera, and in doing so, she'd wield its truth-baring power. She was a sheila with a mission, committed to shining a light on the hidden truths, the silent battles everyone faced. She'd decided to wrangle this unpredictable beast, not for the thrills or the glory, but for the chance to help others understand their own hidden truths. It was a ripper of a job, but someone had to do it. And that someone was Emma, a chick armed with nothing more than her resilience, her Argus C3, and a gut full of determination. The real adventure was just beginning. She was ready, like a jackaroo at his first rodeo, to take the bull by the horns and ride into the unknown.

With the decision made, the Argus C3 was her mate now, for better or for worse. Emma set up her tiny flat for a new shoot. This time, she was both the shutterbug and the subject, preparing to catch a glimpse of her own bloomin' soul.

The room was as silent as the bush at midnight as she positioned herself before the camera. The light from the bulb cast long shadows, adding an eerie ambience to the room, like a spooky yarn spun around a campfire. She peered into the camera, her heart pounding like a cat on a hot tin roof, and clicked the shutter. The flash was blinding, an electric whip cutting through the gloom, capturing her essence within its silent confines.

Back in the darkroom, the smell of developer hung heavy in the air, a bitter symphony that played in tune with her beating heart. Emma watched as her own image appeared on the photo paper, like a ghost materialising out of the night. It was a daunting sight, seeing her own self from an outsider's perspective.

Her eyes held a mixture of grit and vulnerability, the same she'd seen in countless others but never acknowledged in herself. The rawness of her own emotions was as startling as a snake in the dunny. There were layers she'd never noticed, depths she'd never plumbed. It was like diving into the Great Barrier Reef, finding new wonders with every blink.

"Well, I'll be a bluey's uncle," she muttered, her voice a whisper against the stony silence. The realization that she too had her own silent battles was as grounding as the red dust of the outback. The woman in the photo was Emma, but a version she was yet to fully comprehend, as mystifying as a bunyip's tale.

She was a sheila with a wild heart, but also a girl with a swirl of emotions tucked away in the recesses of her soul. She realised she was like an ancient gum tree, with roots buried deep and unseen, bearing the brunt of the seasons, while still reaching for the sky. The rawness of this insight was a slap in the face, a reminder of her own humanity.

As Emma stared at her own image, a sense of understanding blossomed within her. She was no different from those she photographed - just another soul grappling with life's punches, trying to stay afloat. The camera had given her a glimpse of her own struggles, her own story etched in her eyes, and it was a truth she was ready to face. It was high time she showed the world the real Emma, warts and all. Because beneath the rough exterior, she was just a girl armed with a camera and a bucket load of dreams, ready to brave the wild, wild world.

Emma, under the harsh glow of a single, stubborn bulb in her flat, pondered her decision. She was as still as a goanna sunning itself on a rock, the Argus C3 clutched in her firm grip. She was the keeper of a unique power, a window into the souls of others. Her gut twisted, like a croc's death roll, at the thought of it.

There was power in the shutter's snap, in the stark flash, in the hush of the darkroom as images bloomed onto paper, and, crikey, there was power in the truths those images whispered. It was a power that could destroy or heal, depending on how it was wielded. Emma wasn't blind to the responsibility it entailed.

She knew she had a choice. She could use her camera, with its otherworldly knack, as a tool for harm, like a huntsman spider lurking in the shadows, waiting to strike. Or, she could use it to help, to heal, to uncover hidden truths and encourage self-discovery. It was a billy lids' game to guess what she chose.

A flicker of determination sparked in her eyes, the same way dry bush ignites under a fierce summer sun. She would use the Argus, not as a weapon, but as a balm. She would approach her subjects tactfully, as cautious as a wallaby sniffing out a dingo. She knew too well the devastation of having one's secrets laid bare, the shattering vulnerability it induced.

She'd show them their photos, not as a gotcha moment but as a gentle nudge towards introspection, a prompt to start a conversation with their own souls. She'd respect their privacy, tread lightly around their emotional states, because she was not just a photographer now, she was a custodian of hidden truths. It wasn't about sensationalism, it was about healing, about bringing the shadows into the light.

Emma stared at the Argus, its lens reflecting her newfound resolve. A surge of anticipation rushed through her, a wild river after the wet season rains. She was about to embark on a journey, stepping off the beaten track into the unknown. There'd be hurdles, sure as eggs, but she was ready to face them head on. Emma, the girl with the mystical camera, was set to play her part, to tell untold stories, to help people see themselves through a new lens. With the snap of a shutter, her path was set.

Emma had always been a dab hand at taking photos, but now the stakes were different. Now it was more than just playing with lights and shadows, it was about reaching into the soul, about capturing the whispers of the heart. It was bloody terrifying, and, in a perverse way, intoxicating too.

She started off slow, like a roo testing the waters before taking the plunge. She put out a call for models, offering free photoshoots under the guise of wanting to build her portfolio. A harmless lie, she reckoned, a smokescreen to hide the true purpose of her venture. Emma wasn't about to spill the beans about her camera's uncanny abilities; she was no drongo.

Word spread around like a bushfire on a dry day. Free photoshoots, taken by Emma with her old-school Argus C3? You bet your boots, people were interested. They started trickling in, friends, acquaintances, even a few curious strangers.

She watched them as they preened and posed, their smiles frozen, eyes vacant. And then the Argus would click, capturing more than just their well-practiced smiles. It snapped their truth, their pain, their joy, their fears. Emma wondered if she'd be able to bear the weight of so many truths.

After the shoots, she'd retreat to her flat, developing the photos in her makeshift darkroom. Each photo was like unwrapping a present, a surprise, a revelation, a secret told in hushed tones. It was exciting, and yet, there was a gnawing unease, a fear of what she might uncover next.

She found herself knee-deep in a sea of emotions, of revelations she wasn't prepared for. But she held her ground. This was the path she'd chosen, and she wasn't about to wuss out. It was her little mission, to coax the hidden truths out, to show people their own reflections through the lens of her magical Argus C3.

She hoped this first step, as shaky as it was, would lead to something meaningful. Perhaps she could make a difference, however small, in people's lives. As the sun set on another day, casting long, quivering shadows in her room, Emma was both hopeful and scared. The road was long, and the journey had only just begun. But she was ready. As ready as a sheila could be with a mystical camera and a heart full of hope.

Emma was no stranger to the tall poppy syndrome, but the resistance she met from some was like a gut punch. There were snide remarks, offhand comments, whispers behind her back. The camera? That old thing? You've got to be having a lend of me! But she'd expected this. She'd steeled herself for the backlash, the scepticism. Even so, it got under her skin, like sand in her swimmers.

But she didn't let the naysayers get to her. She was like a wallaby on a mission, bouncing back each time, more determined than before. She kept at it, clicking and developing, revealing and unveiling. Each photo a story, each story a life.

The pictures were raw and powerful, the emotions palpable. Some couldn't bear to look, others wouldn't stop looking. There were tears, there were smiles, and then there were those who stared back at her, their eyes holding a question, a plea, a challenge. The camera's uncanny revelations were hard to digest for some, a sucker punch right in the feels.

Emma had to tread carefully, like a surfer navigating a choppy sea, maintaining a delicate balance between showing people their hidden truths and not overstepping personal boundaries. It was a tightrope walk, a dance with the devil. But she learnt, and she adapted. She became as tactful as a diplomat, as gentle as a mother kangaroo with a joey in her pouch.

She was still learning the ropes, understanding the dynamics of her newfound ability. It was uncharted territory, risky and fraught with challenges. She knew she was meddling with something powerful, something sacred. But she also knew that she was onto something, something that could help, something that could heal.

She was showing people what they were hiding from themselves, and in doing so, she was forcing them to confront their fears, their insecurities, their hidden sorrows. It was a bitter pill to swallow, but there was a catharsis in that confrontation, a liberation. It was tough as old boots, but it was necessary.

Emma had taken the plunge, and there was no turning back now. The challenges were part of the journey, the humps in the road that she had to navigate. And navigate she would, with her camera in hand and a fire in her belly. The world could throw whatever it wanted at her, she was ready to face it head on.

Emma found herself in a pub on a Sunday arvo, cold frothy beer in hand, her mind spinning like a waltzer. She'd always been a bit of a wallflower, preferring to observe than to participate. But now, things were different. There was a subtle shift in the air around her, like the first whiff of an oncoming storm, a change so profound yet so subtle it was almost imperceptible.

Each person she'd photographed had left an imprint on her, like footprints on the sand. Their stories, their sorrows, their joys, their secrets, they all intermingled with her own, creating a tapestry that was as complex as it was beautiful. She wasn't just an observer anymore, she was a part of it, a part of them. It was as if she'd swallowed a magic pill, and she could suddenly understand people better, feel their emotions more keenly. It was all a bit dizzying, a bit surreal, like standing on the edge of a precipice, the wind whipping through her hair, the earth seeming to tilt under her feet.

Her heart felt heavier, but it also felt fuller. It was like she'd grown a second skin, one that was more sensitive, more intuitive, more accepting. She had started seeing people beyond their facades, acknowledging their complexities, their quirks, their flaws. She was getting better at reading people, reading their silences, their expressions, their body language. She was understanding people, not just their words, but also their unspoken thoughts, their hidden fears, their secret dreams.

With every click of her camera, every splash of developer on the photographic paper, she was peeling away layers, unveiling the raw, unvarnished truth. It was unsettling, it was revealing, it was liberating. It made her feel vulnerable, yet powerful. She was helping people see themselves in a new light, and in the process, she was seeing herself differently too.

In the solitary confines of her darkroom, Emma felt a sense of peace wash over her. She was right where she was supposed to be, doing what she was meant to do. It was a feeling as comforting as a cuppa on a cold day, as exhilarating as a dip in the ocean on a hot summer's day. She had accepted her role, her responsibility, and she was ready to face whatever came her way. She had learnt to accept the good, the bad, the ugly, the beautiful. She had learnt to accept life, in all its maddening complexities. She had learnt to accept people, in all their glorious imperfections. And above all, she had learnt to accept herself, with all her faults, all her strengths, all her fears, all her dreams. It was acceptance in its purest form.

Emma noticed a subtle change in her subjects as they left her makeshift studio. It wasn't just a hint of satisfaction from a job well done or the lightness of a fun day out, it was something deeper. It was like they'd been carrying a swag full of rocks, and she'd helped them unload, leaving them standing taller, breathing easier. Some even admitted to it, in hushed voices, as if they were confessing to a sin. They said they felt lighter, freer, as though they'd been carrying a heavy load and had suddenly let it go.

It struck her then, like a boomerang returning with full force. She was making a difference. She was lifting veils, unveiling truths, and in doing so, she was helping people understand themselves better. She was helping them lighten their loads, helping them let go of the ghosts that haunted them, helping them confront the demons they had been dodging.

It was an intoxicating feeling, knowing she was making a difference, no matter how small. It was as satisfying as a cold beer after a hard day's work, as comforting as a hot cuppa on a cold winter's night. It was a sensation that filled her up, made her feel like she was glowing from the inside. It was like she was a sparkler on a dark night, lighting up the world around her in little ways, leaving a trail of stardust behind.

She wasn't just a photographer anymore, she was a guide, a friend, a confidante. She was someone who was helping people navigate the labyrinth of their minds, helping them find their way, helping them understand themselves better. The realisation filled her with a sense of purpose, a sense of achievement. She felt like a prospector who'd finally hit gold, a gambler who'd won a jackpot, a surfer who'd caught the perfect wave.

It was a high unlike any other. It was like riding a wild brumby, holding on for dear life, heart pounding, wind whipping through her hair, adrenaline coursing through her veins. It was like climbing a mountain and reaching the summit, gazing out at the world stretched out below, feeling on top of the world. It was like standing in the ocean, letting the waves wash over her, cleansing her, refreshing her, invigorating her.

She felt alive, truly alive, for the first time in a long while. She felt fulfilled, content, at peace with herself. She knew she had a long road ahead, with its fair share of challenges, but she also knew she was ready to face them head-on. She was ready to ride the waves, ready to climb the mountains, ready to embrace the storm. She was ready to live, really live. And it was all thanks to a beat-up old camera and a bunch of beautiful, complex, fascinating people who had trusted her with their stories.

Emma sat alone in her flat, the only sounds the low hum of the refrigerator and the occasional rumble of a car passing by outside. The Argus C3 sat on the table in front of her, its glass eye reflecting the weak light that filtered through the blinds. Its presence was like a wild dingo's—unpredictable and slightly unsettling, yet strangely fascinating.

She'd come to accept the camera for what it was—a revealer of truths, a catalyst for change, a silent companion on a journey she'd never signed up for, but was now fully committed to. It was no longer just a hunk of metal and glass; it had become an extension of her, a part of her identity. It was a part of her story, as integral as the red earth of the outback, the blistering sun, the eucalyptus-scented air.

She thought about the people she'd photographed, the lives she'd touched, the secrets she'd unveiled. It was like gazing into a billabong, its calm surface hiding a world of complexity beneath. It was an emotional rollercoaster ride, one that often left her feeling drained, like a bottle of beer left out in the sun. But it was a journey she wouldn't trade for anything else.

Each photograph was a story, a glimpse into the human soul, a revelation of hidden pains and secret joys. It was like bushwalking in uncharted territories, never knowing what you'd stumble upon next. It was raw, it was real, it was life—in all its messiness and unpredictability.

Emma knew the road ahead wasn't going to be easy. The camera, for all its power, was a ruthless beast. It peeled back layers, leaving her subjects exposed, vulnerable. It took a toll on her too, the emotional weight sometimes becoming almost too much to bear. She felt like a drover, herding a group of skittish cattle, navigating through the rough and the smooth, the calm and the storm.

But as she sat there, looking at the Argus C3, she realized that she wouldn't have it any other way. She had accepted her gift and the responsibility that came with it. It was like accepting the venomous critters and the scorching heat as part of the Australian landscape—challenging, intimidating, but ultimately, a part of who she was.

She would continue to wield her camera, continue to document the undocumentable, continue to reveal the hidden. She was as determined as a thirsty 'roo searching for water, as relentless as the Aussie sun beating down on the red earth. She was ready for the journey, ready to face whatever came her way. She was ready to embrace her gift, ready to embrace her destiny. Emma had accepted her camera's power, and with it, she had accepted her purpose.

With her decision cemented, Emma was awash with a strange mix of emotions – apprehension, excitement, a hint of fear. It was like standing at the edge of the outback, peering into the endless expanse of red dirt and eucalyptus, not knowing what lay beyond the horizon. She was no stranger to the unknown, but this was different, it was a bonzer of a challenge.

The camera, her trusty Argus C3, seemed to mock her with its silent stare. It was the source of her turmoil and the key to her exhilarating journey. It was her ticket to a dance with the raw, undiluted essence of human existence.

She was in for a long haul, and she knew it. She'd be dealing with emotions as volatile as a summer bushfire, revealing truths as hidden as a 'roo in the bush at dusk. She'd be peeling back layers, digging deeper than a wombat burrow into the labyrinth of human psyche. It was a ride she'd volunteered for, one she intended to stick with, come hell or high water.

There was no turning back now. The road stretched ahead, inviting and daunting in equal measure. She was like a wallaby, eyes gleaming in the headlights, frozen with the enormity of the situation, yet filled with a wild, instinctive urge to leap forward.

Her days of being a naive shutterbug were done and dusted. The Argus C3 had opened a door, one she could never shut. It had thrust her into a world where the facade of human pretences was ripped away, leaving only the raw, unvarnished truth.

Emma knew she had to tread carefully, be as stealthy as a saltwater croc stalking its prey. The stakes were high, the consequences potentially devastating. Yet, the allure of the challenge, the thrill of the hunt was too powerful to resist.

As the last of the evening light streamed in through the window, bathing the room in a warm, orange glow, Emma cradled the camera in her hands, her thoughts lost in the journey ahead. She was no longer a mere photographer, but a seer of truths, a navigator of emotions, a custodian of stories.

Yes, the road was going to be as rough as an outback track, and yes, she was going to get her hands dirty. But as she sat there, with the Argus C3 in her hands, she knew she wouldn't have it any other way. She was Emma, the woman with the magical camera, the woman unafraid to step into the unknown. And with that, she welcomed the future, the labyrinth of human emotions, and the myriad of stories waiting to be captured.

The Healer

Emma was feeling as dry as a dead dingo's donger in the emotional department, a void taking up residence where a fire used to be. When she wasn't lost behind the lens of her Argus C3, she was prowling art exhibitions, losing herself in the crowd, a drifter in a sea of artistic pretensions.

That's where she first clapped eyes on him – Man A. Bloke looked like he'd stepped straight out of a bushranger film – dominant, assertive, bristling with a raw sexual energy that made the little hairs on the back of Emma's neck stand at attention. He looked like the kind of man who ate the problems of life like a meat pie – with tomato sauce and without a napkin. A bloke with rough hands and a gaze that felt like it could pin you to the spot. He was as alluring as a waterhole in the outback, and twice as dangerous.

Then there was Man B. As different from the first bloke as a dingo is from a roo. Soft-spoken, kind-hearted, his smile was as comforting as a hot cuppa on a cold morning. His eyes didn't pin you, they enveloped you. His attention was like balm on sunburnt skin – gentle and soothing. His attraction was the quiet kind, like the whisper of the wind through the wattle, but just as pervasive.

Both blokes were gobsmacked by Emma. Not just by her looks – though she was as striking as a sunset over Uluru – but also by her talent. Her photographs held a stark reality that was as uncomfortable as a bindi in a swag, forcing people to confront truths they'd rather ignore. And for some strange reason, these men, these polar opposites, were drawn in by her lens, by her.

There was a raw hunger in her, a need to be filled, to be satisfied, and these men, these two raw slabs of masculinity, offered her a feast. It was a dangerous game she was about to play, as treacherous as a walkabout in the dead heart. But the spark in her eyes, the upturn of her lips, it told a different story. Emma was ready to dance with the devils. It was game on, mates.

Emma found herself caught between the blokes like a roo in the headlights. The raw, pulsing energy of Man A was like a bonfire on a cold bush night, wild and unpredictable, it beckoned her, promising danger and excitement. His every glance was a challenge, a provocation, as blatant as a bogan's mullet, and just as hard to ignore. He was a cyclone, tearing through her thoughts, stirring up a hunger in her that was as old as time.

Then there was Man B, as comforting as a winter's soup, his warm eyes filled with understanding and care. He was the kind of bloke you could share a tinny with under the stars, swapping stories about the one that got away. His quiet intensity was a balm to her restless spirit, a promise of warmth and comfort in the bleak desert of her loneliness.

Emma found herself on the edge of a precipice, caught in the tug-of-war of her own desires. It was as intoxicating as a long pull from a cold bottle of VB after a day in the sun, as tempting as a fresh pie from a roadside bakery. Her body was an opera of anticipation, each nerve ending singing a different tune, the symphony of her desires building to a crescendo.

A wicked idea sparked in her mind, as brilliant as a lightning strike in the outback, its reflection dancing in her eyes. She would take them both, Man A and Man B, let them stoke the fires of her desire till she was burnt out and satisfied. It was a mad plan, as crazy as a drunken galah, but Emma was all in. She decided to go troppo, to let herself be swept away in the flood of her own erotic needs.

She approached them, her gaze as daring as a larrikin on a Friday night, her lips curled in a sultry smile. "Gentlemen," she said, her voice low and husky, "how about we go on a little walkabout together?" Emma was no longer playing it safe; she was betting the house on a pair of jokers, throwing caution to the wind like a boomerang. And like a boomerang, she was eager to see where it would land.

The night was as thick as a black-stump bush, and her flat was the stage for a dance as old as time. Emma, the conductor of this wild symphony, sat perched on the edge of her ragged couch, Man A and Man B flanking her like bookends.

Man A, as brash as a rowdy dingo, was all hands and hungry eyes. He took his pleasure as if it was his right, his greedy touches threatening to set her ablaze. There was a rough, unapologetic eroticism to his actions, a stark contrast to the tenderness of Man B. He was as gentle as a lamb in a spring meadow, his fingers tracing her skin as if she was a treasured work of art, his love and care washing over her like a warm rain on a summer evening.

Yet, amidst this heady whirlpool of desires, Emma didn't forget the golden rule of the bush – the survival of the fittest. As Man A tried to steer the ship, she tossed him overboard with a smirk, taking the reins in her hands. She was no damsel to be saved, but a sheila in control, dictating her own desires.

Man B watched the exchange, his soft gaze steady as a gum tree in a storm, love pouring out from him like sunshine on a perfect beach day. But Emma was no delicate blossom to be pampered, she was the raging bushfire consuming everything in her path, and she set his gentleness aside, making sure her hunger was satiated first.

The night wore on, a dance of desires and power play as heady as some outback moonshine. Emma was in control, a lioness in her den, the men her willing prey. The dance of bodies, the exchange of power, filled the room with a heat that rivalled a summer in the Kimberley's, their primal sounds echoing off the faded wallpaper like a chorus of kookaburras at dawn.

As the morning sun trickled in, streaking the room in shades of gold, Emma found herself tangled in the crumpled bed sheets, the remnants of the previous night's debauchery scattered around her room. The scent of sweat and passion hung heavy in the air, serving as a stark reminder of the dance she had engaged in just hours ago.

But as Emma lay there, she felt as hollow as a gumtree ravaged by termites. The lust that had fuelled her the previous night had burnt out, leaving a charred void in its wake. The intimacy, the shared whispers, the entangled bodies; it all seemed like a surreal dream, fading with the break of dawn.

The space in the bed, flanked by the bodies of the two men, seemed to encroach on her personal territory. A deep, unyielding desire to reclaim her solitude began to gnaw at her. She shook off the bed sheets and slowly extricated herself from the tangle of limbs, the cool morning air against her bare skin bringing a semblance of clarity.

She moved to the kitchen, her every step asserting her dominion over her personal space. The guilt that tried to grip her was swatted away as swiftly as a troublesome fly. This was her life, her rules. She wasn't some bloke's Sheila to be owned, but a free spirit, like a lone galah soaring in the limitless outback sky.

She filled the kettle, the noise breaking the awkward silence. "Time for a cuppa," she said, her voice cutting through the morning stillness. It wasn't an offer, it was a wake-up call. The men, their faces a mix of confusion and annoyance, stirred at her voice. "Once we're done with the brew, it's time to hit the frog and toad, mates," she declared, her tone devoid of any sentiment.

Man A, his arrogance still present under his morning scruff, tried to argue. "Hey, now, Emma," he said, his voice rough as sandpaper. "We just got carried away last night. No need to be all shitty about it."

And Man B, soft as a lamb, attempted a plea. "Emma," he murmured, "surely you don't mean that."

But Emma was as unmovable as Uluru. "Don't try to pull the wool over my eyes," she snapped, her eyes as hard as the opals of

Coober Pedy. "It's time to hit the frog and toad. I'm not your nursemaid or your doll to be toyed with."

With that, she ushered them towards the door, their protests echoing off the flat walls. Despite their blustering and pleading, Emma stood her ground, as tough as a seasoned stockman. This was her life, her rodeo, and she would hold the reins.

And so, with a final shove, she saw them out, the door slamming shut with a sound as final as a judge's gavel. She leaned against the door, her breath hitching as the reality of her actions settled in. But there was no regret, no second thoughts. Just the pure, heady rush of reclaiming her space, her independence.

As she stood there, the silence of the flat seemed to echo back her triumph. She had discarded the remnants of the night before like a snake shedding its old skin, ready to embrace the new day. And in the quiet of the morning, with the past firmly shown the door, Emma felt free, like a bird soaring high in the outback sky, ready to chart its own course.

The flat was her kingdom again, stripped bare of the ghosts of last night's company. Emma took a deep breath, savouring the sense of solitude like a cold brew on a stinking hot day. Her life was back on her own terms. Her lovers of the night had become yesterday's fish and chip paper, discarded and forgotten, leaving only the memory of satisfaction in their wake.

She perched on the edge of her bed, running her fingers over the tangled sheets, an ephemeral trace of her night of passion. The men had been the fire in the cool of her evening, but now they were extinguished, leaving her in her peaceful solitude.

There was a relief, like the end of a long, gruelling footy match. Emma was the lone player, the one who had seized control, defended her turf and discarded the opposition like unwanted clutter. The satisfaction washed over her like the cool ocean waves, raw and intoxicating.

Her gaze found her Argus C3 sitting on the table, a silent observer of her exploits. She felt a strange kinship with it. Like her, it revealed hidden truths, then detached itself, offering no judgment or lingering attachment.

In the stark light of her solitude, Emma made a decision. Her heart was a free bird, untamed and wild, it wasn't to be caged by the needs of another. No man, no matter how thrilling or tender, would be allowed to stake his claim, to cast a long shadow over her solitude. She'd crack the whip, kept them at bay, let them be passing clouds, never the immovable mountains.

With a nod to herself, she rose from the bed, striding across her flat like a queen inspecting her realm. Her life was an open road under the vast Aussie sky, and she'd be damned if she let anyone but herself take the wheel. The world outside waited, teeming with secrets to capture and experiences to savour, Emma, with her camera and her steely resolve, was more than ready to dive headlong into the fray, alone but never lonely. She was an island, strong and untamed, in the vast sea of life.

Emma, feeling cleansed and renewed, swept through her flat like a whirlwind, scrubbing away all traces of the previous night's exploits. Sheets were washed, glasses cleaned, every memory of the men erased as if they were just figments of a dream. It felt like a hard-earned victory, a necessary ritual to reclaim her space, her freedom. She viewed her actions not with guilt, but as a self-fulfilling prophecy. She'd become a sheila who satisfied her own needs without any bloody compromise.

The air in the flat started to change, losing the musky remnants of passion and replacing them with a clean, crisp scent that smelled like fresh beginnings. Emma, the queen of her domain, stood amidst the organised chaos, an artist ready to dive back into her world of unspoken truths and hidden emotions.

Her trusted Argus C3 called out to her, perched on the table like a loyal mate, ready to take on the world again. There was no judgment, no lingering strings of attachment, just the promise of more secrets to reveal, more lives to touch. She took it in her hands, feeling the cool, reassuring weight of her purpose.

Each click of the camera was a heartbeat, each picture a life touched. Her own desires, raw and fleeting as they were, had no place here. She was an artist, a medium between the unsaid and the visible, the emotions and their acknowledgement.

There was a sense of satisfaction, a sense of rightness, as Emma found herself behind the lens again. Her previous night's adventure was a necessary detour, a diversion to fuel her own needs. Now, her path was clear, undistracted by personal desires. She was a professional, her mission unclouded by personal attachments.

As she snapped a picture of the empty flat, the click echoing in the silence felt like an affirmation, a seal on her resolve. The image captured her world in its raw, honest form, free of anyone's lingering presence. She looked at the image, feeling a rush of empowerment.

Emma stood tall, the heaviness of the past discarded like last season's fashion. She was the woman behind the camera, the capturer of emotions, the storyteller. The world outside her door was teeming with unspoken stories, waiting to be unearthed, and she, with her Argus C3, was ready to listen.

Feeling invigorated, a sense of anticipation prickling her skin like the first touch of summer. Emma knew she was embarking on a challenging path, but she was armed with her determination, her camera, and her absolute independence. She had a mission to accomplish, a destiny to fulfill, and she wasn't about to let anything, let alone fleeting personal desires, distract her from it. Emma was ready to face the world, one click at a time.

Miracle Worker

The solitary fortress of Emma's studio, once a hermit's cave of quietude, was now a buzzing beehive echoing with life. Her art, her ability to coax hidden emotions into the light through her camera, had caused a stir. Like a pebble dropped in a still billabong, the ripples of her work swelled and swirled, touching the sandy edges of the vast Australian outback, whispering into the bustling heart of the urban cities, and resonating in the cosy homes of coastal towns.

The old country telegraph, the bush telegraph, was a flutter with tales of Emma's uncanny knack. From the lonely red dust plains where roos and emus shared the vast nothingness, to the coastal pubs filled with weathered surfers and sun-kissed beachcombers, murmurs of the miracle worker stirred the air. News of the bird who could capture your soul, and through that capture heal wounds unseen, spread like a bushfire in the dry season.

"Ever heard of Emma, the sheila with the camera?" one might whisper into his schooner at the pub. "They reckon she can see into your soul; help you mend what's been broken. Worth a shot, ain't it?"

And so, the wild Australian winds carried the tales, woven with awe and hope, and the curious came knocking at Emma's door, like moths drawn to a flame. The studio, which had been her sanctuary, was now flooded with souls bearing the weight of their past, their stories hanging in the air like the scent of eucalyptus after rain. Strangers, yet connected by the thread of shared human experience, they all sought solace in Emma's art, in her remarkable talent to reveal, heal, and help them move forward.

The serenity of Emma's life, once as still and calm as a billabong at sunset, was stirred up into a whirling dust storm. Her studio, a space once dedicated solely to the intimate dance between her and her camera, was now a bustling terminal of human suffering and hope. Blokes and sheilas from every corner of the land made the pilgrimage to her doorstep. Leathered stockmen who'd spent their lives wrestling the harsh outback, city slickers with their quick talk and flash attire, everyone, it seemed, had a hankering for a bit of Emma's healing touch.

It was like the whole country had heard tell of a gold rush, only the gold was not glittering nuggets nestled in the dirt, but a chance at a cleansed soul, a shot at laying bare the wounds they'd been nursing in private, hoping for a touch of healing from behind Emma's lens.

This deluge of human thirst took Emma by surprise. She'd been prepared for the trickles, the rivulets, but this was a flood. It was as if the skies had opened up, and a torrent of longing, pain, hope, and despair was pouring down upon her. But, she wasn't a delicate wattle flower to be washed away by the first sign of a storm; she was as stubborn as a gnarled old gum tree, rooted deeply into the ground. Emma, the woman who'd held her own against both love and lust, who'd chosen solitude over companionship, was not about to be swept away by this tide.

And so, amid the chaos of this unexpected human avalanche, Emma stood tall. Her tranquil life may have been disrupted, her solitude may have been invaded, but she was not going to buckle. She anchored herself in the storm, holding fast to the principles that had guided her life so far – the love for her art, the belief in its healing power, and the resilience of the solitary outback spirit within her. This was her storm to weather, her chaos to navigate, and if the bloody universe thought it could throw her off course, it had another thing coming. Emma was ready. She was ready to face this gathering storm head-on.

Emma was like a boomerang, forever destined to circle back to her beginnings. As she navigated through the maze of her subjects' souls, peeling back layers of grime to reveal their raw essence, echoes of her own past came bouncing back. Like spectres rising from the red dust of the outback, fragments of her personal history surfaced, demanding attention.

It was as if each click of her shutter, each flash of her camera was a beacon, calling forth the ghosts of her past. Faint whisperings of unresolved issues and hidden wounds slipped through the cracks of her fortified defences, staining the canvas of her consciousness with their murky ink. This wasn't just about the souls she was healing through her lens, it was about her own soul, riddled with the scars of yesteryears, that was demanding healing.

Flashes of a dingy flat, the reek of stale beer and disappointment heavy in the air, began to play out in her mind. A drunken father who loved his bottle more than his daughter. A mother who disappeared before dawn, leaving behind nothing but a hollow echo of her once vibrant presence. A young Emma, caught between the crushing waves of abandonment and the sharp rocks of loneliness, learning to swim against the tide.

The memories were like shards of glass, cutting through the protective shell she'd carefully constructed over the years. They seeped into her present, casting a long, ominous shadow over her newfound purpose. But she was no stranger to the darkness. Like a seasoned drover navigating the bush under a starless sky, she acknowledged the shadows and kept moving, her resolve undiminished.

The flicker of her past in the frame of her present left the reader intrigued, a mystery to be solved, a puzzle to be pieced together. The whispers of her past raised questions. What shaped Emma into the woman she was today? What events in her life had bestowed her with this unique ability to heal? What was the source of her own hidden pain? The fragments of her story were scattered like breadcrumbs, teasing the reader to follow the trail, enticing them to delve deeper into the enigma that was Emma. Her journey wasn't just about healing others; it was about healing herself. Each click of her camera, each soul she touched was another step towards confronting her past and reclaiming her own wounded spirit.

Emma, the outback's unlikely saviour, manoeuvred through the murky swamps of her clients' emotions, her camera a divining rod attuned to the underground springs of hidden truths. Each click was an echo in the silent abyss of suppressed feelings, each frame a snapshot of unvarnished reality. Her lens was sharper than a jackaroo's shearing blade, cutting through facades and revealing the bare essence within.

Her subjects varied as widely as the landscape of the continent, each bearing the distinct imprint of their personal Outback. From hard-edged stockmen who'd spent a lifetime wrestling cattle and bottling up emotions, to city slickers in shiny loafers, their smiles as empty as the Nullarbor. The silence of the shutter echoed their untold stories, the film developed in a cocktail of honesty and vulnerability.

But dealing with this deluge of raw emotion was like trying to cradle the waters of the Murray-Darling in her hands. It was overwhelming, a flood threatening to burst the banks of her sanity. The flimsy separation between her clients' emotional chaos and her own serenity had started to erode. It was like she'd cracked open Pandora's box and the unleashed emotions refused to be tamed.

Each shutter release was like a dam break, allowing their pent-up sorrows and secret regrets to crash into her, leaving her drenched and shivering. Her own soul, already grappling with the spectres of her past, now had to serve as a vessel for others' pain. The residue of their suffering clung to her, a phantom weight that dragged her down into the quagmire of her own suppressed traumas.

She was the miracle worker, the healer, but the healing came at a cost. Each soul she helped was another stone added to the burden she bore. It was a lonely road, this journey of empathy and understanding. She became a solitary gum tree in the heart of the desert, providing shade for weary travellers but standing alone under the merciless sun.

At the close of the day, when the last of her clients had been seen, when the final frame was captured, Emma found herself alone with the echo of their pain. Her flat, once her sanctuary, now hummed with the silent reverberations of their stories. Despite her resilience, she felt the fringes of her spirit unravel, leaving her feeling as hollow as a didgeridoo.

But Emma was a fighter, a survivalist. She understood that healing was messy business, a bushfire that levelled the old to make way for the new. So, she clung onto her hope, her tenacity serving as her anchor in this stormy sea of emotions. She bore the brunt of their pain, turning it into art, a balm for their wounded spirits. And at the heart of it all, she found a strange sense of satisfaction, a purpose that fuelled her even when she felt emotionally spent.

Each dawn in Emma's world was like pulling a new grog from the fridge. It promised a certain buzz, but left an unsavoury aftertaste, a hangover that clung to her like a clingy joey to a mother roo. The relentless parade of clients, their stories, their tears, their hopes – it all tumbled into her life like a mob of roos, uprooting her calm and leaving a trail of emotional dust storms.

Her camera, once a medium of artistic expression, had now become an extension of her spirit, a conduit for the sorrows and joys of those who sought her out. The lens mirrored back at them their fears, their yearnings, their hidden selves. The flash illuminating their raw vulnerabilities was a stark contrast to the shadows that began to creep into Emma's heart.

She found herself treading water in the choppy sea of emotions she had inadvertently plunged into. As a lifeline to those teetering on the edge of despair, Emma felt an uncanny kinship with the vast Australian landscape - both sought to nurture, to comfort, despite bearing the scars of past trials and tribulations.

The tales she unravelled through her photos began to mirror her own neglected narrative. With each interaction, Emma found fragments of her past resurfacing, bobbing up like ghostly buoys in a forgotten harbour. Her own pains, once locked away in the vault of her mind, began to peek through the cracks, hungry for recognition.

The silence of her flat, a place that was once her fortress, echoed with the whispers of these forgotten stories. In the solitude of the twilight, her past rose from the shadows, prowling around the periphery of her mind, a feral cat waiting for the opportune moment to pounce.

Yet, in this maelstrom of memories and emotions, Emma found a paradoxical solace. It was in this cacophony that she found her rhythm, a resilience that had always been a part of her DNA. She was a dingo, solitary yet steadfast, navigating the harsh outback of her own past while providing sanctuary for those brave enough to face their demons under her lens.

The solitude of her space allowed her to regroup, to recharge. It was like the quiet after a vicious bushfire, where the seeds of resilience take root amidst the ashes, preparing to bloom anew. And so, each night, Emma would retreat into this silent cocoon, shedding the emotional fatigue of the day and bracing herself for the battles that lay ahead.

As Emma comforted others, the ghosts of her past began to howl louder. Each day was a duel, not only with her clients' demons but also with her own. But this is what Emma was - a fighter, a survivor, an artist who transformed pain into poignant portraits. And as she did, she left her audience, and herself, with a lingering question - What hidden stories lay behind the healer's own eyes?

The wave of humanity that descended on Emma's doorstep brought with it a storm of emotions, each face a testament of life's bitter-sweet symphony. Like sun-parched earth under a sudden deluge, Emma found herself soaking up the tales of heartache and triumph that were etched on the canvas of her clients' faces.

But as the days rolled on, like endless stretches of the Nullarbor, Emma found herself teetering on the edge of being completely swamped. The multitude of faces, their stories blending into a discordant orchestra of pain and relief, began to bear down on her like a scorching Aussie summer. There were moments when she felt as if she were standing in the eye of a cyclone, everything whirling around her, threatening to sweep her into its vortex.

Yet, amidst this whirlwind, she found pockets of peace in the solitude of her quiet moments. Away from the buzz of the studio, away from the expectant eyes and the shutter of her camera, Emma found an oasis. Like a cool billabong in the heart of the outback, solitude offered her respite, a place to quench her emotional thirst.

She was an arid desert, fiercely holding on to its solitude. But even the desert had its moments of bloom, its sporadic bursts of life. And so did Emma. She loved her work, the intimate dance of peeling back layers, of unearthing truths. But she realised, like the desert needing the rain, she needed these moments of quiet. They were not just a want, they were a necessity, as essential to her as the air she breathed.

With each passing day, the need for balance became evident, like the tell-tale signs of an approaching storm. It was a delicate dance between being the beacon for those who were lost and maintaining her own grounding. The healer, she realised, had to guard her own sanity as fiercely as she fought for others'.

Late at night, when the last of her clients had left and the echoes of their stories had faded into the silence, Emma found herself alone in her flat. The space, once a cocoon of her solitude, was now a sanctuary where she could unravel, free from the scrutiny of others. It was here, amidst the comforting embrace of her solitude, that she replenished her strength, ready to face another day of healing, of balancing her own sanity amidst the sea of emotions that was her life.

Each morning, as the first light of dawn washed over her, Emma would brace herself for another day. The weight of her work was a heavy mantle to bear, but bear it she did, with the resilience of a lone gum tree standing tall in the outback. She was Emma, the healer, the miracle worker, and above all, a woman who found resilience in her solitude.

As Emma sank deeper into the billowing sea of her clients' emotions, she began to encounter strange and haunting echoes of her own past. The chorus of voices that sought her healing touch sang familiar tunes of pain and joy, striking chords that resonated within her own soul. It was as if she was looking into a cracked mirror, each reflection bearing marks of her own hidden scars. Her subjects' raw stories turned her studio into an uncanny echo chamber of her own past, each tale puncturing the walls she had built around her old wounds.

There was something brutally honest about this mirroring of emotions. It was like confronting a ghost, a spectral entity bearing the face of Emma from yesteryears. Every rugged stockman that gruffly shared his pain, every city-dweller who tearfully spilled their fears - they all were, in essence, fragments of her own story, pieces of a puzzle she had long since buried in the red dust of time.

Her camera, the tool of her trade, seemed to take on a life of its own, revealing truths not only about her subjects but also about herself. She felt her heart twitch in her chest as each flash of her camera illuminated not just the raw pain and joy in her subjects, but also the haunted corridors of her own past. She was more than just a photographer or a healer; she was a participant in this enthralling theatre of life, playing out her own catharsis amidst the chaotic orchestra of human emotion.

Confronted by these echoes of her past, Emma made a startling revelation: in order to heal others, she had to first tend to her own wounds. Just like a wind-beaten eucalyptus tree, standing tall against the relentless gales, she too had her own set of gnarled scars, hiding under the hardy exterior.

Emma began to look inward, probing the shadows of her past with a newfound courage. The revelation added a new depth to her character, painting her as a lone warrior battling her demons even as she shouldered the burdens of others. The mystery surrounding her character deepened, her tale steeped in intrigue, leaving the readers at the edge of their seats, eager to peel back the layers of her enigmatic persona.

It was in these quiet moments of introspection that Emma truly embraced her dual roles - the healer and the wounded, the listener and the speaker. Every tear she wiped, every smile she coaxed out, was a testament to her own journey, her own healing. Her past, once a hidden spectre, now stood as a beacon of her resilience, a testament of her strength. It was a hauntingly beautiful symphony, a dance of shadows and light, reflecting the age-old truth - to help others, one must first help oneself.

In the crooked alleyways of memory and healing, Emma stumbled upon a revelation that was as bright as the midday sun over the barren outback. She had been balancing on a razor's edge, straddling the line between her personal life and the emotional symphony of others. It was a delicate dance, and she knew it was time to draw a line in the sand, to establish boundaries between her work and her inner world. The time had come for her to don her armour and guard her peace.

Her flat, once a bustling hub of emotional turmoil and healing, began to take on a different persona. Emma turned it into a sanctuary where she could retreat and find solace, away from the insistent gaze of her clients. It was here, amidst the quiet murmur of her own thoughts, that Emma would retreat after a gruelling day of healing others.

With the persistence of a stubborn dingo, she began to carve out moments of solitude amidst the chaos. These moments became sacred rituals, a time to rejuvenate and gather her wits, a lighthouse guiding her through the turbulent sea of emotions she dealt with every day.

She was unflinching, her gaze steady, her resolve firm. She had seen the fires of her own past mirrored in the eyes of her clients. Yet, she stood, as steadfast as the ancient gum trees, bending but never breaking under the emotional gales that blew her way.

Emma, our lens-wielding healer, had begun to understand the rhythm of her existence. There was a season for healing, a season for self-reflection, and a season for rest. And as she danced through these cycles, the readers bore witness to her strength, her resilience. She was more than just a miracle worker; she was a survivor, a beacon of hope in the turbulent sea of life.

Emma's journey, like the dusty outback roads, had its shares of bumps and sharp turns. But she navigated it with the grace of a river carving its path through the rugged landscape. Her past, once a haunting spectre, was now a constant reminder of her journey, her transformation.

Every shutter of her camera, every tear she wiped away, was a testament to her own healing and her undying will to move forward. As the chapter closed, readers were left marvelling at Emma's strength. She was more than a character in a story; she was a symbol of resilience and strength, a testament to the enduring spirit of humanity.

In the theatre of life and pain, she had not just survived, but thrived. Emma was not just a healer, a miracle worker. She was a warrior, battling her own demons even as she shouldered the burdens of others. Her story was a song of hope, a symphony of resilience, echoing across the vast expanse of the outback, inspiring all those who dared to listen.

The underbelly of memory can be a real croc-infested river. You wade in, and the murky past snaps at your heels, ready to drag you under. And Emma, the miraculous shutterbug, was knee-deep in the middle of her personal Murray River. Her past, a motley crew of unresolved issues, now demanded her attention with the persistence of a bushfire on a hot summer day.

She'd realised her gift was twofold. It was a vehicle for the healing of others, yes, but it was also a mirror reflecting back the raw, scarred elements of her own past. Her sanctuary, her safe haven, was now speckled with fragments of a history she'd long buried under the outback sand.

So, she decided, like a defiant kangaroo in a spotlight, to face her past. And in doing so, she found a part of herself she had long forgotten. Like a jackaroo pulling on his boots for a long day on the cattle station, she strapped in for an emotional ride, her heart strumming with a warrior's spirit.

Her past unspooled before her, a raw tapestry of pain and pleasure, joy and sorrow, love and loss. There was the spectre of old love, a charming bloke who'd left her as hollow as a gutted fish. There were traces of abandonment, like the fading echo of a dingo's cry in the wilderness. There was the sting of failure, reminiscent of a bush fly's irritating buzz.

But with each encounter, she found herself standing a little taller, her spirit shining a little brighter. Her own scars, under the glaring light of introspection, revealed themselves to be not just markers of pain, but badges of survival. Emma had been through the wringer, had danced with pain, but she'd emerged on the other side stronger, fiercer.

Readers found themselves leaning into the story, their hearts pounding in sync with Emma's. They bore witness to her warrior spirit, her fearless confrontation of her past. The woman who had healed so many was now healing herself. She had become a duality, a therapist and a patient, and it was an inspiring spectacle.

Emma had found her battlefield, not under the expansive outback sky or in the rugged bushlands, but within herself. And as she charged forward, her past her adversary, her courage her weapon, she was every bit the warrior. She was the miracle worker, the healer, the survivor. But above all, she was Emma, a woman reshaped by her past, emerging stronger from the anvil of her own history.

The outback is a harsh mistress, moulding its inhabitants into hardened survivors. It had done the same to Emma. The girl who once sought solace in the solitude of her photography was now a woman embracing the tumult of her life. She stood strong, feet rooted in the red dirt of her past, eyes gleaming with the unspoken promise of a battle well-fought.

Emma's studio, a hive of buzzing activity during the day, was now quiet in the late-night stillness. The room was lit by the soft glow of a single lamp, casting long, lanky shadows that danced on the worn-out wooden floor. It was in these hallowed hours of solitude that she found herself - not the miracle worker, not the therapist, but Emma. A woman with a past as craggy as the Flinders Ranges, a present as chaotic as a Brisbane peak-hour, and a future as unpredictable as the Melbourne weather.

But Emma was no pushover, no common galah to be ruffled by a bit of wind. The challenges looming on her horizon were more welcome than a cold tinnie on a scorching summer day. They were no longer ominous thunderclouds of uncertainty, but opportunities to demonstrate her resilience.

So, she embraced them, those looming challenges, with the fervour of a footy fan on Grand Final day. She welcomed them with open arms, her heart throbbing with a wild, untamed beat, an anthem of resilience. She was ready to go another round with life, to play the tough game, to get back up even when she was knocked flat on her arse.

Her journey, once a solitary trek through the photographic wilderness, had turned into a tumultuous roller-coaster ride, complete with uphill struggles and adrenaline-pumping drops. And yet, she wouldn't have it any other way. The struggle, she realised, was a part of the dance. A messy, frustrating, exhilarating dance of life.

People were left, not with a neatly wrapped ending, but with an enticing promise of more. They watched, their hearts throbbing in tune with Emma's, as she forged ahead, ready to grapple with whatever life lobbed her way.

As the story arc drew to its close, it did not offer a neat resolution, but rather a clarion call. A beckoning to accompany Emma on her unvarnished journey of self-discovery. A voyage that promised to be as wildly unpredictable, profoundly moving, and breathtakingly beautiful as the untamed expanse of the Australian outback itself.

A Heavy Burden

The world was on Emma's shoulders, no, scratch that – the bloody universe was there, each star a pulsing, burning responsibility that seared through her like a wildfire through the bush. Each face she encountered, each life she glimpsed through the lens of her camera, seemed to etch itself onto her soul. Their pain became hers, their struggles wove themselves into the fabric of her being.

Every night, she'd lie down on her lonely bed, the silence of her studio echoing with the phantom cries of the tormented. The heart-wrenching sobs of the bloke from Brisbane who'd lost his mate in a car crash. The silent screams of the young sheila from Adelaide, barely out of her teens, grappling with the vicious tendrils of addiction. The resigned sorrow of the old man from Darwin, his eyes narrating a story of lost love and missed chances. Their faces haunted her dreams, their sorrow, their hopelessness seeping into her consciousness until they became a part of her.

Emma was like a vessel, a dam holding back a ceaseless tide of raw emotion that threatened to consume her. But the dam was starting to crack, the floodgates were beginning to groan under the relentless pressure. Every morning, she'd wake up, her eyes gritty with unshed tears, her heart heavy with a grief that wasn't entirely hers. She'd sit up, the weight of her burden pressing her into the mattress, and she'd stare out the window at the dawn breaking over the outback. She'd watch the sun rise, its rays chasing away the shadows, and she'd wonder if her own darkness would ever see the light of day.

Her work, once a source of joy, had morphed into an overwhelming beast of emotional burden. She was drowning, floundering in a sea of sorrow and desperation, struggling to keep her head above the waves. The resilience that had once been her lifeline was fraying, her spirit buckling under the constant strain.

Every night, the echoes of her clients' silent cries would invade her sleep, every day the flood of emotions would threaten to drag her under. But she'd grit her teeth, square her shoulders, and continue to tread the turbulent waters. For this was her chosen path, her burden to bear. And she'd be damned if she let it defeat her. But the cracks were there, lurking beneath the surface, and it was only a matter of time before they started to show.

You wouldn't have known it to look at her, that beneath the tough exterior – that bloody staunch facade she'd constructed – Emma was hurting, bloody well dying inside. The brave smile she wore for her clients, the reassuring words she spoke, all of it masked a raw, open wound within. A wound that refused to heal, refusing to scab over, stoked by the constant barrage of pain she was exposed to.

Each day was a battle. A gritty, white-knuckled struggle to keep the demons at bay. The ones that her clients unwittingly dragged into her life, and the ones that were uniquely her own. Emma was waging a war on two fronts, and it was starting to take its toll. Like a stoic gum tree in a fierce bushfire, she stood tall, resolute, bearing the brunt of the flames. But beneath her bark, her heartwood was smouldering, a slow-burning fire of despair that threatened to consume her.

She'd look in the mirror and see a face that didn't seem to belong to her anymore. A face that was slowly being etched with lines of worry and shadows of exhaustion. Her vibrant green eyes, once mirrors to her fiery spirit, now held a weariness that made her heart ache. A silent scream for help that she refused to voice, a plea for respite that she denied herself.

Her studio, once a sanctuary, had transformed into a battleground. Every photograph, every click of the shutter, was another volley in the fight. A fight against the torment of others, a fight against her own spiralling emotions. Emma was at war, and the battlefield was her own mind.

And yet, amidst all this, she found the strength to put on a brave face. She'd paint on a smile, a facade as sturdy as a brick wall, hiding the turmoil within. She greeted each day with a soldier's resolve, each client with a healer's compassion. For all her clients saw was the miracle worker, the confident woman behind the lens. They saw the healer, the saviour, the symbol of hope. They saw everything but the woman wrestling with her own demons, drowning in a sea of sorrow she couldn't seem to escape.

But behind closed doors, in the solitude of her studio, Emma allowed herself to be vulnerable. To be human. To grieve, to cry, to rage against the unfairness of it all. It was a side of her the world never saw, a side of her that she carefully kept hidden behind the brave facade. But it was there, as real as the red dirt of the outback, as tangible as the heartache she carried within. It was the side of Emma that made her resilient, yet so terribly vulnerable. The side of Emma that was quietly breaking beneath the weight of her heavy burden.

The past has a funny way of creeping up on you, a bit like a snake in the grass. You might not see it, you might not even sense it, but one day you'll feel its bite. And it was starting to nip at Emma's heels, a constant, unwanted reminder of the world she'd left behind. A world she'd tried so hard to bury beneath layers of grit and determination, now pushing its way to the surface like stubborn weeds through cracks in the pavement.

Her past was reverberating, resonating on the same bloody frequency as the emotions she was wading through each day. Each memory, each ghost of her former life, it all echoed in the chaos of her daily existence. It was like a haunting melody that you can't quite shake, a tune you didn't particularly fancy but was stuck on repeat in your head. It was starting to unnerve her, this unsolicited symphony of her past, playing alongside the cacophony of emotions she was dealing with.

There was no hiding from it anymore. The boundary between her professional and personal life was becoming as thin as the air atop Uluru. The two worlds were colliding, a violent clash of present pain and past regrets. It was muddying the waters, blurring the lines she'd painstakingly drawn to protect herself. Emma, the stoic miracle worker, the photographer with a heart of gold, was now just Emma. The woman with a past as murky as the Yarra River, a history she'd been running from, but was now catching up with her.

The ghost of a smile she'd seen in a photograph, a laugh that echoed one she'd heard long ago, it all kept pulling her back. Each day, each encounter, each photograph was a voyage into the past she didn't want to take. It was a ticket to a journey she hadn't signed up for. But there it was, the ticket, clutched in her hand, leading her down a path she'd thought she'd left behind.

Her studio, once a place of refuge, was now echoing with the whispers of her past. Each corner seemed to hold a fragment of a memory she'd forgotten, each photograph a window into a chapter she'd closed. The space that had been her sanctuary was becoming a hall of mirrors, reflecting parts of her she'd hidden away, parts she didn't want to confront.

She stood at this precipice, the chasm between her past and present growing wider by the day. Each memory was a gust of wind, threatening to tip her over. She was teetering, struggling to maintain her balance amidst the storm of emotions that swirled around her. Emma, the resilient photographer, the miracle worker, was wrestling with ghosts of her past. And she knew, sooner or later, she'd have to face them head-on.

Emma's life had become a jumbled mess of emotions, like a messy drawer of mismatched socks. It seemed every moment of her waking life was now soaked in the pained gazes and silent cries of her clients. Every heartbeat echoed with their heartbreak. The air around her, thick with the scent of their despair. She was like a sponge, soaking up all that raw emotion. And she was becoming saturated. It was getting too much.

There was one place, though, where she could find a bit of respite. A place where she could dry off, squeeze out the emotions that clung to her like a second skin. Solitude. Solitude was her sanctuary, a safe harbour in the storm of feelings that constantly threatened to capsize her.

In those stolen moments alone, she could breathe. She could disconnect, float away from the tidal wave of emotion that threatened to pull her under. It was in solitude that she could unravel, could let the walls crumble, the brave facade slip. Solitude was her confidant, her ally, the only witness to her vulnerability. It was here that she found her strength, here that she recharged, here that she regrouped.

She'd curl up on the old worn-out sofa in her studio, a cuppa in her hands, letting the silence envelop her. There was comfort in the nothingness, a peace in the stillness that was as soothing as a lullaby. She could hear herself think, could feel her own heart beating, could sense her own breath. It was a chance to reconnect with herself, to maintain her own emotional health amidst the chaos of her work.

In those quiet moments, when the world seemed to pause and the only sound was the soft whisper of her breath, Emma realised the truth. She needed to disconnect. To disconnect from her work, to keep it from engulfing her, from snuffing out the flame that kept her alive.

It was a hard pill to swallow, a bitter realisation. But it was a necessary one. If she was to continue, to keep up the good fight, she needed to find a way. A way to help others without losing herself. A way to care without caring too much. A way to keep the waters of her clients' despair from seeping into the dry land of her own heart.

She needed a shield, a boundary, a firewall. Something to keep the pain out, to keep her sanity intact. She knew the road ahead was going to be a rough one, a path strewn with hurdles and potholes. But she was ready. She had to be. Because in the end, she was all she had. And she had to protect herself. For her sake, and for those who needed her.

Emma was fighting a war, not against the world, but against the shadows that lurked in the dark corners of her mind. Shadows of her past, long-buried memories, resurfacing like ghosts from a forgotten graveyard. They thrived on the chaos, fed off the emotional turmoil she was immersing herself in every day. She could feel their strength growing, feel their cold fingers clutching at her heart, squeezing the life out of it.

There was no running away, no hiding. Not this time. The shadows were a part of her, imprinted onto her soul like indelible ink. They were in her dreams, in her thoughts, in every pulse of her heart. They were everywhere, a constant reminder of what was and what could have been. They were her past, and they were threatening to consume her present.

Her work, once a source of fulfillment and joy, had become a battlefield. Every client, every emotion she captured with her lens, was like fuel to the fire. The fire that was slowly eating her from the inside, gnawing at her sanity, making her question her worth, her purpose.

She was tired. Not the kind of tiredness that a good night's sleep could fix. No, this was a bone-deep weariness, a chronic exhaustion that permeated every cell, every fibre of her being. It was the kind of fatigue that came from fighting a battle she didn't know how to win.

She needed to fight, she knew that. But how does one fight shadows? How does one fight something that's not real, yet as potent as the most deadly poison? How does one fight the past?

But Emma wasn't one to give in. She wasn't one to let the demons of her past dictate the course of her life. She had her own demons, her own skeletons in the closet. But she was not a product of her past.

She was Emma, the miracle worker, the woman who'd been given a gift to help heal others. And she wasn't going to let her shadows destroy that.

Acknowledging the depth of her internal struggle was the first step towards healing. She had to confront her shadows, to face them head-on. It was a daunting task, one that made her heart flutter in her chest like a caged bird. But it was a necessary task, one she couldn't avoid anymore.

Facing her past, she realised, was like diving headfirst into a stormy sea. It was a terrifying prospect, fraught with uncertainty and danger. But it was also a chance for redemption, for healing. A chance to tame her demons, to turn her shadows into allies. A chance to find herself again, amidst the ruins of her broken past.

It was a chance she was willing to take, a risk she was willing to run. Because in the end, it was not about winning or losing. It was about surviving, about emerging from the ashes stronger and more resilient. It was about healing, about reclaiming her life. And Emma was ready. Ready to face her past, to face her shadows, to face herself. Ready to fight. Because that's what survivors do. They fight. And they never give up.

In the raw landscape of shared pain, Emma found an unlikely refuge. Each tear shed in her studio, each quiet sob muffled behind clenched fists, each anguished face frozen in her photographs - they weren't just echoes of her clients' emotional turmoil. They were reflections of her own heartache, mirrored in the eyes of the broken souls that sought her help. They were, in their own obscure way, guiding her towards her own redemption.

Her clients, they were just like her. Bruised by life, wounded by the past, grappling with inner demons. Each one carried their own heavy burden, their faces etched with stories that words could never fully express. Stories of heartbreak and loss, of missed chances and wrong turns. Stories that were as uniquely human as they were painfully universal. They were stories she was familiar with, stories that resonated with her own battle scars.

She wasn't just helping them; they were helping her too. They were helping her face her past, confront her fears. They were helping her find her way back to herself, one shared tear, one shared smile at a time. And for that, she was grateful.

The shared pain, the shared humanity, it brought her closer to her clients. It was a bond forged in the crucible of life's trials, an unspoken pact between wounded hearts seeking solace, seeking healing. A pact that transcended professional boundaries, that transcended social norms. It was a connection that was as real as it was raw, as deep as it was painful. A connection that added another layer to the narrative, another facet to her character.

Her clients, they were more than just faces behind the lens. They were her comrades in arms, her fellow warriors in the battlefield of life. They were her mirrors, reflecting back at her the strength she didn't know she had, the resilience she didn't know she possessed. They were her reminders that she wasn't alone in her struggle, that she wasn't the only one fighting her shadows.

This was the reality of her work, the hidden depth beneath the surface. The reality that each photograph she took, each emotional revelation she captured, was a two-way street. A shared journey of discovery and healing, of facing the past and embracing the future. A journey that was as much about her as it was about her clients.

This was Emma's burden, her cross to bear. But it was also her privilege, her gift. The gift of healing, the gift of empathy. The gift of being able to touch lives, to make a difference. And despite the emotional toll, despite the overwhelming weight, it was a gift she wouldn't trade for anything. It was a gift she cherished, a gift she was willing to carry, no matter how heavy the burden. Because in the end, it was worth it. It was all worth it.

The emotional terrain that Emma was traversing felt like a tightrope. A constant balancing act between immersing herself in the raw, visceral emotions of her clients and preserving her own sanity. It was like dancing on a knife's edge, a precarious waltz with echoes of heartaches, murmurs of unspoken pains, and the remnants of shattered dreams. It was demanding and draining, like trying to catch sand in a sieve. But, bloody hell, if it wasn't exhilarating.

She saw the beauty in the madness. The sense in the chaos. The human connection in the shared pain. But, she was no fool. She knew this tightrope act was unsustainable. She knew she had to find balance, to create boundaries. Or else, she'd be consumed by the torrent of emotions she faced daily, drowned by the sea of tears that flowed in her studio.

Slowly, she started to understand the importance of self-care, the necessity of emotional detachment in her work. Her job required her to dip her toes into the turbulent waters of her clients' emotions, but she couldn't afford to lose herself in the storm. She had to remain anchored, grounded in her own reality, steadfast in the face of the emotional tempest.

Emma began setting boundaries, carving out time for herself amidst the whirlwind of her work. She found solace in the Australian outback, the rugged terrain a balm for her frazzled nerves. The endless expanse of the bush, the quiet hum of the wilderness, it soothed her. Gave her space to breathe, to recalibrate. Gave her the strength to walk back into the storm.

She knew she had to face the music. She had to continue her work, continue the healing. But she also had to heal herself, replenish her reserves. She couldn't pour from an empty cup. She was beginning to realise that. Her work, it was a part of her, but it wasn't all of her. And she had to honour that. Honour herself.

Her journey wasn't just about healing others anymore. It was about healing herself, too. It was about finding that sweet spot between being a professional photographer and an impromptu therapist. It was about navigating the tricky terrain of empathy without losing herself. It was about walking the emotional tightrope, with grace and strength.

So, she took a deep breath, squared her shoulders, and continued her dance on the tightrope. It was a dance only she could perform, a dance that was as enchanting as it was terrifying. A dance that was uniquely hers. And despite the risks, despite the dangers, she wouldn't have it any other way. She was Emma, the miracle worker, the emotional tightrope walker. And this was her dance. Her life. Her story.

The onslaught of emotions she'd been dealing with was akin to trying to surf a bloody tsunami on a plank. Each day, another wave crashed over her, threatening to pull her under, to lose herself in the turmoil. And although she'd been doing her darnedest to stay afloat, she was all too aware that she was slowly but surely sinking. It was a slow, insidious descent into the abyss, one that had snuck up on her, like a dingo on the prowl. But once she realised it, she knew she had to do something about it.

She couldn't keep ignoring the fact that her work was slowly consuming her, gnawing at her like a starved possum. She couldn't keep pretending that she was alright, that she could handle it all, not when she was drowning. The signs were all there – the restless nights, the shadows under her eyes, the fatigue that clung to her like a second skin. She was burning out, and she knew it. She needed to change, and bloody soon.

She took a hard look at herself, at her life, at the direction she was heading. It was a harsh reality check, one that hit her like a freight train. She was no longer just a photographer. She was a therapist, a counsellor, a healer. And she had been carrying the weight of the world on her shoulders, a burden that was not hers to bear.

She had to change. Had to find a way to disengage from the emotional maelstrom she found herself in. Had to find a way to continue her work without it taking over her life. And it wasn't just about self-preservation. It was about being able to continue helping her clients effectively. If she went under, she'd be no good to anyone. Not to her clients. Not to herself.

So, she decided to face the music, to confront the elephant in the room. She couldn't keep running away, keep ignoring the mounting pressure. She had to deal with it, head-on. Had to find a way to lighten the load, to ease the burden. She couldn't change the fact that her work was emotionally draining. But she could change how she dealt with it, how she let it affect her.

The call to change echoed in her ears, a constant reminder of the crossroads she found herself at. It was a wakeup call, a call to arms. She knew it was going to be a tough road ahead, knew it wasn't going to be a walk in the park. But she was Emma, the miracle worker, the emotional tightrope walker. And if there was one thing she had in spades, it was resilience. She was a battler, through and through. And she'd be damned if she let this beat her. She was ready for change, ready for the fight. Ready for whatever life threw at her.

At the coalface of her own turmoil, Emma found something unexpected – strength. It wasn't the kind of strength that came from an easy win or a stroke of luck. No, it was the kind of strength that was born out of struggle, out of hitting rock bottom and clawing your way back up. It was the kind of strength that was forged in the fires of adversity and quenched in the waters of resilience. It was raw, it was gritty, it was as real as the Australian outback.

Emma was learning to wrestle with her own demons, to navigate the treacherous landscape of her past. She was facing down her ghosts, meeting them head-on instead of running away. And with each confrontation, she found herself growing stronger, more resilient. The weight of her burden didn't lessen, but she was learning how to carry it without breaking her back.

The whispers of her past, once ominous and threatening, were starting to lose their sting. They were becoming just that – whispers. The noise in her head was starting to quiet down, and in its place, she found clarity. She found understanding. She found strength.

And she began to realise something profound – her struggles, her vulnerability, they were her strength. They were what made her a better healer, what made her able to truly understand her clients' pain and despair. She was walking the same path they were, was facing the same kind of emotional battles. She was one of them, and that was her strength.

It was a revelation, one that was both terrifying and liberating. She was a healer, yes, but she was also a warrior. A warrior who was fighting her own battles, who was overcoming her own obstacles. She was fighting the good fight, not just for her clients, but for herself.

She was starting to see the beauty in her brokenness, the strength in her scars. She was a tapestry of her past, of her struggles, of her victories. She was Emma, the miracle worker. And she was bloody strong.

And with each day, each client, each photograph, she was becoming stronger. She was discovering new depths to her resilience, new facets to her strength. She was growing, evolving, transforming. She was facing her past, embracing her struggles, and coming out stronger on the other side. She was a fighter. She was a survivor. She was a bloody miracle worker. And she was only just getting started.

Emma was no fool. She knew the cross she bore wasn't about to get any lighter. Her mission, this profound calling she found herself tied to, it wasn't a straight road through some pretty-as-a-postcard bushland. It was a winding path through the harsh outback, an unending expanse of desolate beauty, as brutal as it was breathtaking.

But Emma had no intention of turning tail. She'd made peace with her burden, welcomed it like an old friend, as inseparable from her as her own shadow. The emotional weight of her work was heavy, sure, but it was a weight she'd chosen to carry. It was a weight that had shaped her, defined her, made her the woman she was – a bloody resilient one.

Her work, the daily deluge of raw emotions and naked vulnerability, was not something she could simply put down at the end of the day. It clung to her, seeped into her skin, marked her like a tattoo. But Emma, she took it in her stride, wore it like a badge of honour. She was Emma, the miracle worker, the woman who wasn't afraid to shoulder the weight of a thousand broken hearts.

She knew she couldn't keep going the way she had. The daily grind, the constant tug-of-war between her work and her sanity, it wasn't sustainable. She had to evolve, to adapt, to learn how to navigate this emotional minefield she found herself in. And so she made a resolution – a commitment to herself, to her work, to the people she served. She would evolve. She would adapt. She would find a way to carry this weight without letting it crush her.

But make no mistake, Emma wasn't playing the martyr. She wasn't seeking sympathy or looking for an easy out. She knew she was in for a rough trot, but she also knew she was made of tougher stuff. She was a fighter, a survivor, an Aussie battler. She was bloody Emma, and she was stronger than she'd ever been.

With a steely resolve in her heart and a fire in her belly, Emma was ready to face whatever came her way. She was embracing the challenge, the struggle, the pain. Because she knew that it was in the struggle that she would find her strength, in the pain that she would find her purpose.

This journey, this mission, this life, it wasn't going to be easy. But Emma, she was up for it. She was ready for the fight. Because she wasn't just a miracle worker. She was a bloody warrior, and she was only just getting started.

The Dark Side

E mma had a knack for reading faces, but this bloke was a corker, a veritable book that begged to be deciphered. With a laughter as infectious as the drop bear tale told to unsuspecting tourists, his eyes twinkled with an impish delight that was hard to mistrust. His features were hardened from years under the harsh Australian sun, lines etched deep into his weather-beaten skin. Yet, his laugh was a young one, robust and full of life, like a cockatoo's raucous squawk piercing through the silence of the bush.

She pegged him as a larrikin, a man quick with a joke and quicker with a smile. His joviality seemed to fill her small studio, his bellowing laughter bouncing off the walls, permeating the room with an atmosphere of infectious cheer. It felt like he was the sort to have a permanent grin etched onto his face, someone who laughed in the face of danger, who took life by the scruff of the neck and said, "Strewth, mate! Is that all you got?"

There was a comfort in his mirth, a warmth that seeped through the cold lens of her camera. She saw in him the embodiment of an Aussie battler, a bloke who'd lived life in the fast lane yet still found a reason to crack a joke, to chuckle and laugh uproariously, echoing the spirit of the land down under. But beneath this facade of irrepressible cheer, Emma couldn't shake off a nagging sense of something hidden, something skulking in the shadows. It was a whisper, a subtle note in the symphony of his laughter that didn't quite fit the merry tune.

But, she brushed it off. What could possibly lurk beneath such a cheerful exterior? Emma dismissed the doubt, attributing it to the overactive imagination that had been her companion ever since she discovered her uncanny ability. She kept her focus on the man before her, ready to capture the merry twinkle in his eye, the infectious laughter on his lips, oblivious to the storm brewing beneath the surface.

Under the harsh studio lights, she focused her gaze through the camera lens, the metallic taste of anticipation humming in the back of her throat. The man in front of her was an open book, his joyous facade painted in bold strokes of laughter and broad smiles. It was easy, too easy, to be lulled into his vibrancy, the energy that crackled around him like a raging bushfire. But Emma had learnt over time, every face was an intricate mosaic, the pieces often revealing more than the whole.

His roars of laughter filled the room as she urged him on, the comfortable rhythm of their interactions easing her initial wariness. "Keep it coming, mate," she'd coax, feeding his enthusiasm with a genuine smile and light-hearted banter. Her shutter clicked in quick succession, each snapshot freezing a moment of his merriment for eternity.

His laughter was infectious, spreading through the room like a jolly virus. The man's joy filled every crevice, every corner of the stuffy room, as if determined to banish the shadows that clung to the walls. Emma, caught in his overwhelming mirth, found herself smiling, laughing along, a silent spectator in the theatre of his exuberance.

In between shots, he'd reel off a yarn or two, tales filled with wild outback adventures and harmless tomfoolery. Every word seemed to cement his image as the life of the party, the bloke everyone wanted at their barbie, the soul of any gathering. And with each click of her camera, Emma fell a little deeper into the charm of his cheerful facade.

The hours rolled on, the sunlight outside her studio window dimming as the day aged. Her fingers worked with practiced ease, adjusting the camera's settings, switching lenses, focusing and refocusing until every detail was perfect. The laughter, the stories, the infectious joy, it all continued in a steady stream, the man seemingly tireless in his performance.

As the session drew to a close, Emma couldn't shake off a sense of unease. Her instincts were screaming, a primal warning resonating in the back of her mind. But the cheerful man before her seemed to be nothing but that - cheerful. She pushed her concerns aside, chalking it up to the fatigue of a long day. She was just a photographer, after all, not some sleuth in an old noir film. With that, she decided to wrap up, unaware of the revelation that lay in store.

As she peered through the lens, her fingers lightly dancing over the camera settings, a shift in the atmosphere pricked at her senses. The room, previously alive with laughter and joviality, suddenly seemed dense, the air heavy with an inexplicable tension. Emma hesitated, her finger hovering over the shutter button, her instincts sounding a silent alarm.

The bloke across from her, once an embodiment of raucous joy, now emanated an entirely different energy. His laughter was still there, filling the room with echoes of mirth, but underneath the surface, something had changed. His eyes, once twinkling with infectious joy, held a glint that sent a cold, strange shiver down her spine.

Deciding to trust her gut, she hesitated, her instincts prickling like a spooked wallaby. "Hold that pose," she found herself murmuring, her voice oddly strained. He obliged, the laughter on his face freezing into a disconcerting smile. Emma tightened her grip on the camera, took a deep breath and pressed the shutter.

The camera captured the moment, freezing it in time – a facade of joy, an undercurrent of something darker, a pair of eyes that held an unsettling intensity. The image was a stark contradiction, a man lost between the lines of laughter and lurking shadows, caught in the cruel flash of her camera.

As the camera whirred, processing the image, Emma found herself holding her breath, her mind racing to decipher the cryptic signals her intuition had picked up. When she finally looked at the image she'd captured, her blood turned to ice. The man in the image stared back at her, his mirth replaced by an intensity that seemed to leap off the screen, raw and chillingly real.

The laughter that had filled the room moments ago now seemed distant, a mere echo in the oppressive silence that had enveloped the room. The photo revealed a truth far removed from the joyous facade the man had put on. It showed a soul stripped of pretence, exposing a darker side that Emma could not quite fathom.

She tried to shake off the growing sense of unease, attributing it to the long, tiring day. But the image on her camera screen refused to let her. It was a rude intrusion into the man's soul, a peek into the darker corners of his being, corners that were meant to stay hidden behind the veil of laughter and good cheer. Emma knew she had unintentionally stepped over a line, her camera lens prying into a realm she was not prepared for. She felt a cold chill, a disturbing sense of dread slowly creeping over her. This wasn't just another day at work. This was something else. Something far more sinister.

As Emma waited for the image to develop, she busied herself with cleaning her lenses, a simple ritualistic task that helped ground her. It was just another portrait, she reassured herself, trying to ignore the queasy feeling bubbling up from the pit of her stomach. The printer hummed its rhythmic tune, spitting out the image she'd captured.

As the photo rolled out, she took a glance and felt her heart freeze. The man in the picture, so full of life and laughter, was now a ghost of his former self. The bubbly energy, that contagious joie de vivre that filled the room just moments before was nowhere to be found. Instead, there was something else - a chilling glare that made the room feel several degrees colder.

"Stone the crows," Emma muttered, her breath hitching in her throat. It was the same bloke, but it wasn't. The photograph was a terrifying paradox - the man she'd seen laughing and the man she was now seeing were as different as chalk and cheese. His eyes, once alive with laughter, now had a cold hardness, an intensity that made her skin crawl.

She swallowed hard, feeling the dryness in her throat. The photo seemed to hold an energy that was almost palpable. An icy, menacing aura that sent shivers down her spine, chilling her to the bone. It was as if his soul, the darker, more sinister side of him, had decided to come out and play.

Emma found herself staring at the picture, unable to tear her gaze away from the man's cold, piercing eyes. It was a stark contrast from the bloke who had entered her studio just hours before. The cheerfulness was replaced by a chilling intensity that felt foreboding, dangerous even.

She felt a bead of sweat trickle down the side of her face, the usual comfort of her studio replaced by a tense, eerie silence. The photo in her hands felt heavier, a silent testament to the man's unseen darkness. She took a deep breath, trying to comprehend the enigma the photograph presented. The image was a revelation, a chilling insight into the depths of a human soul. It was a grim reminder of the dual nature of humans, of the darkness that could lurk beneath a surface of cheer and laughter.

Emma's heart pounded in her chest as she looked at the photograph once more. It was no longer just a portrait, it was a haunting revelation. Her hands shook as she placed the photo on her desk, her mind filled with questions and her heart heavy with an unsettling dread. This was more than just an encounter with the unexpected. It was a chilling brush with the unseen darkness that lay beneath jovial exteriors, a stark confrontation with the complex labyrinth that was the human soul.

Developing photographs was typically a ritual of silent satisfaction for Emma. The process had an innate rhythm, as predictable as a beating heart. This time, though, the process was different. It was a baptism of a new reality, a shadowed revelation born out of the chemical soup in the dark room.

There was a stark transformation that had unfolded on the glossy paper - the hearty laughter and infectious energy were gone. They were replaced by something else entirely, something dark and discomforting. The image that lay before her was no longer a man, but a cruel caricature painted by the darkest strokes of humanity. His laughter had turned into a grimace; his eyes, that were once full of joy, were now hollowed out, as if all the light within them had been sucked out.

"Blimey," Emma muttered under her breath, staring at the haunting image. It felt as though shadows dripped off the photograph like ink, staining the cheerful man she thought she'd captured. It was as if the photo had been soaked in a pitch-black ocean, leaving behind an unsettling residue. The shadows didn't just sit on the surface; they seeped deep into the core of the image, warping it into something barely recognizable.

Emma found herself pulled into the vortex of the photograph, unable to break free from the dark allure it exuded. It was as if the man's dark aura had spilled over the edges of the image and was now infecting the very air around her. She felt an icy chill run down her spine, the eeriness of the photo slicing through the solitude of her dark room.

"Cor blimey, what have I got myself into?" she whispered, her voice shaking as much as her hands. The man she'd photographed had seemed like a dinky-di Aussie, full of laughter and light-hearted banter. But now, looking at the photograph, it felt as though she'd crossed paths with a grim spectre, something that masqueraded as human but was steeped in darkness.

The photograph became a sinister puzzle that Emma felt compelled to unravel. The contrast between the man's jovial demeanour and the chilling darkness captured in the photo was hard to reconcile. It was as if she'd peeled back a layer of the man, revealing a hidden, darker version of him. His face, distorted by the shadows, was a haunting reminder of the duality of the human soul. And as Emma grappled with this revelation, she could feel the weight of the darkness pressing down on her, filling her with a sense of dread that was hard to shake off.

It was a gut punch, an unexpected shockwave that rolled through Emma's core, leaving her feeling gutted. Her mind was a thunderstorm of thoughts, swirling and colliding in chaos. The photograph, now seemingly steeped in a deep and impenetrable darkness, was a jarring contradiction to the cheery bloke she had interacted with.

She felt as though she had been sucker-punched by a rogue kangaroo, left winded and disoriented. "What the bloody hell is going on?" she murmured, her voice a mere shadow against the mounting silence. She was spooked, the alarming revelation was like the harsh sting of a bluebottle.

The unsettling photograph was an undecipherable riddle that gnawed at the edges of her sanity. It challenged her understanding of her gift, taunting her perception of reality. She had begun to question everything - her abilities, the credibility of her camera, even the essence of her own judgement. The raw ambiguity of the situation was overwhelming, like trying to find north in a vast desert without a compass.

She felt the heavy weight of doubt settle in, like an unwanted guest taking up residence in her mind. Was she losing her touch, or was her camera seeing beyond the veneer of human pretence, revealing a hidden, dark truth?

Every bit of laughter and light-hearted banter she had shared with the man felt like a deception, a facade for something more sinister lurking beneath. The man's dark energy seemed to have trickled into her world, enveloping her reality in a cloud of eerie uncertainty. It was as though she had ventured into an uncharted bushland, unsure of what creatures lurked in the dense undergrowth.

Emotionally fatigued and mentally derailed, Emma felt a deep-seated dread seep into her bones. It was a cold, chilling fear that made her shiver, a feeling she couldn't shake off no matter how hard she tried. The darkness in the photograph had become a tangible entity, wrapping itself around her, the cold tendrils of fear weaving their way into her thoughts.

In the deafening silence of her dark room, Emma felt a loneliness she had never felt before. She was wrestling with a reality that felt surreal, the boundary between the known and the unknown blurring. As she grappled with the unexpected turmoil, she felt like a lone swimmer lost in a turbulent sea, struggling against the powerful undercurrent of her own anxiety.

This was no ordinary predicament. It was a struggle that tested her resilience, a challenge that was as convoluted as the twisted shadows etched in the photograph. And as she stood there, the weight of the situation pressing down on her, Emma knew she was teetering on the brink of a profound revelation. She was ready to face the harsh reality, even if it meant venturing into the dark, unknown abyss.

A mix of fear and curiosity stirred within Emma, an uncomfortable blend that tasted as sharp as a swig of Bundaberg Rum straight from the bottle. The photograph, steeped in darkness, called out to her, its silent whisper echoing through her mind. It was a mystery she felt compelled to solve, an anomaly she yearned to understand.

With a grim determination, she decided to dig a bit deeper, to unravel the conundrum that was this man with a laugh louder than a kookaburra's and a darkness lurking beneath that was as cold as a winter night in Tasmania. As she delved into the man's past, the investigation felt like wrestling a crocodile in the murky waters of his life.

Each discovery was more unsettling than the last, like finding deadly brown snakes hiding in the most mundane of backyard sheds. She unearthed a past filled with shadows and secrets, each one darker than the one before. They were threads woven into a chilling tapestry that bore an eerie resemblance to the aura she had captured in the photograph.

The deeper she dug, the more the darkness seemed to make a strange, terrifying kind of sense. It was like piecing together a jigsaw puzzle with a grim, horrifying picture gradually forming. His life was a disturbing narrative of twisted actions and horrific events that aligned with the terrifying image the camera had captured.

It was not what Emma had expected. Her hands trembled as she sifted through the labyrinth of information, a chill coursing through her veins as though she was standing barefoot on an icy Outback morning. The sheer rawness of the revelation was a gut punch, leaving her feeling as if she had been thrown off a bucking bronco.

Every bit of information she unearthed felt like a painful jab, an icy stab of dread that sent shivers down her spine. It was as if she had stepped into a chilling horror story, the echoes of the man's past resonating with the aura she had captured through her lens.

The investigation had brought her face-to-face with the stark reality that was more disturbing than the mysterious aura that had initially troubled her. It was an uneasy dance with the truth, one that was as bone-chilling as wading through a pool of blue-ringed octopuses.

The fear was real. It was no longer just an image, a shadow on a photograph. The man's past was a terrifying testimony of his darkness. Yet, the most alarming part was the realisation that the cheerful exterior was merely a facade. And in this chilling dance with truth, Emma was left grappling with a reality she wished she never uncovered. But she knew she had to press on, she had to continue this perilous dance with the truth. It was a journey that had begun, a path she had to tread, no matter how treacherous it might be.

Gathering the courage was like hoisting a bag of cement bricks onto her shoulders. It was a heavy, gnawing weight that refused to ease. Yet, Emma knew she couldn't dodge this confrontation. The dread was like a nasty paper cut – small yet persistently irritating, begging for attention.

With her stomach churning like a choppy sea, she arranged to meet the man. She had to tread carefully, revealing enough to test the waters, but not so much that she'd give away her hand. No need to let on that she'd seen past the facade, right into the murk of his soul.

As the man walked into the meeting spot, his hearty laughter echoing around the room, it was like the rumble of thunder before a storm. Emma felt an icy shiver run down her spine. His jovial demeanour was as jarring as a cockatoo's screech in the silent Outback. Underneath the loud laughter and easy-going banter was a serpent, coiled and ready to strike.

Every word she said was calculated, measured, careful not to stir the sleeping beast beneath the surface. Yet, with every passing second, the tension strung between them, as taut as a guitar string, ready to snap at any given moment. Her words were stones thrown into a still pond, creating ripples that could easily turn into waves.

The confrontation was like dancing with a tiger snake – one wrong step, and it could all go pear-shaped. The tension was thick enough to cut with a knife, her words hanging heavy in the air between them.

Every moment, every second, Emma could feel her fear amplified. Yet, she didn't back down. She held his gaze, not blinking, not flinching, even as the joviality in his eyes started to fade, replaced by a cold, hard stare that made her insides turn.

Despite the fear coiling in her gut like a nest of venomous snakes, Emma stood her ground. Her voice, though it wavered, did not falter. The confrontation was not about bravery, it was about survival, about facing the reality she had stumbled upon, no matter how terrifying it was.

The confrontation ended with no resolution, just a lingering dread. The cheerful mask had slipped, if only for a moment, revealing the cold, dark eyes of the predator beneath. The tension between them didn't ease, but hung in the air, a potent reminder of the dangerous game she had found herself in.

As she left the man, his laughter once again echoed behind her, a chilling sound that sent cold shivers down her spine. The encounter left Emma rattled, her fears not only affirmed but amplified. Yet, she knew she had started something that she needed to see through to the end, no matter how frightening the journey might be.

With the meeting etched like a nasty scar in her mind, Emma found herself dealing with a threat that she hadn't signed up for. This wasn't just an emotional wrestle anymore; it had morphed into a potential danger, as tangible as the Australian summer sun beating down on the bare neck. A bit like being stuck in a bloody boxing ring with a roo, not knowing when it would throw the next punch.

As the reality of her predicament sunk in, she knew she had to be as cunning as a dingo if she was going to navigate this dangerous terrain. It was her against the sinister world her camera lens had exposed, and she needed a solid plan, not just a few kangaroo leaps here and there.

Emma started to piece together a strategy. She couldn't let fear paralyse her into being a sitting duck. Instead, she had to turn that fear into a tool, let it be the sharpened blade that kept her alert, ready to react at a moment's notice.

She knew she needed to keep a safe distance from the man, avoid poking the bear too much, yet continue to gather information, sly as a fox. She was a rat in the dark, moving stealthily around the edges, always wary of the looming cat.

Her plan revolved around cautious movements, subtle probing, and a hell lot of gut instinct. She was as vigilant as a guard dog, her senses heightened, aware that one wrong move could land her in the crocodile-infested waters.

Every step she took, every decision she made, Emma was keenly aware of the unseen danger lurking beneath the surface. She realized that the man was a land mine, his cheerful exterior nothing more than deceptive camouflage.

Her unique ability, once a beacon of hope for healing, had revealed a threat she wasn't prepared for. Yet, Emma knew that running away was not an option. She had to face this danger head-on, tackle it with all the courage she could muster.

But she wasn't foolhardy. She knew that courage alone wouldn't cut it. She needed her wits about her, had to tread as softly as a cat, ready to sprint at the first sign of trouble.

As Emma navigated the potential dangers, she knew she had changed. The carefree photographer healing souls was now a woman on a mission, facing a threat she was unprepared for. Yet, she was determined to rise to the challenge. In the face of danger, she found an unexpected resilience, a strength she didn't know she possessed. This journey was far from over, and Emma was ready to fight every step of the way.

The revelation hit Emma like a thunderbolt on a cloudless day. Here she was, trapped in the confines of her own knowing, a secret so heavy it could bring down the walls of a fortified castle. The man was a hidden devil behind the mask of a jovial, carefree soul. But the damning knowledge was not something she could spill out, not without revealing the strange nature of her powers.

A predicament, she thought, a real bloody bugger of a situation. It was like being caught between the devil and the deep blue sea.

There she was, a Sheila trying to do good, but stuck in a quagmire that was looking darker and stickier with every passing minute.

She spent her days tiptoeing around the edges of the problem, watching the man from the corner of her eye like a kangaroo on a moonlit night, alert to the slightest movement. Her nights were spent tossing and turning, wrestling with the moral dilemma. Her mind was a battle ground, ideas clashing and colliding like ancient warriors locked in a deathly duel.

And yet, the silence was her only companion. She was a lone soldier in the heart of a vast desert, armed with nothing but her ability and sheer determination. A part of her yearned to yell from the rooftops, expose the darkness that lurked beneath the man's cheerful facade. But she couldn't, she bloody well couldn't. It was her word against his, and she had no proof, not the kind that would stand in the harsh light of scrutiny.

Every day, Emma walked the tightrope of her dilemma, trying to maintain her balance, grappling with the weight of the secret threatening to tip her over. She was a bird caught in a storm, tossed around by the winds of fear and uncertainty, desperately trying to find her way.

The clock was ticking, and with every tick, the predicament gnawed at her sanity, pulling her into a vortex of anxiety and fear. She could feel the dangerous nature of the man seeping into her world, a malignant energy tainting the air around her.

And as the chapter came to a close, we left Emma staring into the abyss, her mind a whirlpool of chaos. The predicament was more than just a threat; it was a time bomb waiting to explode, leaving a trail of destruction in its wake.

She was left with a daunting task - how to navigate this treacherous path, how to protect others from the imminent danger, and how to preserve her own sanity amidst the brewing storm. It was a cliffhanger that hung in the air like a sword of Damocles, leaving readers teetering on the edge, waiting with bated breath for the next chapter in this suspenseful saga.

Fear & Doubt

Emma slouched over the bar counter; her gaze fixed on the amber liquid swirling in her glass. She wasn't here for the booze, but for the solace the dimly lit pub provided. A refuge from the world where she could blend in with the grizzled old blokes nursing their beers, grumbling about footy scores. This was her secret sanctuary, away from the prying eyes of her clients and their fractured souls.

"A penny for your thoughts, Em?" The bartender, a burly Aussie bloke named Mick, gave her a knowing glance. The corner of her mouth twitched in a half-hearted smile.

"Nah, mate. Just wondering if I've got my wires crossed," she confessed. Mick shrugged, poured another shot, and left her to her musings.

She picked up her glass, the liquid throwing off hazy reflections of neon signs. With every soul she peered into, every life she interfered with, a gnawing sense of unease had been growing in her gut. Was it her place to intervene? To nudge lives onto paths they never intended to tread? Could she justify her actions simply by what she saw in their souls?

She was not a god. She was a woman who, by some cosmic joke, had been given the power to peer into people's deepest fears, desires, and shames.

This power, this...ability, it was like a murky flood, threatening to drown her in a sea of ethical quandaries. She found herself questioning the very essence of her actions. Was it right to exploit such intimate knowledge? Did these souls give their consent for her to dive into their deepest corners?

She'd started off thinking she was helping. Righting wrongs unseen, healing hidden wounds. But as she delved deeper, the lines blurred. She felt like a puppeteer, pulling strings based on what she thought was best. Yet, who was she to decide?

The shot glass clinked against the counter, the sound echoing her turbulent thoughts. It wasn't the fear of playing god that rattled her; it was the fear of becoming a monster under the guise of a saviour.

Mick sauntered over, refilling her glass. "Whatever it is, you'll sort it out, Em. You always do."

Emma looked at Mick and then back to her glass, her reflection distorted in the amber depths. The line between right and wrong seemed to have lost its rigid clarity. All she was left with were shades of grey and a flood of uncertainty, a challenging path that she had to navigate herself.

Emma found herself in the grungy alleyway next to the pub, the cool brick wall pressing into her back, a stogie perched between her lips. The smell of tobacco and damp asphalt filled her senses, providing a grounded counterpoint to the whirlpool of thoughts churning in her mind.

She'd been down this rabbit hole before, wrestling with morality like a croc wrangling its prey. This power, this voyeuristic window into people's souls, was it a boon or a curse? Was she the diviner or the meddler, the saviour or the spectre?

The stogie's red ember flickered in the night, its hazy glow painting shadows on her face. She watched as it danced, creating bizarre patterns in the dark, a surreal stage mirroring her own chaotic thoughts.

She'd built her whole existence around this gift of hers, but it had never felt so heavy, so burdensome. She was meant to heal, to guide, yet now, she felt like an intruder, a burglar stealing into the sacred sanctuary of souls under the cloak of a healer.

Every face she captured, every soul she saw, they all seemed to stare back at her now, a choir of silent accusations ringing in her ears. What right did she have to expose their darkness, to dissect their lives based on these fleeting glimpses into their souls?

What if she made a wrong call? Pushed someone off a ledge when she thought she was pulling them back from the edge? The potential repercussions gnawed at her, a horde of hungry rats gnashing their teeth at her conviction.

The smoke from her stogie curled up into the night sky, disappearing into the inky void. She remembered the man, his cheery façade hiding a predator beneath. She had acted, intervened, driven by instinct, by the horror of what she'd seen in his soul. But what if she was wrong? What if she'd misread, misinterpreted?

With a heavy sigh, she stubbed the stogie against the wall, watching the ember sputter and die. It was a solitary death, a silent end to a fiery existence. The ethical quandary she found herself in mirrored this lonely end.

A cruel twist of irony indeed, Emma mused, leaning back against the cold bricks. This gift of sight, this extraordinary power, had cast her into a sea of doubt, a tempest of ethical dilemmas that threatened to consume her.

She couldn't deny the fear gnawing at the edges of her consciousness, the echo of her own doubts reverberating in the quiet alley. The weight of her power was a heavy burden, a yoke she wasn't sure she could carry anymore. The line between right and wrong had blurred, dissolved into a nebulous haze of uncertainty.

"Fair dinkum, what a bloody mess," she muttered into the cold night, the words dissolving into the crisp air, a stark testament to her turmoil. The clarity she once had was gone, replaced with the echoing question: Was she healing or was she harming?

Haunted by the weight of her past, Emma sank into the worn-out chesterfield in her living room, its familiar groans offering cold comfort. Flickers from the dying fire in the hearth cast shadows on the peeling wallpaper, an eerie dance of light and darkness mirroring her inner tumult.

She was now stuck knee-deep in the murky quagmire of past decisions, sifting through each memory, each intervention with a clinical detachment that left her feeling raw and exposed. A parade of faces, a montage of souls passed in front of her, each one a testament to her interference, her attempts to steer their lives based on the secrets she had unearthed.

There was Benny, the bloke from the corner pub, his face etched with lines of hardship and despair. His soul, a tapestry of pain, had called out to her, the silent scream resonating with her own inner demons. She'd intervened, tried to pull him out of the pit he was stuck in. But Benny was no more; a tragic end to a story that she had tried to rewrite.

And then, there was Mabel, the old dame from the antique store down the road, her soul radiating a warm, golden glow that belied her frailty. Emma had seen her strength, her indomitable spirit, and had encouraged her to fight her battles. But Mabel had lost her store, her livelihood, in a cruel twist of fate.

A heavy sigh escaped her as she swirled the amber liquid in her glass, the ice clinking against the sides in an irregular rhythm. With each instance she revisited, each memory she pored over, her doubts gnawed at her, a relentless rat chewing at the edges of her confidence.

She had acted with the best intentions, had used her gift to try and steer these lives towards better days. But the road to hell, as they say, is paved with good intentions. Her interference, her meddling, had it brought more harm than good?

The guilt clung to her like an unwanted shadow, a constant reminder of her transgressions. The faces she had tried to help, the souls she had tried to heal, they seemed to stare at her from the darkness, their silent accusations piercing the quiet of her sanctuary.

"Bloody oath, what have I done?" she muttered, the question echoing through the empty room, a chilling reminder of her predicament. Each sip of her drink tasted bitter now, a stark contrast to the sweet solace it usually provided.

Her power, her gift, it had brought her to this crossroads, a junction where the line between right and wrong blurred into a vague haze. Would she continue down this path, continue to intervene, despite the ghosts of her past haunting her? Or would she withdraw, let nature take its course, unaffected by her insight?

These were the questions that gnawed at her now, their sharp teeth cutting through her defences, leaving her naked in the face of her past, her doubts, her fears. The crossroads beckoned, and Emma found herself on the precipice, staring into the abyss of uncertainty.

Doubt, that vile beast, had begun to gnaw on Emma's faith in her own abilities. It had crept in like a cockroach, insidious and persistent, burrowing its way into her mind, casting long, sinewy shadows over the conviction she'd held so dear. As she sat alone in the dim, smoky light of her flat, nursing a bottle of cheap whiskey, the echo of questions reverberated in the silence.

Was she playing god, meddling with the fates of those she'd not the right to interfere with? What gave her the authority to expose, to unveil the buried secrets tucked away in the recesses of one's soul? These questions chewed away at her, relentless as a dingo with a bone.

The images she captured, those intimate reflections of hidden struggles, were they hers to interpret and act upon? She'd begun this journey with noble intentions, a desire to soothe, to heal. Yet, it seemed as though the more she tried, the more entangled she got in the intricate webs of other people's lives. She was a mere mortal caught up in a god's game, a jillaroo trying to wrangle a wild brumby.

She poured herself another drink, the amber liquid hitting the glass with an almost accusatory thud. She was caught in a storm of her own making, the eye of the tempest being her unique ability, her gift. Or was it a curse?

Emma had started this work, believing that if she could glimpse the depths of a person's soul, she could guide them towards healing. But with every soul she touched, every secret she unearthed, the weight of her responsibility bore down on her, heavy as the hot Australian sun in the merciless outback.

She had believed in the sanctity of her mission, viewed her ability as a tool for healing. But now? Now, the same ability seemed more like Pandora's box, each photograph she took, each soul she laid bare, only adding to the turmoil.

Staring into the abyss of her whiskey glass, Emma wrestled with the gnawing doubt. It gnashed at her, tearing away chunks of her self-assuredness, leaving behind a hollow echo of uncertainty.

She was no god, nor a devil. She was Emma, the lass with a knack for capturing souls on film. But the faces of those she'd exposed stared back at her, their eyes reflecting the pain of being laid bare, and she couldn't help but wonder, was it all worth it?

The questions hung in the air, unanswered, a bitter testament to her dilemma. The taste of doubt lingered on her tongue, an unwelcome guest that refused to leave. As the night grew darker, Emma's struggle with her fears and insecurities painted a poignant picture of a woman grappling with the implications of her unusual gift, leaving her teetering on the edge of a precipice, one wrong step away from a fall.

In her cloud of self-doubt, Emma sought out a beacon of wisdom, a mentor. She found herself in front of the shabby door of an old friend, George - an elder bloke who'd seen his fair share of the world's darkness and light. He was a crusty fella, as rough around the edges as a piece of sandpaper, but with a heart as vast as the Outback. He had been her rock in past times of tumult, offering nuggets of wisdom in his raspy voice that belied the deep understanding beneath his grizzled exterior.

She knocked on the door with a nervous intensity, akin to a joey trying to find its way back to its mother's pouch. George opened the door, squinting against the light that spilled in, highlighting the maps of wrinkles etched onto his face. "Emma, it's been donkey's years. Come in, love," he greeted, the usual gruffness in his voice softening at her sight.

Emma tried to navigate the minefield of her thoughts, choosing her words carefully to ensure they wouldn't give away too much about her abilities. Sitting on the worn-out couch, she poured out her soul, voicing her fears and doubts, the words spilling from her like a dam that had burst. The room soaked up her words, offering back a silence filled with understanding.

George listened, his old eyes keen, dissecting the avalanche of words. The quiet stretched between them, a yawning chasm that Emma was too afraid to breach. Finally, he leaned forward, elbows on knees, and with a huff that expelled years of smoked tar, he said, "Life's a bit like a game of cricket, Emma. It ain't about the runs you make, but how you play the game."

He sipped his beer, his gaze steady on her. "You've got this gift, and you're using it to make a difference. But, love, you're not God. You're just... you. You can't control the outcome, no more than a bowler can control where the batsman will hit."

Emma absorbed his words, her mind thrashing around the advice like a croc with its prey. But she knew he was right. She wasn't a divine entity, she was just a sheila with a knack for seeing people's souls. And it wasn't her place to control the narrative of others' lives, only to provide a helping hand when she could.

As she walked out into the night, her thoughts whirling in her head like a wild dust devil, she realized that this fear, this doubt, they were just bumps on her path. She had a gift, yes, but she also had the strength to wield it responsibly.

The shadows of doubt still lingered, but for the first time, they didn't seem as daunting. As the night crickets started their symphony and the air cooled down, there was a new sense of determination in Emma's stride, a resolve to continue using her abilities in a way that respected the humanity of those she sought to help.

Emma found herself standing on the edge of the world, looking down into the abyss. She felt the weight of her gift, heavy as a mountain on her shoulders. It was a monstrous responsibility, a beast she'd unknowingly tamed and now had to live with. She felt like an Atlas, the earth of her gift a mighty burden pressing down, grinding her into the dirt.

It was late, and the Sydney skyline stretched out in front of her like a tired animal. The Harbour Bridge glowed against the black velvet of the night, the glittering lights of the city were as scattered as her thoughts. It was a panorama of life going on as usual, ignorant of the struggles of a single sheila wrestling with the weight of a thousand souls.

Every face she'd ever captured, every secret she'd ever unveiled, it all seemed to suffocate her. Her gift had become a Pandora's Box, letting loose a deluge of emotions that crashed over her like monstrous waves. She felt as if she was drowning in a sea of other people's secrets, their pains, their joys, their lives. It was overwhelming, the realisation that she held the strings to their destinies, that her decisions, as minor as they might have seemed, could echo profoundly in their lives.

She sunk to the floor, her back against the cool brick wall, the city's hum fading into a distant drone. She realised she'd been holding her breath, the air rushing out of her in a loud sigh. She was one woman, not a god, not a saint, just a simple sheila trying to do some good. But the path she'd chosen was strewn with pebbles and boulders, each decision a potential stumbling block, each choice carrying the weight of someone's life.

A sense of loneliness enveloped her, a stark reality of her situation. She was walking a solitary path, a journey none could comprehend fully, nor share the burden of. She felt as vulnerable as a joey left out in a storm, yet as tough as an old gum tree standing tall against the winds of change.

The silence of the night became her companion, echoing her solitude, yet offering a strange kind of comfort. It was in this quiet that she found the strength to bear her burden. She knew she would make mistakes, she would falter, stumble and maybe even fall. But as the sun began to creep over the horizon, painting the sky with shades of pinks and oranges, she realised that she had the power to rise again, to pick up her burden and continue the journey.

With a newfound acceptance of her reality, Emma realised that her gift was not a sentence to a lifetime of fear and doubt, but rather a chance to touch lives in ways others couldn't. It was a daunting prospect, but one she was ready to face head-on, her fears not eradicated, but acknowledged and kept in check. The morning light dawned on a different Emma, still burdened, but stronger, and ready to meet the world, come what may.

The stark dread settled in Emma like a bad omen, a harbinger of an impending storm. It gnawed at the edges of her sanity, threatening to consume her whole. The fear of making the wrong choice, of turning a life upside down with her gift, of becoming a destroyer rather than a healer, haunted her like a nocturnal beast.

The city lights of Sydney seemed to flicker and die in the face of her fear, their once reassuring glow now a haunting reminder of the thousands of souls she could impact. It was as if she was standing in a boxing ring, her fear a formidable opponent, ready to knock her out cold with a sucker punch.

She felt it creeping up her spine, a cold, icy sensation that rooted her to the spot. She was trapped in the spotlight of her own stage, her every move scrutinised, every decision carrying a weight she didn't know if she could shoulder. The thought of making a wrong move, of pushing someone over the edge instead of pulling them back, sent a jolt of terror through her.

Her workroom, once her sanctuary, now seemed like a cave of despair. Her photographs stared back at her, a grim reminder of the lives she could alter. The faces in the images looked back at her, their eyes boring into her soul, their secrets laid bare and their lives in her hands.

She looked at her camera, the tool of her trade, the gateway to souls. It now seemed more like a weapon, its lens an unblinking eye that could unveil the deepest shadows. The fear of what she might reveal, of what her camera might capture, made her hand waver.

The fear wasn't just a whisper anymore; it was a roaring tempest, threatening to drown her in its tumultuous waves. It was a heavy shroud, its dark folds enveloping her, making it hard for her to breathe. It was the monster under her bed, waiting to pounce at her in her most vulnerable moments.

But even in the face of her paralysing fear, Emma held on to a sliver of hope. It was the single spark in the midst of a dense fog, the single note in a cacophony of noise. It was her lifeline, her anchor in the stormy sea of fear.

She remembered the smiles, the relief, the healing she'd brought about with her gift. She thought of the lives she'd touched, the souls she'd soothed, the hearts she'd mended. She wasn't just a bearer of bad news; she was a conduit of healing, a bridge between despair and hope.

In the quiet of her workroom, in the deafening silence of her fear, Emma resolved to wrestle with her dread. She would face it, head-on, acknowledging its existence but refusing to let it dictate her choices. It was a battle she was determined to fight and, in time, she hoped to win. For she wasn't just Emma, the fearful; she was Emma, the brave, the healer, the seer of souls.

As Emma teetered on the edge of a cliff, her fear and doubt howling around her like a gale, she began to realise something. She was bloody terrified, sure, but she was also asking the right questions. She was considering the ethical implications of her gift, and the importance of how it should be used. She was squaring up to her fear, not for herself, but for the sake of the others, those blokes and sheilas whose souls she had the power to bare.

It was an understanding, a realisation that came to her not like a light bulb moment, but more like a dawning, an outback sunrise spreading its warm rays over a cold desert. The fact that she was questioning her actions was testament to her empathy, to her commitment to do the right thing, no matter how hard. It showed that beneath the fear and the doubt, she cared. Cared enough to question, to doubt, to fear.

Each question, each doubt became a rung on a ladder, helping her climb out of the dark pit of fear. She started to draw strength from her doubts, like siphoning petrol from a tank. Her fear was still there, gnawing at her like a hungry dingo, but now she was fighting back. She was starting to understand that her fear was not a weakness, but a sign of strength, of courage.

She began to look at her gift through a different lens, like changing the filter on her camera. Her ability was not a curse or a burden, but a responsibility, a privilege. She had the power to heal, to mend, to help. It was a responsibility she couldn't shirk, no matter how terrifying it seemed.

As she pondered on this, she started to feel a spark, a kernel of strength forming within her. It was like striking a match in the darkness, the tiny flame flickering, struggling, but holding on. It wasn't much, but it was a start, a sign that she wasn't going to let her fear consume her.

Emma wasn't a superhero, she wasn't bulletproof. She was just a sheila with a camera and a gift. But she was strong, and she was brave.

And as she stared her fear in the face, she knew she would find the strength to continue, to question, to doubt, to fear, and through it all, to do the right thing.

The doubts still lingered, the fear still gnawed, but now she was standing firm. She had found strength in her fear, resilience in her doubt. She was no longer a puppet being jerked around by her fear; she was the puppeteer, controlling her fears, shaping them into a source of strength.

As she looked around her workroom, at the faces in the photographs, the souls she had revealed, she felt a surge of determination. She wouldn't let her fear and doubt rule her. She would use them, channel them into doing the right thing, into becoming a better healer. She was Emma, the soul-seer, the fear-fighter, the strength-finder. And she was ready for whatever came next.

Emma sat in the quiet of her darkroom, surrounded by the ghosts of her past photos. A harsh reality sat heavy in the air, but something new was mingling with it. A realization, a new understanding, began to ferment, like homebrew in the warm Aussie summer.

She wasn't cursed, she reckoned. No, she was given something potent, something special. It was no more a curse than a kangaroo's hop. Her ability was just that, an ability. A tool. It wasn't meant to burden her, it was meant to be wielded, like a swagman's billy can, carrying life's necessities. But she had to learn to use it wisely, she had to control it, not let it control her.

There was a depth to her questioning, her self-doubt. It was an introspection that had initially seemed as welcome as a redback in your dunny, but now it was starting to make sense. The very questions she had been wrestling with were a measure of her growth. The doubt, the fear, it was all part of the process, part of learning to use her tool, her ability.

Every query was like a pickaxe striking rock, chipping away at the surface to reveal the lode beneath. She was probing, digging, not content to accept things at face value. She was pushing beyond the boundaries of her understanding, striving to make sense of her unique predicament.

Her photographs, stark in the red light of the darkroom, stared back at her. She'd seen their souls, she'd glimpsed their deepest secrets. It was an intrusion, yes, but also a chance to understand, to empathise. They weren't just images; they were people, each with their story, their pain, their joys. Her gift allowed her to connect on a level that few could.

Every picture, every soul she'd revealed, every time she'd questioned her decisions, it had all led her here. It had all been part of her journey, her path to understanding. To learning to wield her ability wisely, to see its potential, not just its pitfalls.

Emma, a lass who just happened to see people's souls through a camera lens, was finally seeing the value in her own introspection. It wasn't self-doubt that had been creeping in, it was self-growth. Like a gum tree shooting up out of dry dirt, she was finding her footing. She wasn't cursed; she was privileged. Her gift was not a burden, but a tool. A tool she was learning to wield wisely.

With that, she felt a shift, a realignment. It was as though she'd been squinting in harsh outback sun, and now the brim of her Akubra had been adjusted just right, the world coming into sharper focus. Emma, the soul-seer, the fear-fighter, was becoming the wisdom-wielder, and it was about bloody time.

Emma found herself in the quiet sanctuary of her thoughts, alone with her resolution. It was as though she was standing at the edge of the Great Victoria Desert, gazing at the endless expanse, knowing there was a trek ahead, full of unknowns, full of surprises. But this outback lass was no stranger to journeys, no stranger to forging her path in the scrub.

Her gift, once a bloke at the bar who wouldn't leave her be, was now a travel mate she'd decided to befriend. There was a new-found acceptance, a fresh pact between them. She would continue to use her gift, to gaze into the souls of others through her camera lens, but with care, with empathy.

In her gut, she knew there was no map for the journey she was on, no trusty swagman's guide to lead her way. She was wandering into uncharted territory, a wanderer in the grand landscape of human souls. But she was not without direction. She had her moral compass, her sense of right and wrong, and it was sturdy, as robust as an old Holden barrelling down a dusty track.

She pledged to continue her mission, to keep looking into people's souls, to keep revealing what lay hidden. But she'd do it with care, respect the privacy, tread softly on the tender terrain of other people's inner worlds. Her camera, once just a tool of her trade, had become her compass, guiding her on this extraordinary journey.

There was fear, sure, a sense of trepidation. She was like a wallaby caught in the spotlight, frozen for a second, knowing it had to move but unsure which way to leap. But fear wasn't going to stop her. If anything, it would fuel her, like eucalyptus oil fuels a bushfire, intense but purifying.

The fear, the uncertainty, the moral dilemmas, they were not deterrents; they were merely signs that she was on the right track. They were the checks and balances of her journey, her internal auditing system ensuring she didn't become complacent, didn't lose sight of the significance of her mission.

Emma wasn't just a photographer; she was a seer of souls, a holder of secrets, an explorer of human psyche. And she knew she had much to learn, much to understand. But she was ready, determined to continue, to keep striding forward, one foot in front of the other, with the vastness of the outback as her backdrop and the guidance of her moral compass as her ally.

There was a mission ahead, a fascinating journey into the wilderness of human souls. And Emma, brave as a dingo defending its turf, was ready to venture forth, her camera in hand, her resolution as solid as the red earth beneath her feet. The journey of the soul-seer was just getting started. And bloody hell, what a ride it was going to be.

Taking A Stand

S he found herself wrestling with a kangaroo in her mind, the bloody fear of the whole ordeal was gnawing at her. Emma, the sheila who took photos of souls, preparing for a confrontation that'd have most shaking like a shitting dog. A deep breath, a gulp, a quick swig of the old amber fluid – liquid courage, she thought, trying to lighten the weighty moment.

The fear, it'd been hanging around like a bad smell, taking up too much bloody space, cramping her style. But then, there was also something else. Something like determination, a bit of a bulldog's grip that wouldn't let her leg go. The bloke, the bloke she was about to confront, had a soul that'd given her the shivers. His energy was like a cold beer gone flat, all cheer gone wrong, a nasty surprise behind the sparkly façade.

She found herself remembering the squint-eyed focus as she had snapped his picture, the lens becoming the window into his soul. The camera, her trusty tool, was now a conduit of fear and it rattled her to her roots. But there was more than fear, there was an obligation, a responsibility that came with the ability to see the unseen, to capture the hidden. She had seen the alarm bells in his aura, and she couldn't just bloody well ignore it, now could she?

She looked at her reflection in the window, a silhouette against the burning orange sunset of the outback. She saw fear, but she also saw something else – a sheila who was not about to let the fear boss her around. She was Emma, the bird with the camera, the one who had seen souls whisper and scream through the silent film of her lens.

Her heart was thumping a wild rhythm against her ribs, her palms sweaty against the cold glass of the bottle. She took another gulp, the bitter ale burning a trail down her throat. She was scared alright, scared as a roo in the headlights. But she was not about to bloody well let that stop her. The man, the man with the shadowy soul, he needed confronting, and she was just the sheila to do it.

Emma was no dill, no two-bob drongo. She'd seen a lot through her camera, a lot more than most ever would. This confrontation, she knew it had to be handled like a bloke handling a brown snake – with bloody careful precision. Couldn't go barging in, letting on about her unique gift, that'd be as useful as a bum full of smarties. No, she needed a plan, a bloody good one.

She found herself drawn to the pub, the warm glow of the cheap chandelier lighting up the worn-out bar stools, the smell of stale beer mingling with the night air. It was no Ritz, but it'd do for now. She scribbled down on a beer-stained napkin, a mental chess game playing out – his move, her countermove, a potential checkmate. The bloke she was dealing with wasn't your average Joe, he was a smoky mirror of a man, cheer on the outside, darkness lurking within. She had to prepare for every possible reaction.

Her mind whirled, like a bloody cyclone, thoughts whipping around, a mental tug-of-war. She decided she wouldn't reveal too much about her gift, that'd be like handing over the keys to the kingdom. She'd hint at it, dance around the edges, throw him a bone but keep the steak for herself. Her gift was a sacred thing, not something she could trust with a bloke who had more shadows than a ghost gum at twilight.

She saw her plan taking shape, saw the potential pitfalls and planned for them too. This wasn't her first rodeo, but it sure was her most dangerous. She was going up against the unknown, the unseen, armed with nothing more than her camera and her guts.

The pub grew quieter as she planned, her mind a battlefield, her heart a warrior beating the drums of war. Her decision was firm, her resolve stronger than steel. She knew she was stepping into the lion's den, knew the danger that awaited her. But she was Emma, the sheila who saw souls through her lens, who faced the unseen and lived to tell the tale. She would not back down. She would face him, confront him, and whatever happened next, she'd handle it. The lens of her camera had shown her the dark, and she was about to shed some light on it.

Emma sat on her unmade bed, an island of chaos in the sterile room. The hour was fast approaching, the moment when she'd come face to face with the man, her own personal bogeyman. Her heart pounded against her ribs like a desperate prisoner, each beat echoing her growing uncertainty. The plan she'd crafted seemed shakier, frailer. A flicker of doubt began to snake its way into her mind, a rattling question - was she bloody mad for going ahead with this?

She stared at the crumpled photograph of the man, his jovial face and its sinister aura. The image seemed to taunt her, seemed to hiss, "You're in over your head, Em." She ran her fingers through her unkempt hair, recalling past instances when her well-laid plans had gone down the gurgler. The way faces changed when the laughter faded, the way trust morphed into betrayal. The shadows of her past snaked around her present, choking her with the chains of 'what ifs'.

Like that bloke from Perth, full of sunshine smiles and good cheer, his soul a rotten graveyard that had almost claimed her. Or the young woman from Adelaide, sweet as honey, her aura dark as an outback night, that encounter leaving Emma shaken for days. Her ability, it seemed, was a double-edged sword, a boon and a curse, a blessing and a bloody nightmare.

She gripped the photograph tighter, her knuckles white as bone. The seconds ticked away on her faded wall clock, its monotonous rhythm matching the thumping in her chest. A part of her screamed to call it off, to bury her head in the sand like an emu. But a stronger part, the part forged in the fires of her trials, roared back in defiance. It whispered of her duty, of the people she could help, of the wrongs she could right.

Torn between her fear and her conviction, Emma found herself stuck in no man's land. She was walking a tightrope, a precipice on either side, the rope swaying with her indecision. Each past failure felt like a gust of wind, threatening to unbalance her, to send her tumbling into the abyss of doubt. But with each gust, she found herself steadying, found her resolve hardening.

Looking at the man's photograph one last time, she shoved her doubts away. She was not the same Emma who'd failed before. She was stronger, tougher, a bloody bush ranger in a world of ghosts. Doubt could take a backseat, fear could go jump. Emma was confronting the man, come hell or high water. She'd look into the eye of the storm and dare it to blink first.

The sun was setting, splashing the sky with hues of burnt orange and plum, as if Mother Nature herself was giving a nod to the storm brewing inside Emma. The clock on the wall continued its merciless march, ticking away the seconds that stood between her and the impending confrontation. Doubt still gnawed at her, a relentless blowfly in her mind, yet she felt a burgeoning resolve, a determination fiercer than a pack of hungry dingoes.

Sitting on the edge of the worn-out mattress, she allowed herself to be swallowed by the deafening silence, her eyes closed in a quiet contemplation. She tried to conjure the faces of those she'd helped in the past, every face a testament to the potential good she could do, every face a defiance to the creeping doubt. The way their eyes lit up with relief, the way they clung onto hope like a lifeline – it all served to reinforce her conviction, to feed the flickering fire of her resolve.

There was Tommy from down the road, his life a spiral of bad decisions and lost chances. Emma had seen the remnants of goodness in his soul, obscured by shadows of regret. He'd turned his life around, now helping others tread the narrow path of sobriety. There was also little Lily from the block, trapped in a cycle of abuse and despair. Emma's intervention had been her lifeline, her way out.

Memories, like snapshots in an old photo album, unfurled in her mind. The past was both a well of heartache and a beacon of hope. The uncertainty, the fear, they were real and tangible, but they were not the sum of her existence. Her gift had the power to make a difference, to pull people back from the brink.

In the midst of this whirlpool of contemplation, Emma reaffirmed her mission, her moral obligation. It was not just about her, not anymore. Her doubts, her fears, they were battles she had to fight, for herself and for those who couldn't. Her gift had chosen her, for reasons unknown, and she had an obligation, a duty even, to wield it as a force of good.

Opening her eyes, Emma stared back into the fading daylight, the ghost of a smile tugging at her lips. Her doubts, they still lingered, like the faint aroma of burnt eucalyptus, but they no longer consumed her. She'd weathered storms before, she'd weather this one too. Reassured, resolute, she was ready to face the man. Ready to stand her ground, ready to push through, come what may. It was not just about confronting the man, it was about confronting herself, about standing up to her own demons. And for Emma, that was a fight worth fighting.

In the creeping twilight, Emma found herself face-to-face with the bloke. His facade as normal as an Aussie barbecue, hiding what she'd seen - a soul that was more shadow than light. He stood there, chewing on his toothpick, and gave her a nod, his eyes as unreadable as a platypus playing poker.

His voice cut through the sultry night air, an odd mix of charm and chill. "G'day, Emma. Fancy meeting you here." His casual greeting danced on the edge of Emma's nerves, flicking them like a nasty case of the twitching jitters. This was a wily old fox, she could tell, and she was tiptoeing into his den.

"Thought we needed a chat," she said, keeping her voice steady, her accent broad and her words direct.

The bloke cocked an eyebrow. "Oh? You got something on your mind?"

This was the moment of truth. She felt like a kid caught in a riptide, out of her depth and struggling. But she had to forge on, had to keep a lid on the churning in her guts. "Something ain't right," she said, her gaze never leaving his face.

The man chuckled. "What are you on about, Emma? You've been knocking back a few tinnies too many?"

Emma held her ground, despite the sweat gathering on her brow. "I don't reckon so," she shot back. "Just wanted to let you know... I see you."

The man's smile faltered, his demeanour shifting like sand beneath her feet. Emma had hit a nerve. The air around them crackled with tension, a storm threatening to break.

But Emma stood strong. She'd voiced her concerns, managed to keep her secrets while pricking his conscience. She'd confronted the darkness she'd seen, had taken the fight to its doorstep. The tension of the moment was as sharp as a bushranger's blade, but she didn't buckle.

She'd said her piece. It was up to him now, up to the shadows that clung to his soul. Whether he chose to heed her words or ignore them was his choice. But she'd done her bit, had taken her stand. Emma had faced her fear and, for now, that was victory enough.

A cold smirk spread across the man's face, like a fog rolling over the harbour on a frosty winter morning. His dismissive laugh echoed in the stillness, a grating sound that gnawed at Emma's resolve.

"Well, aren't you a larrikin, Emma? Seeing things, are ya?" His voice was a layer of ice over a deep, murky river.

She looked at him, this bloke with the soul of a gargoyle, feeling a surge of defiance. No, she wouldn't be silenced, wouldn't be swatted away like an annoying fly. She had seen something. Seen something in him that was darker than the dingy backrooms of a seedy pub.

"I'm not bloody joking," she spat back, her tone steady. His smile didn't falter, but she saw a flash of something in his eyes, a glint that was sharper than the shards of a shattered bottle.

"Pull the other one, it's got bells on," he retorted with a sneer, his arrogance as thick as the humidity of a Queensland summer.

This wasn't going the way she'd hoped. His dismissal felt like an unexpected slap, stinging and disorientating. But Emma wasn't the kind of sheila to back down. Her teeth gritted, she dug her heels in, her gaze locked on his. "I'm not pissin' in your pocket," she said, her voice unyielding. "You need to have a hard look at yourself."

His dismissive snort filled the air between them, a mocking sound that tried to diminish her words, her warning. But she had said it, had voiced her concern, her truth. He could deny it, could scoff at it, but he couldn't unhear it.

Emma stood her ground, stood tall in the face of his scorn. She'd thrown down the gauntlet, had confronted the man whose soul hid a sinister secret. His cold reception only cemented her suspicions, adding fuel to her resolve. Whatever happened next, Emma knew she'd done the right thing. She'd faced the fear, the uncertainty, and hadn't flinched.

Yes, there was a chill in the air, a frostiness in his response. But it didn't reach Emma. She was aflame with purpose, burning bright with the conviction of her actions. His coldness could try to quench her fire, but it wouldn't succeed. She was Emma, the sheila who saw souls. And she would not be dismissed.

The tension in the room grew thicker, filling the air with a sense of danger as palpable as the acrid smoke of a raging bushfire. The man's eyes hardened, his body language shifting from dismissive to aggressive. There was a venomous hostility in his gaze, the look of a taipan about to strike.

"You're starting to really piss me off, sheila," he spat out, his tone biting as a mid-winter's gust through the Outback. Emma's heart pounded in her chest, but she kept her expression steady, refusing to show fear.

The man leaned in closer, his aura casting a dark shadow, a dangerous rip current threatening to pull her under. "You're skating on thin ice, Emma," he warned, his voice low and threatening.

Despite the rising fear, Emma managed to hold her ground. The threat was now as tangible as the hard, sun-baked soil of her homeland. She had rattled the snake, and it was ready to strike.

But Emma wasn't one to turn tail and run. She was a dinkum Aussie, as stubborn as they come. The hostile twist to the man's mouth, the menacing glare in his eyes; they didn't deter her. They only fuelled her determination.

"I'm not scared of you," she said, her voice as steely as a miner's pickaxe. It was a bluff, but sometimes you had to put on a brave face, even when your insides were quaking like the aftermath of a quake.

His gaze was predatory, a clear warning of the danger she had stepped into. But Emma was resolute, her resolve hardened by the magnitude of what she had seen and the threat it posed. If he chose to retaliate, she was prepared to weather the storm.

Her mind started racing, planning her next moves, considering all possible outcomes. She might've stepped on a hornet's nest, but she wasn't going to stand around and wait to be stung.

The air grew colder, the hostility more pronounced. But Emma wouldn't back down. She was in the eye of the storm, and the only way out was through. She would face this threat head-on, no matter how dangerous it got. She was Emma, the woman who could see souls, and she wouldn't be silenced. Not by fear, not by threats, not by the chill in his gaze.

The confrontation had turned sour, but Emma wasn't done yet. She was ready to navigate the threatening seas ahead, ready to stand against the storm. After all, she wasn't just any sheila, she was a battler, and she'd fight tooth and nail if it came down to it.

Emma could feel the situation spiralling, like a cyclone picking up speed, ready to unleash its fury. The man's rage was an oppressive heat, a bushfire ready to blaze. She was in the belly of the beast now, facing off against a predator, far from any semblance of safety.

But she was no daft galah. She knew when to make a tactical retreat, when to step back and reassess. "Righto," she said, her voice barely above a whisper, as steady as she could muster. "I'll be on my way, then."

She turned to leave, every instinct in her body screaming at her to get out, to run as fast and as far as she could. But she resisted the urge to bolt, kept her movements slow and measured. Show no fear, she reminded herself.

His glowering presence was like a ravenous dingo at her back, making her skin prickle with unease. The whole scenario was as unsettling as finding a redback in your dunny. But Emma held her nerve, each step carrying her closer to the exit, further from the immediate threat.

As she reached the door, she risked a glance back. His eyes bore into her, a clear promise of danger, a promise as certain as the Aussie sun beating down on the red earth. A shudder ran down her spine. This wasn't over. She had kicked a hornet's nest, and the hornets were buzzing.

But she managed to escape, at least for now. As she walked away, she could feel the weight of his gaze, the threat of his anger. But the direct danger had passed, like the eye of a storm moving on, leaving devastation in its wake.

Walking down the street, the hustle and bustle of city life a stark contrast to the tense standoff she'd just experienced, Emma couldn't shake off the feeling of foreboding. She had seen the darkness within him, had stirred it up, and now it was fully awake, fully aware of her.

The confrontation had gone pear-shaped, but she was still in one piece, still standing. But the air of danger lingered, a thunderstorm on the horizon, a promise of turbulence yet to come.

Emma knew she had to rethink her strategy, to come up with a game plan. This was more than just a friendly warning gone awry. This was serious, and she had to be prepared.

The world moved on around her, oblivious to the storm brewing. But Emma, she knew. She could see the thunderheads building, could feel the static in the air. She was in the eye of the storm, but she wasn't going to be swept away. Not without a fight. Not without taking a stand. She was an Aussie, after all. And Aussies, they didn't back down from a challenge. They faced it, chin up, ready to take on whatever life threw at them. And Emma was no different.

Left alone with her thoughts, Emma found herself lost in the aftermath of the encounter. The confrontation had been as uncomfortable as a sunburn, as unpredictable as a bushfire. Yet, there she was, standing on her own two feet, as resilient as a gum tree after the storm.

The echoes of their tense exchange rumbled around her mind. She could still feel the icy chill of his dismissive gaze, see the flicker of darkness in his eyes. It was as if she'd come face to face with a saltie and escaped its jaws by the skin of her teeth.

"Was it worth it?" She asked herself, her mind a flurry of doubt and questions. Was her approach too confrontational, too aggressive? Should she have tiptoed around his dark aura instead of charging head-on?

But even as the doubts gnawed at her, she knew deep down she had done what needed to be done. The darkness in his soul wasn't just a shadow, it was a black hole, a void threatening to consume all the light around it. If she had turned a blind eye, who would've faced it?

Alone in the silence, Emma felt the echoes of her own fears. But she was no wimp. She wasn't about to leg it at the first sign of trouble. As shaky as she was, she didn't regret her actions. Because, sometimes, you have to stir up a bit of trouble to bring the baddies to light.

The confrontation had rattled her, yes, but it also fanned the flame of her determination. The bloke had a menace about him, a darkness that could hurt others. And if she didn't act, who would? She had a responsibility, a duty, that she couldn't just shirk because of fear.

She was like a dingo in a hen house, stirring up all sorts of chaos. But if it meant protecting others from the man's predatory aura, she'd kick up as much dust as necessary. She was an Aussie, a battler. And she wouldn't back down.

In the stillness of her solitude, Emma made a silent promise to herself and to those she vowed to protect. She would face this danger, confront this threat, regardless of the cost. She had opened Pandora's box, but she wouldn't let the darkness spread uncontested.

The aftermath of the confrontation left a bitter taste in her mouth, a sour note that lingered. But it didn't deter her. Instead, it served as a stark reminder of the fight she had ahead of her. It was a fight she was prepared to take on, ready to face, not for herself, but for those who couldn't defend themselves against the darkness she had seen.

Emma was far from a hero, but in that moment, she realised she had what it took to stand against the villainy that lurked beneath the surface. She wasn't fearless, but she was courageous. And sometimes, courage was all you needed to make a stand. And stand she would.

With the confrontation etched into the canvas of her mind, Emma found herself teetering on the precipice of a new resolve. Her heart felt heavy, like a kangaroo had taken up residence in her chest, its thumping beat an urgent reminder of the stakes she was dealing with.

Despite the nerve-racking encounter, a spark flickered within her, a stubborn flame that refused to be extinguished. Emma knew, deep down, that she couldn't abandon her mission now, no matter how dangerous the road ahead looked. She was like a roo caught in the headlights, stunned but determined not to be another roadkill.

The man had been as welcoming as a bluebottle jellyfish, his hostility pushing her further out into unknown waters. The danger wasn't just lurking anymore, it was staring her right in the face. Yet, even as fear gnawed at her, a stubborn resolve emerged.

Emma had always been a bit of a larrikin, a risk-taker. But now, she understood she needed to be more than that. She had to be a strategist, a careful observer, a chess player in a game where the pieces were people's lives.

And so, she decided to re-strategize, to plot her moves like a grandmaster. She needed to be as crafty as a fox, as shrewd as a cockatoo, if she was to navigate this new world of threats and danger. And though the idea sent shivers down her spine, she knew it was the right path.

She sat in the quiet stillness of the night, the only company the hushed whispers of the wind and the distant hoot of a night owl. Her thoughts were her roadmap, each one a steppingstone to a better strategy, a more informed approach.

She needed to be prepared for the bloke's next move, for his unpredictable reactions. She couldn't afford to be caught on the hop. The knowledge of people's souls was a powerful tool, but it was also a double-edged sword. And she had to learn to wield it without cutting herself in the process.

So, she plotted and planned, like a general preparing for battle. Her past actions, her mistakes, they were lessons to be learned from, steppingstones to a better strategy. Her unique ability was a boon and a bane, a tool to protect and a weapon to be careful with.

Alone, her thoughts her only company. The future was uncertain, filled with possibilities both terrifying and exciting. But one thing was certain - Emma was ready. She was ready to face the dangers, ready to confront the darkness, ready to protect those who couldn't protect themselves.

Her mission was clear. Her resolve, stronger. The journey ahead was daunting, as perilous as walking barefoot on a beach full of bindis. But she was willing to take on the challenge, to step into the fray. Because she was Emma, and she wouldn't back down, no matter what.

Unforeseen Consequences

Emma's confrontation had torn through her community like a kangaroo on the hop, stirring up dust and leaving a trail of confusion in its wake. The immediate repercussions were as clear as day, as bright as the Aussie sun on a scorcher of a summer's afternoon. The small town, once a refuge of familiarity and tranquillity, was now awash with unease.

The ripper of a confrontation, the bare-knuckled words and the blazing fire in Emma's eyes had set in motion a series of events that she'd not forecasted. It was like chucking a pebble into a still billabong, the ripples distorting the smooth surface, extending out in concentric circles until they reached the furthest bank.

The community, once as tightly woven as a well-used cricket net, was starting to fray at the edges. The townsfolk started to walk with a different gait, like they had a joey in their pouch they weren't quite sure how to handle. The friendly nods of recognition were fewer, conversations shortened, and the smiles didn't reach the eyes anymore. A bloke could feel it in the air, thick as a swarm of flies in the outback.

People she'd known all her life, who'd shared beers and barbies, gossips and grins, were now looking at her askance. The blokes at the pub who'd once shared a yarn with her were now whispering behind their schooners, their gazes shifty. And the sheilas who'd always been up for a chinwag were now exchanging worried glances, their words scarce.

Emma felt it all, the shift in the air, the change in the rhythm, and the mounting tension. Like a dingo who'd just walked into a flock of cockatoos, she felt out of place, watched, and on edge. The confrontation had indeed stirred the pot, and now the bloody stew was threatening to boil over.

A swift and silent change had rolled over the community like a southerly buster, whisking up every last trace of harmony in its wake. Emma watched it unfold, the reactions of the people around her growing as chilly as an Aussie winter morning. Like wombats holed up in their burrows, they had turned inward, defensive, barely coming out for a g'day or a yarn.

She noticed the way they sidestepped her on the street, their gazes focused anywhere but on her. The laughter at the pub was more forced, the atmosphere more fraught, and the jokes felt emptier. The blokes who used to slap her back in camaraderie now only offered her tight nods, their eyes glinting with a mix of unease and accusation.

The local sheilas, who'd once spilled their hearts out to her over cups of billy tea, now clutched their secrets close to their chest. Their friendly banter had been replaced by tense silence, broken only by the occasional forced laugh. They gathered in huddled groups at the supermarket or the salon, their voices dropping to a whisper when Emma passed by.

It wasn't just suspicion that was brewing. Paranoia had reared its ugly head too, spreading through the community like wildfire through dry bush. People started to jump at shadows, becoming overly protective of their kin, casting wary glances at their neighbours. A sense of distrust was seeping into the fabric of the community, staining the once friendly bonds with shades of fear and uncertainty.

Every glance that missed her, every forced smile, every hushed conversation, reminded Emma of her actions, a ghost that had taken up residence in her mind. Her confrontation with the man had set off a chain of events she hadn't anticipated. She had stirred the nest, and now the hornets were buzzing, ready to strike.

Emma felt the chill of isolation creeping over her, as icy as a gust of wind off the Snowy Mountains. She'd wanted to protect her community, but all she seemed to have done was make them cagey as cats around a dog. And as the days wore on, she found herself on a lonely path, her actions having cast her as the outsider in the community she had wanted to safeguard.

Emma was a damned magnet. Not the kind that drew good luck or fortune, but the type that yanked unwelcome attention her way. Since the confrontation, she'd become the bloody epicentre of a storm she didn't want any part of. The man wasn't her only problem; his mates, strangers, and even the roos seemed to have taken a keen interest in her.

The rumour mill was grinding hard. Every trip to the pub, every walk down the high street, she could feel eyes drilling holes into her back. Tongues wagged faster than a blue heeler's tail, and stories spun out of control like a whirly-whirly lifting dust off the dry outback dirt. She'd become the town's topic du jour, an unwanted fame that made her feel as comfortable as a joey in a dingo's den.

Everywhere she went, whispers clung to her like burrs on a bushman's swag. People had started making connections, linking her to the man and the ensuing shift in the community's mood. The bloke at the fish 'n' chip shop wore a concerned frown, the old coot at the newsagency eyed her with more curiosity than the crosswords, and the local gossip mavens didn't even bother pretending they weren't talking about her.

She was like the damned Pied Piper, but instead of rats, she was leading a parade of nosy parkers, keen on digging up the truth. The man's hostility had spooked her enough, but this new level of attention was worse than a pack of blowflies at a barbie. Emma, once the town's confidante, the one everyone went to with their stories, was now the subject of hushed speculation.

In the spotlight, every action scrutinised, Emma felt the weight of the town's gaze. She was trapped in a cyclone of her own making, whipped up by her well-intentioned actions. She'd wanted to protect her mates, her community. She hadn't meant to set the whole bloody town on edge.

Emma realised she was now wrestling a bigger beast, a storm that was spreading fast, circling her like a pack of hungry dingos. And in its eye, she stood alone, the focus of an unwanted, escalating attention that threatened to bring her world crashing down.

Under the harsh Aussie sun, Emma felt a cold front rolling in. The town had turned on her, or at least that's how it seemed. She was stuck in a bind tighter than a Atherton Jungle Python's grip, the hostility against her rising faster than a southerly buster.

Speculation was her only ally now, a cruel mate that left her mind spinning like a willy-willy. She suspected the bloke she'd confronted had his dirty mitts in the mix, stirring the pot against her. If there was a snake in the grass, it was him alright. He was likely behind the whispers, the rumours, the shifting eyes in her direction.

But suspicion was as solid as the Nullarbor was lush. Worthless without evidence, about as handy as an ashtray on a motorbike. She needed proof, but how do you catch a redback in a web of deceit? All she had was a gut feeling, sharper than a bushman's knife, telling her that the bloke was as crooked as a dog's hind leg.

Emma was no dill; she could see what was happening. She was being isolated, targeted. It was a game of backyard cricket, and she was suddenly the stumps, waiting for a hit that could send her flying. The man she had confronted was, in her mind, no doubt playing the batsman, swinging wildly and making her the scapegoat for his own troubles.

But there was nothing concrete to pin on him. No smoking gun, just smoke and mirrors. Rumour and suspicion were poor bedfellows, making her nights restless and her days an uphill battle. She was stuck in an outback dust storm, squinting through the murk for any solid form.

Her once simple existence was now a merry-go-round of speculation and doubt. The soul-seeing gift that she'd once taken for a blessing felt more like a curse. The very tool she'd hoped to use for good was being turned against her, pushing her further into an arid desert of uncertainty. The man was a dingo in the shadows, waiting, watching, his snarl echoing in the hollow spaces of her sleepless nights.

The town was turning as cold as an outback winter's night, leaving Emma out in the frost. She was copping it sweet, all right. The sour aftermath of her confrontation was like a pint of the roughest brew, and it was sitting as uneasy as a bush tick in her gut.

Isolation, that was her new mate now, clinging to her like a leech to a bushwalker's leg. The people she'd known for donkey's years were now a mix of frosty glares and hushed voices. She was about as popular as a red-belly in a sleeping bag. Everyone keeping their distance as though she was a bushfire ready to spark.

And fear, that sneaky bugger, had wriggled its way into her heart. It crept in like a bloody huntsman spider, all legs and menace. Fear of the repercussions, of what the bloke might do, of what the townsfolk were thinking. Emma was questioning her actions, tossing them around in her head like a game of two-up. Had she ballsed it up, confronting the bloke like that? Was she the galah in this play?

Every sound seemed ominous, every shadow a potential threat. Paranoia was her constant companion, whispering doom in her ear like a relentless magpie at dawn. Each day became a marathon, a bloody long haul through a landscape of doubt and regret.

And the regret, crikey, it was eating her up. Regret for the confrontation, regret for the storm it had kicked up. It gnawed at her like a rat in the rafters, unrelenting, leaving her feeling like she'd been hit by a road train.

She felt like she was trapped in the never never, a place where peace had become as elusive as water in the desert. Doubt was gnawing at her, turning her choices inside out, making her feel as useful as a chocolate teapot.

She'd thought she was doing right, that she was doing good. But the current turn of events had her doubting her actions, second-guessing her own intentions. In the mirror of hindsight, she couldn't help but wonder if she'd been a few roos short of a top paddock in her decision to confront the man. But there was no turning back now, only the rough road ahead.

The repercussions of her decisions were raining down on her like a sudden summer storm in the outback, and the strain was enough to make anyone want to chuck a sickie. Emma's gift, her ability to peer into the deepest recesses of a person's soul, felt more like a curse now.

Had she been as naive as a joey, thinking she could harness this power for good? The community she was once a part of was now as welcoming as a brown snake in a dunny. They'd turned on her like a pack of rabid dingoes. It was her gift that put her in this predicament. No, it was more than a predicament, it was a bloody mess. And as she sat there, nursing a tinny, she wondered if it was her abilities that were the real mongrel here.

Looking at people's souls - it seemed such a noble cause when she started, as wholesome as a meat pie at the footy. But now, she wasn't so sure. The dust storm her actions had stirred up was making her question the value of her gift. Was she just stirring the pot, creating more harm than good? Was her gift nothing more than a sharp claw in a kangaroo fight, destined to inflict wounds instead of helping?

People's souls were sacred territory, as vast and complex as the outback. Who was she to traipse about in there like a lost tourist? She was beginning to feel like she'd bitten off more than she could chew, like a kangaroo in a death roll with a salty. Had she overstepped? Overreached? Misjudged?

Her gift, it was like a wild brumby – beautiful, powerful, but bloody hard to control. She wondered if it was better to leave it be, to let it run wild instead of trying to saddle it up and steer it. Maybe, just maybe, it wasn't meant to be harnessed. Perhaps, it was meant to remain as wild and untamed as the outback itself.

Emma was caught in a rip, torn between the desire to do good and the harsh reality of her circumstances. The constant questioning, the guilt, the fear - it was all a bit too much. She was stuck in a stickybeaks dilemma, wondering if her gift was a blessing or a curse, and whether she had any right to use it at all.

Emma sat alone, cloaked in the harsh silence of her flat, nursing a middy of beer that had long lost its froth. There was a coldness in the air, an icy reality that seeped into her skin and burrowed into her soul. Her mind was whirring like an old Holden engine, clouded by regret and a crippling sense of despair. The kind that held you down like a crocodile in a death roll.

Her confrontation with the man, it had been her decision, her judgement. She'd gone at it full pelt, believing her intentions were as pure as the waters of the Great Barrier Reef. But life wasn't a fair dinkum fairy tale, was it? Now, she was staring at the stark aftermath, the consequences of her actions unravelling like an out-of-control road train.

The community, her community, was up in arms. There were murmurs, sideways glances, cold shoulders – as chilly as a winter's night in the Snowy Mountains. They looked at her now with a suspicion that clawed at her heart, a raw, uncomfortable reality she never thought she'd have to face.

Her intentions had been as golden as a sunset over Uluru, her desire to protect and warn as genuine as the southern cross in an outback sky. Yet, here she was, at the heart of a cyclone she never intended to whip up.

She'd played with fire and, by crikey, she was getting burned. The fallout from her actions loomed around her like a thunderhead ready to burst, a dark cloud that threatened to consume her. She'd kicked the ant nest, and now the little buggers were swarming, biting, stinging. And amidst the chaos, there was him - the man - the eye of the storm, calm and steady, ready to strike.

Guilt crept into her mind, burrowed into her thoughts like a cane toad in a sugar cane field. It wrapped its ugly arms around her, squeezing her with the relentless grip of a python.

She'd intended to be the good sort, a guardian, a protector. But instead, she was the sheila who'd shaken up the beehive, and now the bees were out and buzzing, their stingers pointed at her. She felt like a drongo, her actions leading her down a dark and twisted road, her gift more of a liability than a beacon of hope.

Emma felt like a cockatoo in a flock of galahs, out of place, her gift now a source of chaos instead of clarity. As the beer in her glass grew warm and stale, so did the hope in her heart, leaving behind a bitter aftertaste of regret and despair.

Emma was alone in her flat, the weight of the world heavy on her shoulders. It was as if she'd gone ten rounds with a roo and ended up on the wrong end of a kangaroo kick. The room was dim, the only light trickling in from a lone streetlamp outside the window. Its yellowish hue cast eerie shadows around the room, mimicking the haunting fear that gnawed at her insides.

She felt isolated, a bit like a goanna on a deserted beach. Her eyes drifted towards her phone, her fingers itching to dial the one number she knew she could trust. She was sick of feeling like a billy boiling over with no one to take it off the fire.

It took a moment of mental wrangling before she punched in the number. It rang once, twice, and then a familiar voice drifted through the speaker, like a cool breeze on a scorching day in the Red Centre. It was her mate, her true blue, who'd stuck by her through thick and thin.

"G'day," she began, her voice unsteady like a rusty windmill creaking in the outback. Emma danced around the bush a bit, not wanting to spill the beans on her unique abilities. It was a part of her, as wild and unpredictable as a summer storm in the tropics.

Emma spoke of the confrontation, of the man with the aura as dark as a moonless night in the bush, and the ripple effect that seemed to have the whole community acting as skittish as joeys in a dingo's den. She told her mate about the isolation, the suspicion, the fear that clung to her like burrs on a bushman's sock.

Her friend listened, the silence on the other end of the line acting as a lifeline. It wasn't advice Emma sought, but a sense of understanding, a sympathetic ear to lend her strength. Her mate was like a gum tree in the bush, a constant, sturdy presence amidst the chaos. Emma didn't reveal the full depth of her abilities, instead painting her worries in broad strokes, like an artist unwilling to reveal her masterpiece just yet.

Emma didn't expect her friend to understand everything, but hearing her voice, feeling the sincerity, it was like standing under the outback stars – expansive, grounding, real. Her problems hadn't disappeared but sharing them had made the load a bit lighter, a bit more bearable. As she hung up the phone, she felt a sense of resolve swell within her, like the tide rising in the bay. She wasn't alone in this fight, and with a little bit of luck, she might just come out of this mess unscathed.

Sitting alone in her flat, Emma cradled the phone in her hand, its warmth a silent testament to the connection she'd just shared. It was the dead of night now, the world outside wrapped in a black as deep as the bottom of the Murray. But inside, the darkness was beginning to ebb, chased away by the light her mate had unwittingly ignited within her.

She closed her eyes, letting her mate's words swirl around in her head like the dust devils of the outback. Her friend hadn't understood the depth of Emma's dilemma, the real terror that clawed at her insides, but it didn't matter. The words of encouragement had done their job, provided a moment of solace amidst the storm brewing in her life.

Her mate's words were like a raindrop in the desert, precious and rare. "You're a good sheila, Em. Don't let anyone make you doubt that. And remember, no matter what, we've got your back." It was a lifeline tossed out in the sea of fear and regret that Emma had been drowning in, a promise of support she desperately needed.

With every breath she drew, Emma could feel the fear losing its grip on her. It was still there, lurking in the shadows, but it wasn't the boss of her anymore. Her fear was no match for the raw grit and determination rising within her like a mighty Murray flood. Emma knew she had to navigate through this cyclone she'd unknowingly stirred up. She had to see it through, not just for her own sake, but for everyone else's too.

The thought was as sobering as a cold shower on a sweltering summer's day. But along with it came a sense of purpose, a reaffirmation of her mission. Her gift, her ability to see a person's soul, wasn't something to be feared or regretted. It was a tool, her tool, and it was about time she learned to use it wisely.

As the sun began to peek over the horizon, Emma felt a renewed sense of conviction course through her. This wasn't going to be an easy ride, but then again, nothing worthwhile ever was. Like an intrepid explorer charting unknown territories, Emma knew she had to brace herself for whatever lay ahead.

And so, as a new day dawned, Emma was ready. Ready to face her fears, ready to stand her ground, ready to tackle whatever this bloke had to throw at her. She was no longer just Emma, the girl with the extraordinary gift. She was Emma, the woman taking a stand against the storm. For the first time in what felt like forever, Emma felt ready. Ready to fight, to protect, to weather the storm. And this time, she knew she wouldn't be doing it alone.

Night fell like a shroud over the city, turning the usually bustling streets into silent, shadowy silhouettes. But within the walls of her small, weather-beaten flat, a storm was brewing, its intensity only rivalled by the wildest of tempests that swept the Outback. Emma, caught in the eye of this storm, felt the full weight of the chaos that her actions had wrought, pressing against her chest, threatening to choke her.

The churning thoughts in her mind mirrored the turmoil around her. She had tipped her hand too far, drawn too much attention, and now was caught in a bind tighter than a croc's jaw. The fear that once lay dormant within her, like a beast waiting to strike, had now reared its ugly head, filling her world with trepidation and uncertainty. Every conversation, every look directed her way carried a note of suspicion, a reminder of her confrontation and its consequences.

As she lay on her worn-out couch, the dim light from the solitary lamp casting long shadows over her face, Emma couldn't help but question her actions. Was she reckless? Should she have thought things through more carefully? A torrent of doubts washed over her, but within this whirlpool of thoughts, a strong current began to take shape.

Her gift, her unique ability to peer into the very souls of people, wasn't something she had asked for, but it was a part of her. It wasn't a curse, as she had often deemed it, nor was it a tool to brandish recklessly. Her gift was a responsibility. And she had to learn to wield it wisely.

With the echo of her friend's encouraging words still lingering in her mind, Emma felt a flicker of determination kindle within her. She may have made a dog's breakfast of things so far, but she was far from done. She couldn't simply toss it in and disappear into the shadows. There were people to protect, a community that she couldn't abandon to the mercy of the bloke she had tried to confront.

The thought bolstered her resolve. Emma sat up, pulling her legs beneath her, her hands clenching into fists. This was her mess, and she would clean it up. She would face the consequences of her actions head-on, no matter how daunting. She would learn from her mistakes, become better, more strategic.

As the first light of dawn seeped through the thin curtains of her flat, Emma felt a renewed sense of purpose fill her. She was not just a woman with a unique ability, she was a protector, a fighter, ready to take a stand for her community.

The road ahead was filled with challenges and uncertainties, but Emma knew one thing for sure: She was going to face it with her chin up, with courage in her heart, and a resolve of steel. With a final glance at the approaching dawn, Emma shut her eyes, her mind already planning her next move. The fight was far from over, and she was ready.

Isolation

The afternoon sun slunk behind the beer-bottle-green blinds, casting slivers of dying light across the flat. Emma sat crumpled on the edge of the bed, a mess of tangled thoughts, bloody knuckles white on the edge of the bed frame. The Argus C3, once her passport to the deepest reaches of humanity, sat ominously on the table. A burden now. A boulder she'd been shouldering, like some bonza Sisyphus.

With the weight of the world in her gut, she rose, her bare feet skating on the cool wooden floors. Her glance lingered on the camera. Once, it had been her eyes, the key to the bloody essence of people's souls. A tour guide on a long, winding journey through joy and sorrow, love and pain, all at the press of a button.

But that sense of wonder was long gone, evaporated like cheap grog under the harsh Aussie sun. In its place was a gnawing fear, a bloody snake coiled around her heart, its venom seeping into every corner of her life. The bloke from the pub, his hostility, the community's cold shoulder... it was all too much, like a roo in the headlights.

"Bugger it," she spat, slapping the dust off her jeans. She'd decided. The camera was to stay off. She wasn't going to play God anymore, peeping into souls, stirring up a hornets' nest with her well-intended meddling. It was over.

But as she walked away, the camera's unblinking eye bore into her, a silent accusation that twisted her guts. Her once cherished gift had become an albatross around her neck, a curse. A bloody raw deal, that's what it was.

The evening was setting in, and the shadows were long. And as the last beam of light gave up its ghost, the stark reality set in. Emma was alone, forsaken in the outback of her fear and guilt. The night stretched ahead, unforgiving, and her heart echoed with the quiet click of the camera shutting off, swallowed by the weight of the impending dark.

The world moved around Emma, a fast-paced waltz she was no longer part of. Her camera, her way into the inner sanctums of people's hearts, now lay abandoned, a monument to her misplaced courage. Without it, she felt like a bloody alien on her own turf, disconnected, out of sync with the rhythm of life pulsating around her.

Days fell into weeks, each one a clone of the one before, a dismal carousel of monotony. Work, home, sleep, rinse, repeat. Even the flaming galahs outside her window, once a source of joy with their raucous antics, now seemed to mock her with their freedom.

Her flat, once vibrant with laughter and life, was now just four drab walls pressing in on her, a gloomy echo chamber for her own thoughts. The dust collected on the once-loved knick-knacks, just as regret and guilt gathered in the corners of her mind.

She missed the human connection, the raw emotion that the lens had once revealed. Now, all she had were the mundane greetings at the local Woollies and the cold, polite nods from the blokes at the garage. A bloody pathetic excuse for a social life.

The isolation was crippling, wrapping its icy tendrils around her like a cold southerly buster. And in the midst of it, she was just Emma – no longer the insightful artist, the courageous crusader. Just plain ol' Emma, trudging through the days, holed up in her flat like a possum in its den.

Every night she'd listen to the lonely hum of the refrigerator, its white noise replacing the once lively chatter of friends. She'd stare at the blank TV screen, the static reflection staring back, a silent testament to her seclusion.

As the silence of her flat pressed in around her, it seemed to echo her own solitude. The isolation was not just in her flat, but within herself, a chasm of loneliness that stretched wider each day. She was an island in an urban sea, the cries of gulls replaced by the dull drone of city traffic. And in the centre of this solitude, she was learning the true price of her noble intentions.

The guilt was a weight on Emma's shoulders, a hefty sack of bloody spuds she had to lug around. With every tick of the clock, with every passing day of not using her camera, it was as if she was turning her back on a mate in need.

It wasn't just the fear that gnawed at her. It was the guilt of potential salvation untapped, of souls spiralling in their darkness while she hid, cowering behind the curtains of her flat like a frightened wallaby caught in the headlights. There was a certain guilt that comes with power, the kind of power that could change lives, mend broken hearts, reveal truths - and Emma was neck-deep in it.

Everyday chores became a battleground, her mind the site of a bloody stoush between the morality of her decision and the fear of consequence. She wrestled with the ethics of it all - the fact that she could help, that she could lend a hand to those lost, yet chose to sit idle, a by-stander to a parade of unseen torment.

It felt as though she was betraying her purpose, her gift. Like she'd been given this incredible tool, this bloody ripper of an ability, and she was just tossing it aside. The sense of guilt was suffocating, a wily python coiling tighter around her conscience with each passing moment of inaction.

Every empty street she walked down, every face she passed by, held a mirror to her guilt. She imagined the struggles, the silent pleas for help echoing through their souls. And all the while, she held the key to their salvation, tucked away in the dusty recesses of her flat.

And then there were the nights. They were the worst. The moonlight pouring through the window seemed to taunt her, casting long, accusing shadows that danced on her bedroom walls. They whispered tales of those she could've saved, the lives she could've changed. And there, in the cold loneliness of her bed, the guilt gnawed and gnawed, a relentless possum tearing at the roots of her resolve.

But in the midst of this crippling guilt, she remained paralysed, a kangaroo stuck in the blinding brightness of an oncoming truck. She was caught in a tug-of-war between her sense of duty and the fear of what might come, leaving her stranded in a purgatory of guilt and indecision.

The edges of reality had begun to blur for Emma. Her mind was a dodgy cricket pitch, causing her thoughts to spin and jump in unpredictable directions. Odd occurrences started to fill the gaps of her day, like a grotesque jigsaw puzzle that made no bloody sense.

There were the strange noises that seemed to claw at the silence of her flat, harsh whispers, the creaking of floorboards that had no right to creak. And then there were the shadows, the bloody shadows that danced on her walls as if putting on a performance of some macabre ballet. The subtle shift of darkness in the corners of her eyes made her skin prickle, made her heart race like a greyhound on the track.

Emma was no stranger to living alone. She'd had her fair share of creaks and groans in the dead of night, the kind that played tricks on a mind shrouded in darkness. But this was different. It was as if the shadows whispered her name, the creaks following her footsteps. A cold shiver would trickle down her spine every time she turned off the lights, a sense of unease gnawing at her gut.

And the feeling of being watched, that was the cherry on top of this messed-up pavlova. It clung to her like a second skin, prickling her senses, as though a thousand eyes were pinned on her. She felt it when she was huddled on her worn-out couch, when she tossed and turned in her bed, and when she trudged back home after a gruelling day of work.

She'd catch herself glancing over her shoulder on the quiet streets, her heart pounding in her chest like a furious drummer. At first, she dismissed it as a byproduct of her isolation and guilt. She was alone, spiralling down a rabbit hole of self-blame and regret. Paranoia was a fitting roommate in such circumstances.

But as days melted into nights and the oddities persisted, she began to question the reality of it all. Was it all in her head, her own personal horror show birthed from her guilty conscience? Or was there something more to it? A stalker, perhaps, lurking in the shadows, preying on her vulnerability?

Was she the prey in a sick game of cat and mouse, or was she just losing the plot? Either way, the fear was real. The fear of the unknown, of the possible threat, snaked around her like a venomous serpent, injecting its poison into every crevice of her sanity. Paranoia or not, Emma was drowning in a sea of fear, struggling to keep her head above the dark waves.

Everything seemed to be tinged with menace. Emma's world, once a field of blooming daisies and sunlit paths, had turned into a bloody battlefield. Everyday things morphed into monsters and the simple walks home turned into treacherous journeys through an imaginary minefield.

She'd saunter down the same streets she used to traipse on, only now they felt different. A sinister silence seemed to hang in the air, thick as pea soup, wrapping itself around the dilapidated buildings and narrow alleyways. Every footstep echoed like a gunshot, every rustle of leaves made her heart lurch in her chest. The world was hostile in her mind, her own city a beast waiting to swallow her whole.

Every bloke she passed on the street was a potential enemy. Every sideways glance, every stranger lingering a tad too long was a possible threat. Even the old Mrs. Patterson, the sweet octogenarian living next door who'd lost most of her marbles, seemed suspicious in Emma's paranoia-ridden mind.

Her usual stop at the local café turned into a nerve-wracking ordeal. The barista's innocent smile seemed to have a hidden meaning, his question of 'the usual?' suddenly carried an underlying menace. And the patrons, oh the bloody patrons, every one of them seemed to be in on the conspiracy. Their idle chatters, their secret glances, everything seemed staged, orchestrated.

And just like that, her world shrunk. It was reduced to her small, cluttered flat and the office cubicle where she spent her day in monotonous drudgery. She kept her interactions minimal, her smiles forced. Fear had woven a cocoon around her, a prison she willingly trapped herself into.

Her isolation was not a byproduct of the lockdown anymore. It was self-imposed, an attempt to protect herself from the unseen and unknown. She was the lone sheep, cut off from the herd, and there might have been a bloody wolf in the shadows.

The paranoia had seeped into every aspect of her life, turning everything hostile. She was always looking over her shoulder, always waiting for the other shoe to drop. Even in the safety of her flat, she'd flinch at the smallest of noises, her mind conjuring images of a shadowy figure waiting to pounce.

The world outside her four walls was a battlefield, and Emma was a soldier without a weapon. Her camera, her only defence against the impending darkness, had been abandoned. She was a sitting duck in a pond full of crocs, and the threat of a possible stalker was amplifying her isolation, the echo of her own fears bouncing off the lonely walls of her flat.

Fear does strange things to a person, especially when you're carrying the weight of an unspoken secret. It becomes a chasm, widening with every breath you take, separating you from everyone else. This was Emma's reality. A reality wrapped up in layers of anxiety and paranoia, her once vibrant life muted to grayscale monotony.

She tried reaching out again, to her mates, to anyone who'd listen. But it was bloody hard, even dialling a simple number felt like a Herculean task. Every time she picked up her phone, her heart would race, anxiety clawing its way up her throat. She'd hover over the call button, her mind a whirlwind of worst-case scenarios. What if they don't believe her? What if they thought she was just off her rocker?

She felt as far away from her friends as a dingo from the sea. Every interaction was laced with a distinct feeling of being on the outer, a painful awareness of a chasm she'd unwittingly carved. Her voice faltered during phone calls, her messages filled with hasty typos, her anxiety pouring out in every word she spoke or typed.

Her friends tried to bridge the gap, but it wasn't easy. Every invitation to hang out was met with vague excuses and a promise of 'next time'. Even simple catch-ups over coffee felt like a massive mountain she couldn't possibly climb. Emma was an island, cut off from the mainland by a sea of fear and paranoia.

The weight of her secret, the camera and its supernatural abilities, lay heavy on her tongue every time she conversed with a friend. It was a ghost hovering over every interaction, a truth she couldn't disclose. And so, she tiptoed around it, danced around the bush, offering fragments of her anxiety-ridden reality without revealing too much.

Her friends could sense the change. They saw the shadows under her eyes, heard the fear in her voice, noticed her absence. They tried to help, but how could they when Emma herself was a wall, unyielding and distant.

It was a bitter pill to swallow. To know she had people who cared, who'd stand by her, but couldn't help because she couldn't find the words. The feeling of isolation grew stronger, gnawing at her insides, a constant reminder of the lonely road she had to tread. She had cried wolf, and now she was on her own, navigating through a wilderness of fear and paranoia, waiting for the unseen stalker to make the next move.

Guilt's a slippery bugger. It seeps into the cracks, tainting every thought, every decision, every bloody moment. Emma found herself wrestling with it, unable to shake off the nagging voice in her head that insisted she'd mucked up. She'd tossed her camera aside, abandoned her gift and what for? A quiet life turned into a silent scream in her head.

Her flat, once a sanctuary, was now just four walls hemming her in. The camera lay there, gathering dust in the corner, as if it were just an old toy she'd grown tired of, not the miracle machine that showed the essence of souls. It was a reminder of the world she'd turned her back on, the people she'd promised to help.

In the deafening quiet, doubts swirled in her mind like a perpetual dust devil. Had she been wrong to abandon her camera? Was she doing a dirty to those who needed her, hiding away like a joey in a pouch? What about the dark energy she'd seen in the man? Wasn't it her responsibility to protect others from it?

Each question stung, like a salt-encrusted wound, churning and festering in her mind. The guilt was like a relentless crow, pecking away at her conscience. She'd once seen her gift as a blessing, a divine means to help those around her. Now, it was just a reminder of her perceived failure.

The fear was still there, a steady drumbeat in the back of her mind. It clawed at her insides, whispered threats in her ear, kept her on edge. The paranoia had turned everyday encounters into potential threats, turned the city into a battleground.

But amongst the fear and the guilt, another feeling began to bubble to the surface. It was subtle at first, a whisper that grew louder with each passing day. It was the stubborn grit of determination, the need to stand up and confront the fear instead of cowering away from it.

She'd let fear dictate her life, box her into a corner. Was that who she was? A coward? Or was she the woman who'd once embraced a divine gift, used it to help others, stood up to a man who emanated darkness? Emma realized she was at a crossroads, with one path leading further into fear and isolation, the other towards confrontation and potential danger.

Her decision loomed over her, a mountain she'd need to climb. She found herself thinking about the camera, the weight of it in her hands, the way it revealed the beauty of souls. The fear was still there, yes, but so was her courage, lying dormant, waiting to be tapped into. She was stuck in a tangle of regret and guilt, of fear and determination. Emma knew she had a fight on her hands, a fight that would decide the path her life would take.

The world felt like it was bearing down on Emma, each breath a struggle, each moment shrouded in paranoia and isolation. She felt like a rabbit trapped in the blinding headlights of life, frozen in the face of an oncoming storm. But in the midst of the darkness, a flicker of light emerged. It was faint at first, like a lone star fighting through the thick blanket of night.

It was a memory. A memory of her mate's words, spoken with warmth, infusing her with strength she hadn't realised she needed at the time. Words that pierced through the darkness, offering a glimmer of hope in the shroud of fear. The echo of the conversation started to take root in the soil of her mind, blooming into a radiant bloom that illuminated her thought.

"Emma, you're stronger than you think, mate. You've got a gift, and it's not just about seeing people's souls. It's about the heart you've got, the courage to do something about it."

The words washed over her, a soothing balm to the raw, open wounds of her guilt and fear. She began to ponder, her mind whirring as she retraced the steps she'd taken, the decisions she'd made. Perhaps there was a way to use her camera, her gift, without it consuming her life, without it inviting unwanted attention.

She spent hours nestled in her flat, her thoughts playing tag with the memories of her friend's comforting words. The guilt and paranoia started to loosen their icy grip, replaced by a burgeoning sense of determination. It was like finding a creek in the outback, the hope trickling in slowly, winding its way through the rocks of her fears, offering her a way out.

The realisation dawned on her, like the morning sun breaking the monotony of a pitch-dark night. She could navigate her gift, her camera, her own bloody life. She didn't have to relinquish her abilities out of fear or let them consume her. She could strike a balance, tread the delicate tightrope that was her life.

Hope began to percolate through her veins, coursing its way through her body, infusing her with newfound strength. It pushed back the shadows of her fear, the clouds of her doubt. In the quiet solitude of her flat, amidst the echoes of her friend's words, Emma found a beacon of hope. She clung to it, like a lifeline thrown to a woman drowning in a sea of fear. The fog began to lift, the world becoming less intimidating, less hostile. The fight was far from over, but Emma was ready. She had a battle plan, and a flicker of hope to light her way.

Living under the oppressive blanket of fear and isolation had turned Emma's world into a dreary expanse of grey. The vibrant colours of life were replaced with stark shadows and gloomy clouds. She'd been wallowing in this desolation for far too long, her spirit dwindling, her zest for life sapped away.

One day, sitting on her battered armchair and gazing out the window of her flat, she found her reflection staring back at her. Her eyes, once brimming with enthusiasm, were shadowed and weary. It hit her then, like a kick from a roo, the stark reality of what she'd become. A recluse. A shell of her former self. She was living in fear, becoming a prisoner in her own home. She'd allowed the paranoia to control her, let the guilt gnaw at her soul, and turned a blind eye to the ominous threat looming over her life.

"Bloody hell, enough of this!" she muttered to herself, her voice echoing in the silence of her flat. She was bloody tired of it all. Tired of the constant anxiety, the isolation, the gnawing guilt. This was no way to live. She was no bloody coward.

Her decision formed slowly, simmering in the back of her mind, before exploding into a full-blown resolve. She would face her fears. She wouldn't let the paranoia strangle her spirit or the guilt weigh her down. She'd deal with the potential stalker, head-on. She was a sheila made of tougher stuff, and it was about bloody time she proved it to herself.

With a newfound sense of purpose, Emma straightened up. She would take control of her life, navigate the murky waters of her gift, and handle her camera with the respect and responsibility it deserved. She would shed the debilitating fear and guilt and emerge from this ordeal stronger.

"Bring it on," she said aloud, a fierce determination seeping into her words. Her heart pounded in her chest, but it wasn't from fear this time. It was anticipation, a sense of impending action, a sense of reclaiming control. The fear still lingered in the corners, of course, it did, but it was no longer the dominating force. She was.

She wouldn't be running away anymore. She wouldn't be cowering in fear. She would stare the beast right in its bloody eyes and let it know she wasn't an easy target. The world was still a daunting place, but Emma was ready to face it, head held high and spirit aflame with determination.

The chapter of her life marked by fear and isolation was coming to an end. The next one was waiting to be written - a chapter of courage, resilience, and face-to-face confrontations. It was time to confront her fears. It was time to live again. And she was bloody well ready for it.

With the ominous walls of her self-imposed isolation ready to topple down, Emma finally made her stand. She felt that she had balled up into the smallest possible version of herself, like a hermit crab without its shell, exposed and defenceless. But now, there was a spark within her, a spark that refused to be snuffed out. The sort of spark that made you say, "Bugger it all, I'm not going down without a blue."

The life she'd been living, with her camera locked away and herself being an outsider, was akin to being on the run. She'd run from the responsibilities that her gift had thrown upon her, she'd run from the impact she'd had on her community, she'd run from the unsettling shadows that seemed to be dogging her every step. But it wasn't doing her any good; she was just a kangaroo caught in headlights, paralysed by fear and guilt. The realisation of this made her feel as sick as a parrot.

She thought back to the few mates she'd tried to reach out to. Even to them, she'd come off as distant and uneasy. She'd kept the truth from them, only revealing half-truths. But it was time to own up, to stop hiding, and to start living her life on her own terms.

Emma knew the decision to pick up her camera again wouldn't be a walk in the park. There would be potential backlash, repercussions. The dark energy she had seen around that bastard could still be lurking in the shadows, waiting to pounce. But she had come to terms with that. She was no longer the fearful girl who would buckle under pressure. She was the sheila who had looked into the heart of darkness and decided to fight back.

She was ready to tell the world, "You think you can intimidate me, you reckon you can make me feel small? Well, you've got another think coming, mate. I'm not the one to be trifled with. You want to see what I'm made of? Well, keep your bloody eyes peeled, cause I'm about to show you."

That night, Emma sat in her flat, her camera in her hands. The instrument that had once brought joy and then fear now felt like a promise of strength. She felt a kinship with it, a partnership. It was her tool, and she was ready to use it to wage a war against fear, against oppression, and against that nasty piece of work that had been terrorising her.

Emma gazed at her camera, a new sense of determination welling up within her. She'd be damned if she let anyone — be they a friend, a foe, or some seedy cunt with bad energy — strip her of her life and her abilities. She was ready to own up to her gift and to the responsibilities that came with it.

From now on, the world would have to deal with Emma, camera, gift and all, without any apologies or fear.

The Antique Store Again

E mma felt the morning heat beating down on her as she walked down the familiar lane. An uneasy familiarity hung in the air, like stale beer at the pub in the morning. The antique store stood there, unassuming, yet laden with secrets. The cobweb-ridden facade hadn't changed, still buried under a layer of time that only added to its mystical aura.

Walking in was like plunging headfirst into a time capsule. A waft of musty, old books and decaying wood washed over her, its familiarity strangely comforting yet daunting. The store, bursting at the seams with relics of the past, was as eclectic as ever. From rusty pocket watches to threadbare Persian rugs, every item had a story to tell. It was in this unassuming chaos that she'd found her camera, the instrument that had turned her life upside down.

Her mind's eye flashed with images of souls she'd captured, their deepest vulnerabilities laid bare by her lens. It was like peeling back layers of wallpaper, each more garish than the last. The faces and emotions were as varied as the antiques in the store. Some moments were heart-wrenching, others, profoundly beautiful. But the price of this raw exposure had been isolation and fear.

The echo of her boot heels on the wooden floor seemed louder today, reverberating around the cluttered room, her heart pounding in rhythm. Emma felt the heavy weight of trepidation hanging around her like a thick fog. She hadn't returned to the source to reminisce. She was there to dig deeper into the well of her own courage, seeking answers that only the keeper of these ancient secrets could provide.

The store's door closed behind her with an echoing creak, dust motes scattering in the sunlight that sliced through the grimy window. The familiar clutter of the store felt like a chaotic symphony of the past, items whispering stories of their long-gone owners. But it

wasn't the long lost trinkets that held Emma's attention today; it was
the store owner himself, old mate behind the counter, an antique in
his own right.

A wrinkled monument to a bygone era, the man seemed as old
as the relics that surrounded him. His weathered face held deep-set
eyes, the colour of burnt umber, that held an unspoken depth — a
depth she now knew how to read. His gravelly voice, thick with the
Aussie twang, rumbled from a chest lined with decades of wisdom
and heavy smoking. "Back again, are ya?" he asked, his sharp gaze
taking her in.

He seemed different this time, or maybe it was her. Last time she
was here, he was just another crotchety old codger, shuffling around
the store. Now, she saw him as the gatekeeper to the cryptic journey
her life had taken. His knowing eyes and gnarled hands held a story
she needed to uncover. He wasn't just an old bloke running a dusty
shop; he was the custodian of the cursed instrument that had strung
her life into a symphony of chaos and isolation.

Her past visits had been brief and transactional, like two ships
passing in the night. But this encounter was different. This time, she
was here for answers, answers she hoped he held. For all his prickly
demeanour and gruff exterior, she couldn't ignore the glimmer of
understanding in his gaze. It was as though he knew more about her
journey than he let on. Maybe he was just an old cunt playing games,
but she had to find out.

The old man looked up at Emma, his rough-hewn fingers
pausing over the aged book he'd been thumbing through. His eyes,
framed by creased skin and grey wiry brows, squinted to take her in,
his craggy face etching itself into a bemused smirk.

"Well, I'll be stuffed. Didn't expect to see you back here, love," he
mused, his voice thick with the grit of years, yet somehow carrying
a note of warmth. He rested his gaze on her, eyes tracing the lines
of worry etched into her face. "You're different," he noted, blunt as a

sledgehammer. His eyes bore into her, piercing through the bravado she'd mustered for this encounter. The gravity of her gaze, the stern set of her lips, she had the air of a sheila who'd been through the ringer and come out the other side tougher, more hardened.

There was a depth in her now, a palpable intensity that hung around her like an aura. It was a far cry from the wide-eyed, curious girl who'd wandered into his store months ago, fawning over the vintage camera. His eyebrows furrowed as he took in her transformation, curiosity piquing.

"You alright, love? You're looking a bit how ya goin'," he asked, his tone shifting from the usual gruffness to a rare hint of concern. There was something disconcerting about this version of Emma, the one who stood before him, a stark contrast to the vibrant girl he remembered. She had the look of someone bearing a weight, carrying a secret that felt heavier than the world.

He chewed on the inside of his cheek, a habit he'd picked up in his long years of observing people. She didn't just look different; she felt different. There was a change in her energy, a shift in her demeanour that he couldn't quite put his finger on. He could smell a story brewing around her, thick and heady as the scent of old paper and varnish that filled his store. If anything, the old cunt had a nose for these things. But he could tell this wasn't any ordinary tale. Emma was tangled in something that had changed her, and he suspected it had everything to do with the camera she'd bought.

His gaze followed Emma as she fumbled with the worn-out leather bag, revealing the camera. She held it out to him, her fingers trembling just a bit, her eyes filled with a quiet desperation. "This bloody thing...tell me, mate. What's the real story?"

The store owner studied the camera, his eyes darting between the vintage contraption and Emma. His fingers brushed against the worn leather, tracing the engraved initials 'A.B.' at the base. It was a relic from the past, harbouring secrets from a time he'd all but forgotten.

He finally relented, leaning back against the worn leather chair, his gaze never leaving the camera. His voice was softer now, almost wistful as he began to unravel the tale. "This old clicker," he began, "used to belong to a bloke by the name of Arthur Blackwood. He was a fair dinkum photographer, controversial as all hell."

Blackwood, he explained, was an odd fish, a recluse who'd created a world out of lenses and shutters. He'd been a photographer with a gift, or a curse, depending on who you asked. There were whispers about his portraits, claims that they captured more than just the human form, that they were windows to the soul. "Rumour has it, he could see into a bloke's soul, not just their faces. Sounds like a load of bull, right?" he mused, a crooked smile tugging at his lips. "But looking at you now, I'm starting to reckon there might be more to that story."

As the words spilled out, painting the picture of a man whose talent had teetered on the edge of a supernatural abyss, Emma felt a cold dread creep into her veins. The camera wasn't just an antique, it was an inheritance, a passing down of an enigmatic and terrifying ability that she had unknowingly taken upon herself.

The store owner fell silent, his words hanging in the air like spectres. Emma was left grappling with this revelation, the story of Arthur Blackwood echoing in her mind. The man, the camera, the power - they had all led her here, to this moment of understanding and terrifying clarity.

Emma was left with a gnawing sensation of connection with Blackwood. Two strangers, bound by a hunk of metal and glass and the eerie ability to peer into souls. The old bloke was no longer there, just a faded photograph, a legacy, and a camera that had passed into her hands. But with every click, she was starting to feel his presence, feel the weight of his legacy, and the shared burden they carried.

She was part of something larger now, part of a story that was as compelling as it was disturbing. But Emma was no weak-kneed lass, she was a tough cunt and she'd get to the bottom of this, come hell or high water.

Sitting in that creaky old shop, surrounded by relics of forgotten lives, Emma felt like she was riding the crest of a wild wave. Her mind swirled, a cacophony of thoughts and feelings crashing around inside her like a cyclone. She wasn't alone. The relief that brought, it was like a cool change on a scorching summer day. But it was laced with an undertow of unease, a rising fear that nibbled at the edges of her newfound comfort.

Her hand absently traced the leather casing of the camera, her fingers brushing against the cold metal body. It wasn't just an object, not anymore. It was a piece of her, her destiny tangled up with its lenses and shutters. It was as much a part of her as her heartbeat, an extension of herself that she couldn't deny or escape.

Her mind kept flickering back to the store owner's words, to the tale of Arthur Blackwood. She felt a kinship with him, a connection that sent shivers crawling up her spine. This man, this lonely, misunderstood bloke, had lived with the same terrifying gift. He'd seen people's souls just like she could. The thought was as comforting as it was unsettling. It vindicated her feelings, her experiences. She wasn't mad, wasn't imagining things. But it also raised a question, a gnawing uncertainty. Was this her fate? Was she destined to live her life as he had, alone and haunted by what she could see?

The room felt smaller, the walls closing in as the weight of her fear began to mount. What would this mean for her life, her relationships? Could she live a normal life knowing what she knew, seeing what she saw? The magnitude of it all threatened to crush her, to drag her under. But she was a stubborn sheila, wasn't going to go down without a fight.

Sitting there, the worn-out camera in her hand, Emma made a silent promise to herself. She wasn't going to let fear dictate her life. She'd navigate this storm, steer her life in the direction she wanted. She was Emma fucking Davis, not some shrinking violet. Her life, her rules. And anyone who had a problem with that could get stuffed.

The road ahead was murky, filled with uncertainties and the spectre of a destiny she wasn't sure she wanted. But Emma was a battler. She'd fight tooth and nail, and emerge out the other side, bruised maybe, but not broken. No bloody camera was going to defeat her. She was a tough cunt, and the world was about to find out just how tough.

Staring across the counter at the old codger, a white-hot fury surged through Emma's veins. She felt as if she'd been sold a pup, given a raw deal, and the rage of it all left a bitter taste in her mouth.

"You knew!" She almost spat the words, her voice ricocheting off the dust-laden corners of the antique store. "You knew about the fucking camera, and you never thought to warn me?"

The store owner, the sagacious old bugger, just shrugged, a sheepish look playing on his wrinkled face. "Now, listen here, love," he began, his voice sounding weary and somewhat defensive, "I heard the yarns, but never took 'em seriously. They were just rumours, ghost stories."

Emma's nostrils flared as she leaned in, her hands flat against the counter, her eyes locked onto his. "Ghost stories," she echoed, her voice a low growl. "Ghost stories that turned out to be true. And what? You thought it would be a bloody laugh to keep mum?"

He was unfazed, his gaze steady under her fury. "Look, Emma," he said, his voice dipping low, serious. "I sold it to you because you seemed drawn to it, like it spoke to you. I thought...I thought it was right. If I'd known how much strife it'd cause you, I would've chucked the damn thing in the bin."

The confession, the remorse in his voice, it did little to douse her anger. But as she stood there, glaring at the old man, she felt something shift inside her. This wasn't his burden to bear; it was hers. She'd chosen the camera, chosen this path.

"Yeah, well, you're one cunning cunt," she muttered finally, pushing off the counter and straightening. But there was a steeliness in her gaze now, a determination that hadn't been there before. "I'm not backing down. Not running away. This is my fight, and I'll be damned if I let it beat me."

The old man watched her in silence, a strange light twinkling in his eyes. As she turned to leave, he called after her, "Emma, remember, every curse can be a gift, depends on how you use it."

She didn't look back, didn't respond. His words echoed in her mind as she walked away, their weight settling into her bones. Every curse could be a gift. She would remember that. Because she was Emma Davis, and she was ready to turn this curse into her bloody gift.

In the throes of the dispute, Emma's fury burned as fiercely as a wildfire tearing through the bush. Her mind was a whirlwind, her heart pounding like the throb of an Aussie summer's heat. Her words, sharp as a shearer's blade, were fuelled by the raw emotion coursing through her veins.

"You cunning old cunt!" she snarled, each word wrapped in venom as her Aussie roots took hold of her tongue. The antique store seemed to hold its breath, a silent observer of the storm brewing within its walls.

The store owner merely blinked, his eyes peering through the round spectacles perched on his nose, their calm a stark contrast to Emma's storm. He'd heard the term before, seen it hurled like a missile in countless arguments at the local pub, but coming from Emma, the petite photographer with the strange camera, it held a different weight.

"Easy, Emma," he warned, his voice steady. "You're fair dinkum about this, and I respect that, but there's no need for name-calling."

She laughed then, a bitter, hollow sound that echoed off the musty wooden shelves lined with relics of the past. "Need? You don't get to tell me what I need. You've got no bloody clue what I've been through, what that fucking camera has done."

"Maybe, maybe not," he replied, holding her fiery gaze. "But I do know that you're stronger than you think. You're here, aren't you? You haven't thrown in the towel."

Her anger ebbed then, replaced by a tide of fatigue. But beneath that, simmering in the depths, was a newfound resolve. She shot him one last look, her eyes ablaze with fierce determination. "This isn't over," she warned, her tone unyielding. "And you – you should've been bloody honest from the start."

With that, she turned on her heel, leaving the old store owner behind. As she stepped out into the unforgiving Aussie sun, she felt a sliver of relief. She had confronted her fears, faced her anger head-on. And she'd lived to tell the tale. That alone was enough to fuel her forward.

Emma was no longer a lost girl playing with a magical camera; she was a woman at war, ready to face whatever the world – or the camera – had in store for her. And she was far from being beaten.

Emma stood there, every ounce of her boiling with righteous indignation. The antique store's hushed, dust-filled air was heavy with her anger. She was still trembling, the echoes of her outburst hanging in the air like a cloud of static. The old bloke merely watched her, an unreadable expression behind his spectacles.

"Thanks for the bloody truth, mate," she muttered, her words saturated in sarcasm. Her hands clenched and unclenched, craving the comforting weight of her camera, the solid reality it represented. But the camera was at home, lying dormant, an innocent-looking object that held the power to alter lives.

Walking towards the exit, the wooden floor creaked under her weight, every step taking her further away from the source of her turmoil. She cast one last glance over her shoulder, catching the store owner's gaze. The silence between them felt like an abyss - wide, vast, and loaded with unsaid words.

The door swung open, letting in the harsh Australian sunlight. It slashed through the dust motes, slicing the gloomy interior of the shop into fragmented beams of light. Blinking against the glare, Emma stepped out, leaving behind the dimly lit world of the past.

Outside, the city was coming alive. Cars zipped by, honking, people chatted, and the world went on, oblivious to the storm that raged within her. As she navigated the busy streets, the weight of the camera's history bore down on her, making her steps slow and deliberate.

Despite the midday sun, a cold wind blew, sweeping the streets of Sydney, rustling her hair, and chilling her heated cheeks. Emma welcomed it, letting the icy gusts of wind whip around her, grounding her in reality.

She was out here, alone, carrying a burden too complex to share with anyone. She felt the isolation creeping back in, the walls of her world constricting. But this time, she wouldn't let it defeat her.

Reaching her flat, Emma paused, looking at her reflection in the glass window. The woman who stared back at her was different. She looked harder, her eyes had lost the spark of naive curiosity. In its place, a determination flared, a stubborn defiance in the face of adversity.

This knowledge she'd gained today, it was a double-edged sword. It had cut her, yes, but it had also armed her. There was power in knowledge, in knowing the past, in knowing that she wasn't alone in her strange ability. And Emma, she planned on using this power, wading through the murky waters of uncertainty towards the clarity she sought.

And so, Emma walked away. From the antique store, from her earlier self, and towards a future where she would wield her camera not out of fear or curiosity, but with the awareness of the power it held. A future where she was no longer a spectator, but a fighter. The battle had just begun.

Emma found herself back at her flat, standing in the middle of the room, surrounded by the half-hearted attempts at making it home. But the art prints on the walls, the vase of fresh flowers on the coffee table, and the throw pillows neatly arranged on the couch felt like part of a different life, one that had been upended by an antique camera and a peculiar gift.

She stood there, rooted, the quiet hum of the fridge the only sound cutting through the silence. Her mind was a whirl of thoughts, a chaotic orchestra playing the symphony of her turmoil. She could still hear the store owner's voice, telling the story of the camera's original owner. A photographer who was said to capture souls. It was madness, but wasn't her life a testament to that madness?

Swallowing, Emma moved to the window, looking out at the city sprawled below. The lights sparkled in the twilight, each one a story, a life, a world of its own. It was a sight she'd captured through her lens a thousand times. Yet now, it felt different. More real. More raw. It was no longer just a pretty picture but a testament to life, its joys and sorrows, its mundane routines, and its extraordinary moments. And she, Emma, had the ability to capture it all.

A bitter laugh escaped her lips. She felt like a cosmic joke. Given a gift that felt like a curse, entrusted with a power she didn't ask for. But life wasn't about asking. It was about dealing with the hand you were dealt. And she'd be damned if she let this break her.

Turning from the window, Emma's eyes fell on the camera, lying unassuming on the table. It was just a thing, an object. It held no power that she didn't give it. This was her gift, her curse, her challenge. And she was not about to be controlled by it.

Taking a deep breath, Emma picked up the camera, its familiar weight a comfort. She looked at it, not with fear or dread, but determination. There was a story to be told, a mission to be accomplished. She had the power to make a difference, and she wouldn't let fear rob her of that.

Let the world throw what it may at her, she was ready. She was Emma, the woman with a camera, the woman with a gift, the woman with a story to tell. She wouldn't run from it anymore. She was no longer a lost girl unsure of her path. She was a woman who knew her power and was ready to wield it. Let the bloody world watch out.

It was a calm, still night. Outside, the world was going on about its business, unaware of the storm brewing in the heart of one Emma. She was standing there, right in the middle of her bloody flat, every part of her echoing the reality of the word she had spat out at the antique store owner earlier. 'Cunt'. It was a crude word, raw and undiluted, exactly like her life had become.

There was a chill in the air, but it was nothing compared to the icy resolve that was taking over her. She'd had enough of being pushed around by her own life, by circumstances beyond her control. It was high time to do some pushing back.

She stared at the camera lying on the table, an innocuous piece of metal and glass that had completely changed her life. It was a tool, not a curse. It didn't have control over her, she had control over it. She had been swimming in the turbulent ocean of fear and uncertainty for far too long. It was time to turn the tide.

Shaking her head, she chuckled. "You've really gone off the deep end, haven't you, Em?" She said to herself, a wry grin on her face. But that was okay. Sometimes you needed to go off the deep end to understand just how strong you could be.

She picked up the camera, feeling the cold, metallic weight of it in her hands. Her fingers traced the edges, the contours, almost lovingly. It wasn't just a camera anymore. It was a part of her, as integral to her being as her very heartbeat.

"Alright, you bastard," she said to the camera. "Let's do this."

It was a small step, acknowledging the power she held. But as she stared at her reflection in the mirror, the camera hanging from her neck, she could see a change. Her eyes held a spark they hadn't before. There was steel in her gaze, a determination that came from having looked into the abyss and choosing to fight instead of cower.

With a final glance at her reflection, she turned away. The world was waiting. Waiting for her to make her mark, to use her gift for something greater. And she would. Because she was Emma. She had a camera, a gift, and a mission. And she was bloody well ready to face it all.

"Bring it on, you cunts," she murmured, an uncharacteristic smirk playing on her lips as she switched off the lights and crawled into bed. Tomorrow was a new day. And she was ready. The echoes of that one crude word rang in her ears, a sharp reminder of her determination. The game had changed. She was in control now. And she wasn't going to let go. No matter what the bloody universe threw at her next.

The Previous Owner

A sense of something haunted stalked Emma as she sat at her computer, a stubby of beer at her side, fingertips rattling on the keyboard. She was on a mission, a bloody hunt into the past, like some twisted archaeologist. The camera's previous owner was her target, the one who'd been the first to dance with the power she now held. She was tracking this phantom through the digital wilderness, scattered breadcrumbs of existence, the web that caught the dead and the living alike.

Every click took her deeper into a labyrinth of information, a twisted maze filled with whispers of an elusive cunt who had first discovered the monstrous beauty of the camera's power. Emma couldn't help but feel a strange bond with this shadow from the past, like looking at a warped mirror reflecting a grotesque version of herself.

Each byte of data she uncovered felt like a piece of a jigsaw, another shard of glass in a shattered mirror. This fella was like her, or she was like him – both bound by the same supernatural force, yoked by the same uncanny fate. Only this bloke, this predecessor, had wielded the camera's power like a cudgel, a weapon of control and intrusion.

It was eerie, like walking through a ghost town, or reading a long-dead poet's verse - there was a sense of recognition, a sickly familiarity. A connection, like an invisible umbilical cord, stretched across time, tying her to this faceless man. The power that once fascinated her, now felt like a weight, a responsibility she'd inherited from a man she didn't even know.

The longer she spent immersed in her search, the more the lines blurred. The past bled into the present, the real into the unreal, and Emma found herself caught in this spectral waltz. She drank more, the beer's bitter sting a tether to reality.

The room around her became silent except for the buzzing of her laptop, the occasional sip of beer, and the steady drumming of her heart. She felt a rush of adrenaline, a kind of morbid fascination that propelled her forward, deeper into the rabbit hole. It was a thrill, this chase, a dangerous dance with the past, a rendezvous with a ghost. And she was bloody well ready for it.

Diving deeper into the digital quagmire, Emma began uncovering the sordid history of the camera's previous owner, this anonymous cunt from the past. His name surfaced like an oil slick on water - a tarnished reputation following an infamous photographer renowned for his controversial work. His name had left a foul taste in the mouths of many in the art world, and Emma could almost taste the bitter resentment as she read further.

His art had been invasive, violating even, a testament to a man who pushed boundaries, not just of creativity but of decency. He was a rogue in the world of photography, a renegade whose technique was to invade and capture, to trespass into the lives of others with the eye of his camera.

Emma poured over old interviews, each word shedding more light on the man she was starting to despise. His responses were audacious, unrepentant. He saw his work as a brave new direction in photography, a challenge to the status quo. He was a king in his mind, a bloody dictator in reality, wielding his camera like a sceptre, bending people to his will.

His subjects were not just captured; they were exposed, their privacy stripped away, laid bare for all to see. He had used the camera's power to peep into their souls, to dissect their private moments, to serve his twisted version of art. Each click of the shutter, each flash, was a violation, an intrusion that left an indelible mark on their lives.

Emma felt a sickness in her gut as she learned more. The keyboard felt cold under her fingertips, each new revelation casting a darker shadow on her predecessor. She was left with a picture of a man who had misused the gift she now held in her hands, a rogue photographer who thrived on controversy and invasion.

In her small flat, she sat alone, staring at the screen, her mind buzzing with disgust and a grudging admiration for the man's audacity. She saw what the power could do if it went unchecked, if it fell into the wrong hands. She saw a warning, a chilling cautionary tale, a fate she was determined to avoid.

Emma burrowed into the depths of the internet, uncovering the haunting tales left behind by the photographer's victims. She read through testimonies, one after another, all echoing the same sentiments - a feeling of violation, a sense of being stripped down to their bare selves. Each account was a bullet, and Emma felt each one piercing her insides, a harsh realization of the legacy she had unwittingly inherited.

There were stories of subjects left feeling bare, violated after their sessions with him, their stories thrown around the internet like dirty laundry for everyone to see. The more she delved, the darker the rabbit hole became. Each testimony was more gruesome than the last. Each victim had a face, a life they once knew, only to be shattered by the man wielding the camera with malice instead of respect.

The photographer was no artist, Emma thought, he was a predator, a bloody cunt who used his lens not to capture beauty but to expose the intimate secrets of his subjects. His art was not just controversial; it was invasive, predatory. She could almost feel their violation as she pored over their accounts, each word a grim reminder of the power the camera held.

The more Emma read, the more she felt a rising tide of anger towards the previous owner. The man she had tried to empathize with was turning out to be a monster, a wolf in sheep's clothing. He was a misuse of power personified, a testament to the corrupting influence of unchecked power.

This understanding, as harsh as it was, was necessary. Emma needed to see the man behind the camera for what he truly was - a warning, a signpost on her journey pointing towards what she could become if she let the power consume her. The revelations were as much a haunting echo of the past as they were a guide for her future.

By the time she closed her laptop, the room felt colder, the air heavy with the weight of her newfound knowledge. She was far from the naive girl who first walked into the antique store. Now, she understood more than she had bargained for, more than she had ever wanted. Yet, in the face of the truth, her resolve hardened. Emma knew what she had to do. The man's shadow would not darken her path. She would wield the power with responsibility, with empathy, unlike the cunt before her. The past was a haunting revelation, but it was also a wake-up call. Emma was ready to answer it.

As Emma trawled through the remnants of the photographer's life, she came face to face with the twisted allure of power. Each photograph, each victim's account, was a testament to the darkness lurking in the corners of her gift. Each revelation shook her to the core, but it also sparked a flicker of defiance in her heart. She saw what unchecked power could do, the damage it could inflict, and it scared the bloody hell out of her. Yet, fear wasn't the only emotion churning within her; a sense of responsibility was kindling too.

His work was a terrifying showcase of the dark side of power. Images captured with a predatory lens, each shot reeking of manipulation, violation. She saw faces frozen in time, their eyes mirroring the horror of their exposure. Each photo was a glimpse into a soul stripped bare, twisted into a grotesque form of art. It made her skin crawl.

The more she delved into the bastard's work, the more her heart pounded against her chest. This was the path she could have tumbled down, led by curiosity and the intoxicating thrill of seeing the unseen. She shuddered at the thought. What if she, too, ended up misusing her gift? The mere thought was enough to send waves of nausea rolling through her.

Despite the fear clawing at her, Emma felt an odd sort of gratitude. If not for these disturbing revelations, she could have turned into another version of the cunt with a camera, taking more than she had any right to. But she was not him. She would not let her power distort her into a monster. She would control her gift, not let it control her. She would navigate this tightrope of power with care, not the reckless abandon of the previous owner.

In the harsh light of her laptop screen, Emma made a solemn promise to herself. She would harness her power responsibly, she would respect the sanctity of every soul she captured. The fear and disgust kindled a renewed determination within her. The twisted legacy of the camera would not repeat itself. She would not let it.

Every gruesome image she encountered, every victim's tale she read, became part of a silent oath. An oath to tread lightly, to respect, to protect. And most importantly, to never, ever become the cruel cunt that the previous owner had been. Power had a dark side, indeed, but Emma decided then and there that she would spend every waking moment ensuring she didn't succumb to it. She would shine a light into the shadows, turning her gift into a beacon of empathy instead of a tool of violation.

In the harsh, quiet solitude of her study, Emma turned to stare blankly at the screen that blared out the sins of the previous camera owner. The stories, the accusations, the shattered lives that bore testimony to his misuse of the camera's power. This cunt had taken a gift and warped it into a weapon of violation. Emma's fingers clenched on the edge of the desk, her jaw setting in a grim line. The rough Aussie slang rolled off her tongue in a low mutter, "Cunt..."

He was a cunt, alright, the previous owner. A thieving, soul-stealing bastard. No respect for privacy, no respect for people. He'd taken his gift and used it to pry, to expose, to strip people bare. He'd seen the same intimate truths Emma could see, the raw realities that lay beneath the skin. But unlike her, he had capitalized on it, feasted on it. He'd used his power not for understanding, but for control and manipulation.

She took a slow breath, trying to quiet the tumultuous thoughts and the churning of her stomach. The term she used was not one she took lightly. But here, in the unyielding grasp of night, it felt right. It felt fitting. This wasn't about polite language or good manners; this was about truth. And the truth was, the man was a right cunt, one that had let his power run away with him, careening down a path of destruction.

Emma felt the weight of her anger and disgust pressing against her chest. She'd come so close, danced on the edge of the same precipice. Yet, she'd seen the fall now, seen the carnage that lay at the bottom, and she would not tumble down the same cliff. She would not be that kind of cunt.

Her mouth twisted around the word again, the taste bitter yet empowering. It was a label, a line drawn in the sand. She wasn't using it lightly; it was a reflection of her resolve, a harsh reminder of what she was up against. It was a crude word for a crude reality.

This cunt had tainted the power of the camera, twisted it into something ugly. But Emma wouldn't let his legacy define her journey. She wouldn't be another predator, another violator. She was stronger than that. She was better than that. And as the dawn crept over the horizon, washing away the remnants of the night, she vowed to prove just that. No matter what, she would not become the cunt the previous owner had been.

She sat in the soft glow of the laptop screen, surrounded by the fading twilight and the creeping chill of evening. The ghost of the previous camera owner hovered around her, his spectre cast in the lurid tales of his exploits. His shadow seemed to stretch out and touch her, a haunting reminder of the path she could so easily tread. It was a grim thought, walking in the footsteps of a cunt like him. She could almost feel the slippery slope under her feet, the precipice of misuse looming in her periphery.

There was an uncanny resemblance in their abilities, a twisted kinship born of the camera's power. It was an uncomfortable thought, sending a shudder down her spine. Emma caught her reflection in the screen, the light casting strange, dancing shadows on her face. She couldn't help but notice the hardness in her eyes, the grim determination set in her jaw. The same grim determination that might've graced the face of the previous owner.

But then, there was also a difference. She wasn't him. She was not that cruel, unfeeling bastard. She had the power, yes, but she didn't have his ruthless nature. She had seen the damage he'd done, the lives he'd disrupted. And she knew, in the marrow of her bones, she wasn't capable of such atrocities. She would not, could not, be that kind of cunt.

He had let the power control him, warp him into something monstrous. But she wouldn't. She couldn't. She had seen the damage, had even tasted a little of it herself. She wasn't going to let that happen again. She wouldn't walk in his shadow, wouldn't allow his taint to touch her life, her gift. No, she would carve her own path, one of understanding, not intrusion; empathy, not exploitation.

The air was heavy around her, thick with thoughts and the remnants of the past. The spectre of the cunt with the camera lingered, a cautionary tale painted in stark relief. She knew she had a choice to make - to step out of his shadow, or to remain entangled in his sins. And as the night deepened, she made her decision. She would not be controlled by her fear. She would not become another pawn to the camera's power.

Instead, she would stand tall, casting her own shadow, stark against the tarnished legacy of the previous owner. She would use the camera, yes, but not as a weapon. She would use it as a tool, a bridge between souls, a beacon of empathy and understanding. No, she wouldn't walk in the shadows of a cunt. She would stride into the light, her heart firm, her resolve unyielding. The path of a cunt was not hers to tread. She had a different journey, and she was ready to begin.

In the quiet of her apartment, the echo of past transgressions hanging heavy in the air, Emma took a deep, shaky breath. The stories she'd unearthed, the unsettling echoes of the past, clung to her like smoke, seeping into her consciousness. The invasive, violating photographs taken by that cunt of a predecessor were etched into her mind. It was a chilling reminder of what she could become, the potential monstrosity lying in wait.

"Emma, you won't become him," she whispered to herself, her voice a ghost in the dim room. The walls, lined with photographs of her own, felt comforting in a strange, ironic way. They were different from his, those invading, violating images. They had depth, substance, but none of the intrusive intimacy that marked his work. It was a stark contrast, a line she had drawn without even realising it.

Yet, the promise wasn't just for herself. It was for the faces on the screen, the people whose lives had been stripped bare, their secrets spilled out like cheap wine for the world to gawk at. The ghosts of those violated by the camera's power, they deserved this promise. A silent vow to all those souls, to every person she would photograph in the future.

"I won't become him," she murmured again, the words solidifying the pledge in her heart. She wouldn't be a voyeur, a violator. She wouldn't use her camera as a weapon. She wouldn't be the next cunt with a lens, invading lives with an unblinking, mechanical eye.

Her fingers traced the camera resting on the table beside her. It was cool to the touch, a solid presence against the surreal reality she found herself in. It was her tool, her gift, and her curse, all wrapped up in an innocuous package of metal and glass. And she decided, there, in the silent company of her own thoughts, that she would wield it responsibly.

Her camera wouldn't invade, wouldn't rip apart lives and display them for morbid curiosity. It would serve a different purpose under her watch, a higher purpose. It would capture emotions, tell stories, not steal them. She'd use it to build bridges of understanding, not walls of intrusion.

Emma's oath hung in the air, a silent but potent promise. Her vow to the past, to the future, to herself. No more would the camera be an instrument of violation. Not while she held it. Not while she could control it. As the night deepened, she held on to that promise, a beacon in the dark. She wouldn't become the cunt with the camera. She'd be something else, something better. She'd ensure it.

Emma sat there in her dimly lit room, the air thick with a sense of unsettling resolve. There was something liberating about confronting the past, looking it in the eye and not blinking. The previous owner, that cunt with a camera, had served as a mirror of a darker self she could have become. A grotesque reflection she was determined to avoid.

She was at a crossroads, a junction between a path darkened by misuse of power and a road less travelled, illuminated by her own principles. The choice was as clear as the Aussie sky on a cloudless day. She'd carve her own path, unmarred by the bloody footprints of the man who'd walked before her.

With the chilling echoes of the past still reverberating within her, Emma took a deep breath, allowing herself to momentarily sink in the discomfort. The past wasn't something to be shaken off like a dog shedding water. It was a necessary discomfort, a constant reminder of the consequences if she strayed off her chosen path. The old bloke with the camera was now a ghost in her rearview mirror, a haunting spectre whose mistakes would guide her future.

Yet, beneath the discomfort, there was an undercurrent of strength, a river of resolve that flowed with a quiet but steady force. Emma felt it build within her, a dam of determination holding back the tides of fear and uncertainty. The haunting shadows were beginning to recede, replaced by a burgeoning dawn of courage. She'd learn from the past, not live in it.

Lacing her fingers around the cool, metallic body of the camera, Emma made a silent promise to herself. She'd take this power, this uncanny ability, and put it to good use. The photographer of the past had used it as a weapon to pry open the lives of his subjects. But Emma, she'd wield it as a tool, a means to capture the unspoken, the unseen, in an intimate yet respectful manner.

Her photographs wouldn't be invasions, they'd be collaborations. They wouldn't strip away the dignity of her subjects but enhance it, amplifying their voices through her lens. She'd honour the sanctity of their experiences, their emotions, capturing them not as objects but as humans in all their complex glory.

With a final glance at the dusty mirror hanging on the wall, Emma rose from her chair, her reflection staring back at her. It wasn't a haunting reflection anymore. It was a reminder of the woman she had become, a woman who had looked into the abyss, acknowledged the power she wielded, and chose to rise above it. She was ready to carve her own path, a trail of respectful images and heartfelt stories, distinct from the one laid down by the cunt with the camera.

That bloke was a part of her past, an echo fading into the abyss. Emma was now the author of her own future, the photographer of her own journey. And as the chapter closed, a new one began, a narrative guided by her courage, her resolve, and her camera.

Resolution & Exploration

It was one of those dull, dreary arvo's where the sky looked like a grey old bloke's beard, but Emma didn't notice. She was all tangled up in her thoughts, in the enormity of what she had in her hands. The camera, a relic, a bloody Pandora's box. She stared at it, thinking of the power it held, the lines it had crossed. It was a tool, a weapon, a fucking curse - all rolled into one.

It felt heavier now, loaded with all the truths she had uncovered, all the violations committed by the previous prick. She had been thrown head-first into the bloody deep end, forced to grapple with the murky grey areas between right and wrong, the ethical boundaries that came with wielding such power. The camera had revealed her its secrets, and now, it sat in her hands, waiting for her next move.

"Alright, cunt," she muttered to herself, summoning a resolve as sturdy as a roo's backbone. "We play by my rules now."

Emma set herself some strict guidelines. No invasion of privacy, no stripping of dignity, no exploitation. She was going to respect her subjects, their boundaries. The camera was going to be a bridge of understanding, a conduit of empathy, not a fucking peeping Tom. She was going to use it to capture stories, emotions, the raw unfiltered beauty of life - not to prey on vulnerabilities.

She readied herself to take the first shot, her finger trembling slightly over the trigger. It felt like standing on the edge of a cliff, a mad mix of fear and anticipation churning in her guts. The air crackled around her as she held her breath, the moment stretching out like an elastic band before she pressed down on the button.

The camera whirred to life, capturing her first picture under her new resolve. A quiet street, bathed in the soft, diffused light of the overcast day, void of people, but brimming with stories waiting to be told.

Emma exhaled, her heart thundering in her chest. The first step was always the hardest, but she had taken it. She had stepped back into the water, ready to swim this time. With her rules, her values. The camera was no longer a haunting ghost but a part of her journey, a part of her growth. Emma was ready to rewrite its history, starting with her own.

The outback sun had packed it in for the day, giving way to the blanket of night that lay heavy across the sky. The celestial stretch was a ripper tonight, stars twinkling like mischievous eyes winking down at her from the great beyond. Emma sat out on her veranda, her old camera cradled in her lap, staring into the cosmos as if seeking answers or perhaps absolution.

There was a heaviness in the air, a tension that wove its tendrils around her, binding her in deep contemplation. The camera, its existence, was an enigma wrapped in a dilemma. But she wouldn't let it be her ball and chain anymore. It was time to make the rules, set the bloody boundaries. The power it held could either make her or break her, and she'd be damned if she let the latter happen.

"No more mucking about," she mumbled to herself. She laid out the rules, clear as the southern constellations above her. There was to be no invasion of personal spaces, no rooting through people's lives like they were some reality TV show. There would be no exploitation of vulnerabilities, no stripping people bare to their souls without their consent. It was going to be respect, understanding, bloody empathy.

These rules were set in stone, as immovable as the Great Dividing Range itself. There was no wiggle room, no grey area. She had grown, matured, come to see the camera for what it was - a tool, not a weapon. And she wasn't about to use it like that bloody drongo before her.

Emma looked down at the camera, its lens gleaming in the pale light of the waxing moon. It wasn't a beast to be tamed anymore but a companion on this journey. It was no longer about capturing moments but understanding them, cherishing them.

The stars watched silently as she rose from her seat, determination etched in every line of her being. The bloke before her had misused this power, turned it into something rotten. But she wasn't him. She was Emma, the sheila who'd wrangled with this bastard of a power and made it her own.

With a final glance at the infinite stretch of twinkling stars, she walked back into her house, ready to face a new dawn. The rules were laid, the course set. This camera, her camera, was ready for a second chance, and by God, she was going to give it one.

There she was, Emma, her guts churning like a stormy sea. It had been a fair dinkum struggle, fighting off the fears, the nightmares of what that bloody camera had been used for in its past life. But now, with her new set of rules inked in her soul, she was ready to face the beast once again. The morning sun rose, lighting the canvas of the outback, casting long shadows and painting the world in warm hues of hope and renewal.

She walked out into the unpretentious beauty of the Australian bushland. The scent of eucalyptus wafted in the air, mingling with the dusty tang of the red earth. There was an honesty about it, something raw and primal. It resonated with the way she felt. It was the perfect place to start again, to take the first step into this new journey.

She took a deep breath, feeling the crisp morning air fill her lungs, wash over her nerves. She had the camera in her hands, the familiar weight a reassuring anchor against the turbulent sea of her emotions. It was just a tool, she reminded herself, its power lay in the hands that wielded it. And she wasn't going to be that bloody wanker who'd had it before.

Her eyes scanned the landscape, her photographer's instinct kicking in. She was looking for a subject, something that would symbolize this fresh start. There, on the twisted bark of an old gum tree, was a vivid splash of green - a new leaf sprouting. Perfect. A symbol of life, resilience, new beginnings.

She framed the scene in her camera, the leaf prominent against the rough bark. Her heart pounded like a kangaroo on the hop as she clicked the shutter. The camera whirred, capturing the image, the moment forever frozen in time.

She felt a wave of relief wash over her as she looked at the result. It was a simple picture, a leaf on a tree, but to Emma, it signified more. It was a step forward, an affirmation of her resolve to make this power her own and not let it consume her.

The sun now high in the sky bathed her in its warm embrace. She'd done it. She'd faced her fears, set her rules, and taken her first shot. There was a grin plastered on her dial that would've outshone the bloody Sydney Harbour Bridge.

With the camera hanging from her neck, she walked back home. It was a new day, a new beginning for her. The first picture, a symbol of her renewed journey, marked the start of an ethical era in her photography. She'd shown that she could control the power, not be controlled by it. She'd shown she wasn't the past owner, she was Emma, and she was going to do things her way.

The shadows were growing long as Emma sank into the worn couch, an old, dog-eared book on polyamory resting heavily in her hands. It felt like holding the key to Pandora's box, and yet there was a buzz, an excitement simmering within her that felt like downing a couple of stubbies too fast.

She'd always fancied both the blokes and the sheilas. That was a truth about her as old as the southern cross tattoo etched into her shoulder. But, it was this new bit, this polyamory, that was giving her a bit of a spin. It wasn't just about having a swing, it was about love, about relationships that were as complex as a riddle wrapped in an enigma. The thought of it was like a hot coffee on a cold morning, terrifying and tantalizing all at once.

So, she'd decided to do a bit of a squiz, to learn more about it. This wasn't just some bloody game; people's hearts were at stake. If she was going to do this, to walk down this path, she needed to understand it, to know the rules.

The book was like a tour guide, leading her through the labyrinth of polyamory. She read about the dynamics, the philosophies, the ethics, and the bloody hard work it entailed. It wasn't just about getting your rocks off with more than one person. It was about honesty, about communication, about balancing the needs and wants of multiple partners.

As she read, Emma felt a bit like she was standing at the edge of a cliff, the sea of polyamory stretching out before her. It was vast and daunting, full of sharks and riptides, but also full of promise. She could see the possibility of love, of relationships that would allow her to be herself, to express her love without boundaries or limitations.

The hours passed, the words swirling in her head, muddling and clarifying in turns. It was a lot to take in, to process, but she felt a sense of rightness, a sense of truth that she hadn't felt in a long while. This was her, this was Emma - a bisexual, possibly polyamorous woman who was just trying to navigate her life and love as authentically as possible.

The sun had long set when she finally closed the book, her mind abuzz with thoughts and emotions. It was like she'd just put on a pair of glasses, and the world had snapped into focus. It was scary, it was thrilling, but most of all, it was liberating. It felt like coming home.

Emma looked at the camera resting on the table, the book on polyamory lying next to it. Two journeys, two paths laid out before her - one professional, one personal, both intertwined in a dance as old as time. She knew she had a long way to go, a lot to learn, but she was ready for it. Ready to embrace her power, her sexuality, and her capacity for love. And with that thought, Emma stepped into her new life, a life full of promise, full of potential, full of her.

Emma's mind was a battleground, a fierce tussle between the preconceived notions she'd held and the new perspectives she was beginning to understand. She was smack in the middle of it all, like a joey caught in headlights. It was a bloody tough place to be, grappling with her own biases, wrestling with societal norms that felt as binding as chains.

She'd grown up believing in a certain way of life, a certain understanding of relationships - monogamy, heteronormativity. It was as much a part of her as the Southern Cross on her skin, a silent law etched into her psyche by years of societal conditioning. But now, she was beginning to question it all, to pull at the seams of these norms.

What if she didn't want just one partner? What if she wanted to share her love, her life, with more than one person? What if she was attracted to both men and women? It was a whirlwind of questions, an internal storm that was as thrilling as it was terrifying.

It wasn't easy, bloody hell it wasn't. There was a part of her that wanted to bury these thoughts, to shove them under the rug and go back to living a life of ignorance. But there was another part, a stronger, braver part, that urged her to explore, to understand, to accept who she truly was.

She felt like a digger in the trenches, battling with the contradictions within her. It was a war of acceptance against denial, of truth against pretence, of love against prejudice. It was her own Anzac story, a battle of identity, a struggle for freedom.

Through it all, Emma learnt that understanding oneself was not a destination but a journey. It was a winding, treacherous road full of blind spots and speed bumps. But it was also a road of self-discovery, a road that would lead her to authenticity, to a life lived in truth and love.

There were nights she spent sleepless, her mind an unending whirlpool of thoughts. There were days she spent reading, understanding, processing. It was hard, it was gruelling, but it was necessary. Necessary for her to become who she was meant to be.

And so, Emma, in all her courage and tenacity, dived into the tumultuous sea of self-discovery. She fought her demons, confronted her biases, questioned her norms. It was a battle, a struggle, but it was also a journey of acceptance, of understanding, of love.

As the chapter closed, Emma wasn't the same woman anymore. She was a woman in progress, a woman who had dared to question, dared to explore, dared to be herself. And in that struggle, in that acceptance, she found her true strength, her true identity. She was Emma - a woman of power, a woman of courage, a woman of love.

Acceptance. It's a simple word, really. Eight bloody letters. But it carries weight, enough to shift the bloody universe. And for Emma, it felt like she was carrying the Southern Cross on her shoulders, heavy and profound. She'd spent so much time grappling, wrestling with the enigma that was her sexuality, that acceptance felt like the hardest riddle to solve. But the storm was beginning to clear, and in its wake, it left a landscape of understanding, a path of acceptance.

Bloody hell, it hadn't been easy. Unravelling her attraction towards both genders, towards multiple partners, felt like undressing her very soul, raw and vulnerable. But each layer she peeled back revealed a truth, a piece of the puzzle that was her identity. And every piece mattered, every piece was her.

The world loved to fit people into boxes, neat little compartments that conformed to societal norms. Straight or gay, single or taken. But Emma? She was discovering that she was a bloody kaleidoscope. There were so many shades to her, so many sides, and they were all bloody beautiful.

She was attracted to men, yes. Their strength, their ruggedness. But she was also drawn to women, their grace, their fire. And it didn't end there. She wanted to love and be loved by more than just one person. She craved the complexity, the intimacy, the chaos of polyamory. It was anarchy to the societal norms, but it was her anarchy.

Emma's heart was a wild thing, untamed by societal expectations, unbound by conventional rules. She loved fiercely, broadly, without restraint. Her love wasn't limited to a single gender, a single person. Her love was a wild expanse, a vast ocean ready to embrace whoever dared to dive in.

And the deeper she dove, the more she accepted. Accepted that she was bisexual. Accepted that she was polyamorous. Accepted that she was different. And bloody hell, it felt liberating. Like she'd shed a skin that wasn't hers, and was finally baring her true self.

It wasn't a road paved with gold. There were hurdles, stones, bloody boulders. There were times she stumbled, times she fell. But every time she picked herself up, dusted herself off, and continued on. It was her journey, her path, and she was bloody well going to walk it.

As the chapter closed, Emma stood at the edge of her new life, poised to leap. The fear was there, yes, but so was the excitement, the anticipation. She was ready to embrace her bisexuality, her polyamory. She was ready to live her truth. And as she jumped, she didn't just fall, she soared.

She was Emma, a woman who loved freely, a woman who loved broadly. She was a woman unbound by societal norms, a woman unabashed in her sexuality. She was a woman of power, a woman of courage, a woman of love. She was Emma, and she was bloody proud of it.

Resolution, a declaration of intent, a stamp on the passage of time. For Emma, it marked the close of one chapter and the beginning of another, each one promising its own trials and tribulations, its own bucket load of joys and sorrows. But with the taste of acceptance still fresh on her tongue, she was ready to face whatever came her way. With a bloody-minded determination that was as Aussie as a meat pie, she was set to carve her path and live her life authentically.

The camera, her partner in crime, once a source of trepidation, was now an instrument of expression. Emma, the bloody artist that she was, committed to using it ethically. No more violations, no more invasions. Her work would be marked by respect, empathy, and integrity. She was here to capture stories, not to exploit them. Each click, each frame, was a testament to her growth, a testament to her evolution as a photographer.

Bisexuality, polyamory - terms that once sent her into a whirlwind of confusion, were now part of her identity, her bloody badge of honour. She wore them with pride, with a grin that was as defiant as it was freeing. No more questioning, no more doubts. She accepted her attractions, embraced them with an openness that was as wide as the Outback.

She was Emma, in love with the beauty of both men and women, with the complexities of loving more than one person. Society be damned, she had her own norms to live by. Love was love, and she had plenty of it to give. She had the heart of a lioness, vast and wild, ready to love and be loved, unbound by the conventionalities of the world.

This wasn't just a resolution; it was a revolution. A revolution of the self, a shaking of the roots, a bloody upheaval. Emma was rewriting the rules, not just for herself but for everyone who dared to be different, who dared to be true.

The chapter ended, but Emma's journey was far from over. With her camera in one hand and her newfound truths in the other, she was ready to face whatever lay ahead. The path may be rough, the journey might be tough, but Emma was tougher. With her head held high and her spirit undeterred, she was ready to take on the world.

She was Emma, a woman of courage, a woman of conviction. She was a photographer with a heart full of love and a camera full of stories. She was a beacon of acceptance, of authenticity. She was Emma, and she was bloody well unstoppable.

Shadows & Encounters

Sweat dripping down her brow, Emma found herself back at the heart of the game, camera held close to her face, her blue eyes focusing behind the lens. The pub was buzzing, laughter and banter filled the smoky room, the loud jangling music adding to the quintessential Aussie charm. She could taste the anticipation, feel the electricity of the place pulsating through her veins. Aye, she was back alright.

She'd set her rules, staunch and unwavering. She'd be no bloody voyeur, no bottom-feeder preying on the unsuspecting. Her subjects had dignity, stories, pain, love - raw, untamed emotions that deserved respect. Her camera, that magical bloody box, was to be an instrument of empathy now, a bridge between souls.

With a newfound reverence for her craft, Emma started capturing moments - laughter lines etched deep in wrinkled faces, smoky gazes full of unspoken secrets, the twinkle in the eyes of a bloke as he spun a yarn. She focused not on the faces but on the emotions they carried, each click a testament to human resilience, love, joy, and sorrow. Her photographs were no longer just images, but narratives - heartrending, heartwarming sagas frozen in time.

Soon, word began to spread. Her work started to turn heads, conversations began to whirl around her. The appreciation she received was not just polite applause this time, it was genuine admiration, respect. Her journey, having been through dark alleyways and grim, shady corners, had finally taken a positive turn.

But she was no fool, she knew the world had teeth, and it could bite you if you weren't careful. The past still haunted her sometimes, but the ghostly whispers were growing fainter with each passing day. With every snapshot she took, every story she told through her photographs, she felt a part of the old Emma shed, making way for the new.

The roughed-up, gut-punching past was now a faded memory. The darkness had served its purpose, taught its lessons. Now was the time for light. As the photographs she took started to reflect the resilience of the human spirit, Emma felt a resurrection within her too. Her life wasn't just about capturing light anymore; it was about being the light. And blimey, it felt good.

With every shutter click, she was drawing herself out of the shadows, back into the world that was waiting to embrace her, one photograph at a time. The game had changed, and she was playing by her rules now. Emma was back, and she was here to bloody stay.

Life was a wild sheila, unpredictable, kicking you in the guts one moment, cradling you the next. But it was times like these, watching people engrossed in her work, that Emma reckoned it was all worth it. Her photographs, no longer mere imagery, but windows to human souls, were stirring up the dusty ol' town.

The local café, The Billy Boil, had started showcasing her work. Day after day, she watched from the corner, nursing her long black, as blokes and sheilas from all walks of life stared at her photos, their eyes sparkling with intrigue, brimming with questions.

One photograph stood out. A portrait of a gnarled, grizzled old Digger, eyes like hardened steel, jaw etched with lines of battles fought, both on land and within. It wasn't just the striking reality of age and survival that drew people in. It was the raw emotion, the unspoken tales that his eyes whispered. The old, stoic warrior was a beacon of resilience, of strength and fragility coexisting. The photograph stirred emotions, sparked conversations. Some blokes found solace in his strength, some found their struggles reflected in his eyes. The old Digger's tale wasn't just his own anymore, it became a mirror to many souls.

Her work began to impact lives. Emma, the quiet lass with a camera, was subtly transforming her community. She captured life as it was, raw, unfiltered, challenging the old views, offering a fresh perspective. The heartache, the joys, the struggles, the victories, every photograph was a testament to the human spirit.

It was not just about the aesthetic anymore. Her camera had become a tool of change, a medium to foster understanding, to create a bond of shared empathy. The power of the camera was no longer an intoxicating poison; it was a healing balm, a spark of positivity. The ripple effect of her work was visible, tangible. She wasn't just taking photographs; she was touching lives, changing perspectives.

Emma felt a sense of fulfillment, a sense of purpose she hadn't felt before. The girl who once doubted her place in the world was now an agent of change, a storyteller, an empath. Her photographs were impacting lives, stirring emotions, her journey as a photographer had begun to illuminate not just her life, but the lives around her. It was a feeling that beat any high, any adrenaline rush the camera once gave her. Emma had stepped into the light, and she was lighting up her world. The feeling was bloody brilliant.

It was a busy arvo at The Billy Boil café-cum-gallery, filled to the brim with folks appreciating Emma's work. As she watched the crowd, she saw them— a couple who stuck out like roos in the middle of the CBD. They had an air about them, one that was quite different from the rest of the crowd.

They weren't just looking at her photographs; they were absorbing them, living the emotions that she had captured. The man, broad-shouldered with salt-and-pepper hair, and the woman, a firecracker with lively eyes, they seemed more alive than anyone she'd seen in a while. Emma found herself drawn to them, their aura pulling her in like a rip current.

She shuffled over to them, her heart thumping like a bodhran, her nerves buzzing like bees around a bottlebrush. She introduced herself, and the spark of recognition in their eyes set a series of tingles down her spine. They'd heard of her, of her work, of the shift she'd brought about in the community. Their genuine interest in her and her photography filled her with a warmth, a connection she hadn't felt in a long time.

The couple, they were in an open relationship. They explained it to her, their philosophy of love, their journey of understanding and acceptance. Their words wove a story that challenged her preconceived notions of relationships, opening up new dimensions of love and attraction that she'd been exploring herself. Their openness about their polyamorous relationship was as refreshing as a splash of cool water on a sweltering Aussie summer day.

Emma found herself drawn to both of them, their energy, their story. It wasn't just physical. It was something deeper, an intellectual and emotional pull that sparked a flame of curiosity within her. The couple had disrupted her world, compelling her to question, to explore further.

Emma had stepped into the light with her photography, impacting lives and her community. Now, her life was poised for another shift, another exploration into the unknown. The encounter at the gallery had not just given her new friends but also opened doors to new possibilities, new understandings of love and relationships. Emma, the girl with the camera, was stepping into a broader, brighter world, ready for all the challenges and experiences it was set to throw her way.

There was something about that couple that had Emma stumped. Their aura, an odd mix of sun-kissed surf and arid outback, was as intoxicating as a pint of Victoria Bitter on a sun-baked arvo. Their love was different, open, fluid, flowing like the waters of the Murray, touching banks, nourishing life, but never getting tamed. They were proof that love wasn't confined to a lonely desert track; it could spread, it could flourish, and it could be as expansive as the Aussie bush itself.

Their dynamic was like watching a footy match between rivals who knew each other's every move, every pass, every dodgy tackle. They bantered, teased, their voices intertwining in the air like tangled eucalyptus branches. Yet, there was a palpable respect and admiration, an understanding that went deeper than the Mariana Trench.

In them, Emma saw a physical manifestation of all those nights spent trawling the depths of internet forums, absorbing stories of polyamory and bisexuality. Here it was, not just a theory or a risqué Wikipedia page, but something as tangible as the camera hanging around her neck.

The couple's love was like a campfire on a chilly night, radiant, warm, crackling with life. It was love that didn't need to fit within the white picket fences. It was like an Anzac biscuit - rough around the edges but sweet and comforting at its core. Their relationship was an open book, a stark contrast to the sham that the previous owner of her camera had orchestrated.

Their existence challenged her understanding of love. It shook her notions, stripped away her biases, like a fierce cyclone uprooting a eucalypt. They were a living testament to the idea that love didn't come in one-size-fits-all; it was as diverse as the inhabitants of the Great Barrier Reef.

The meeting felt like a Ripper of a moment, as if she'd stumbled upon a gold nugget amidst the rubble. This was not just another day in the Outback; it was a turning point, the start of a trek towards an unexplored landscape of love. Emma found herself grappling with the sheer novelty of it all, a feeling akin to a roo caught in the headlights.

Her thoughts twirled like a dervish. Could she too, love like this? Could she share her heart with more than one, her feelings flitting between partners like a lorikeet between eucalyptus trees?

The questions buzzed in her head like a swarm of cicadas on a hot summer evening.

Their love story was as raw and real as it could get. There was no sugar coating, no attempt to fit into societal expectations, just a naked show of their love. It was a whole new world for Emma, a world she was ready to delve into, armed with her camera, and her newfound understanding of love and relationships. Emma knew, this was the fair dinkum deal, the moment she'd been waiting for. And as she grappled with these newfound insights, she knew she was on the precipice of a significant transformation.

Emma found herself caught in a rip tide of attraction for the couple. This wasn't the simple, straightforward pull she was accustomed to. No, this was a dual attraction - a bloke and a sheila pulling her in their unique ways, their combined allure more potent than the raw power of an Outback storm.

The man was a tall glass of water, sun-tanned and rough around the edges. He had an earthy aura about him that reminded her of the dry red earth of the Aussie outback, resolute and unyielding. His eyes, the colour of eucalyptus leaves, held an honesty that drew her in, the flicker within them promising stories untold.

The woman, on the other hand, was a breath of cool sea breeze on a sweltering summer day. Her laughter rang around the room like a kookaburra's call, infectiously light and vibrant. She was a riot of colour in a drab world, her vivaciousness as alluring as a blooming jacaranda in the heart of spring. Her eyes, as deep and mystifying as the Great Barrier Reef, held a certain allure that made Emma's heart flutter.

The unexpected attraction to both of them hit Emma like a road train barrelling down a desert highway. She found herself drawn to them, each in their unique way. There was something about the man's rugged charm and the woman's effervescence that ignited a fire within her. A fire she had only read about in the wee hours on the internet, a flame that she'd been stoking ever since she'd started questioning the conventional.

Emma had been toying with the idea of bisexuality and polyamory, trying to comprehend these words that had bounced around her mind like kangaroos on a hot tin roof. And now, standing there amidst her photographs, feeling the unanticipated pull towards the couple, she realised that these weren't just abstract concepts. They were real, visceral feelings that had taken root in her heart, growing and blooming like wildflowers after a heavy rainfall.

The couple, with their easy acceptance and transparent love, were a revelation to Emma. They made her recognise her capacity to love, not confined by gender. They reflected the raw, unfiltered, polyamorous love that she'd been contemplating. This was not some academic exercise anymore. It was here, staring her right in the face.

Her heart pounded in her chest like the bass at a Friday night gig. It felt strange, exhilarating, and a tad terrifying. She was simultaneously adrift and anchored, caught in a maelstrom of emotions that tossed her around, yet kept her grounded. It was like riding the waves on a Gold Coast beach, thrilling and daunting, all at the same time.

This wasn't just an affirmation of her bisexuality; it was a crash course in understanding the complexities and the simplicity of love. It made her question, ponder, and finally accept the fact that she was capable of loving, and being loved by, more than one person. And as the wave of realisation washed over her, she felt a strange sense of peace. She had, in the most unexpected way, stumbled upon a pivotal moment in her journey, one that would forever reshape her understanding of love and relationships. It was a ripper of a moment, indeed.

In the silence of her room, Emma found herself grappling with the idea of polyamory. It was no longer a nebulous concept floating around in the realm of theoretical possibility. The couple at the gallery had breathed life into it, turned it into a living, breathing entity, as real and tangible as the beer stains on her carpet.

They had come into her life like a gust of wind, kicking up dust and rattling her tin-roofed assumptions. Their seamless, fluid love for each other had challenged every notion she'd ever had about love and relationships. It was like seeing the world in colour for the first time after years of monochrome. Dazzling and disorienting, all at the same time.

Sitting alone with a stubbie in her hand, she mused on their connection, their mutual respect, their open and uninhibited love. It was like a three-legged race, where you're only as fast as the person you're tied to. You fall together, you get up together, and you cross the finish line together. It was complex yet beautifully simple. A synchrony she'd never thought possible.

They seemed to fit together like puzzle pieces, complementing each other's edges. He, with his rugged charm, was like the untamed outback – a bit rough around the edges but honest and dependable. And she, with her infectious laugh and vivacious spirit, was the refreshing sea breeze that softened his rough edges. Together, they were a symphony of contrasts, a picture-perfect portrait of polyamorous love.

Emma contemplated her own place in this newfound landscape. Could she be a part of such a dynamic? Could she love two people simultaneously, without jealousy, without reservation? It felt like walking on a tightrope, a test of her balance, her understanding, her ability to love and be loved.

She played with the ring pull on her beer can, her thoughts racing like roos in the bush. Her heart throbbed with anticipation, an odd excitement fluttering in her chest. But there was a tinge of apprehension, too. The unknown often had a way of sending a shiver down the spine, making the guts churn. But then again, she had always been one to dive headfirst into the uncharted, to chase the adrenaline rush, to embrace the thrill of the unknown.

Her mind buzzed like a cloud of flies on a hot Aussie summer day, thoughts whirling around in a frenzied dance. This was new, uncharted territory for her. The stakes were higher, the dynamics more complex. But as she sipped on her beer, contemplating the unfamiliar path that lay ahead, she felt an odd sense of exhilaration. This was her chance to rewrite her own rules, to define her own boundaries, to embrace her desires without fear or guilt.

With a sigh, she tossed the empty can into the bin. The night had slipped away while she wrestled with her thoughts. As she climbed into bed, she couldn't help but think of the couple, their easy camaraderie, their shared love. Polyamory, she realised, was no longer a foreign concept. It was a possibility, a viable one at that. And as she drifted off to sleep, she found herself looking forward to the dawn, to the promise of new beginnings, to the exploration of uncharted territories. It was an exciting prospect, as thrilling as a wild ride through the untamed Aussie outback.

Bloody hell, it was like stepping into the great unknown, a land untouched and mysterious. Emma found herself standing on the edge, peering into a vast expanse filled with possibilities, uncertainties, and questions. But, like the pioneers of old, there was a spark in her eyes – a spark of curiosity, of determination, of a thirst to explore uncharted territories.

She knew it was no bloody picnic. Stepping into a polyamorous relationship was like venturing into the Outback without a map, navigating unfamiliar terrain with nothing but instinct and a shot of courage. She would need to tread carefully, respect the boundaries, adapt to the rhythms. She'd need to dodge the pitfalls, fend off the biting flies, weather the unpredictable storms. But as daunting as it was, the idea of this exploration filled her with an invigorating sense of anticipation.

She wasn't some naive Sheila, mind you. She knew the road was pockmarked with challenges. Jealousy, for one, was a green-eyed beast lurking in the shadows, waiting to rear its ugly head. Not to mention the societal norms, those long-standing constructs that had a way of making you feel like a bloody drongo for not toeing the line. But she also knew that these constructs were nothing more than paper tigers – intimidating, yes, but inherently fragile and capable of being torn apart.

There was something beautiful, something liberating about the couple's dynamic that had lured Emma in. Their love was like the boundless Aussie sky – vast, infinite, enveloping all under its azure expanse. It defied labels, scoffed at boxes, laughed in the face of societal conventions. It was unapologetically authentic, deeply resonant, boldly defying the confines of a monogamous world.

The prospect of being a part of such a love was exciting. It was like being offered a taste of the famed Aussie freedom – unfiltered, unadulterated, unconstrained. It was a freedom to love, to express, to explore without the shackles of conformity. It was a call to a new adventure, a journey of self-discovery, a voyage into the depths of her desires and capacities.

"Bugger it," she muttered to herself one night, her eyes reflecting the fiery resolve that had begun to smoulder in her heart. She was ready. Ready to explore this connection, to test these waters, to take the plunge into the whirlpool of polyamory. It was a leap of faith, a daring dive into the unknown, but she was no stranger to risks. She was a thrill-seeker, a storm-chaser, a trail-blazer.

With this resolution, Emma found herself standing on the brink of a new chapter in her life. It was a chapter that promised discovery, growth, exhilaration. It was a chapter that dared her to dream, to dare, to dive. And as she looked ahead, she knew it was a chapter she was ready to write. After all, she was Emma, a woman of the land down under, a woman of strength, a woman of adventure. A woman who was unafraid to traverse the uncharted, to kiss the unknown, to dance with the new. And with that, she stepped into the new day, ready to embrace what lay ahead – the challenges, the surprises, the love.

Emotional Echoes

A sudden change had come over Emma, a profound shift in the way she viewed the world. It was like seeing in colour for the first time, the world no longer composed of merely black and white, but a blooming explosion of hues, each revealing a different facet of humanity. Having come to terms with her own bisexuality and the notion of polyamory, she could now look beyond the broad strokes, the superficial categorisations, and peer directly into the raw, unfiltered essence of human souls.

She was no longer confined to the rigid binaries the society had constructed. The straitjackets of 'normal' had fallen away, replaced by an acceptance of the beautifully intricate spectrum of human emotions and relationships. A bloke, a sheila, they were labels, mere words. It was the soul beneath that drew her in now, a soul's truth, its pure, radiant authenticity. It was all a bloody marvellous mosaic of diversity, and she stood in the centre of it, taking it in.

Now she understood. Love, attraction, they were not just words, but emotions that could flow freely, unhindered by societal norms, just like the Murray during flood season. It was a liberating revelation, one that left her feeling as if she had broken free from an unseen, oppressive shackle. Love wasn't bound by a binary code, but was as limitless as the outback under a crystal-clear night sky, waiting for those brave enough to explore it.

Her lens, an extension of her soul, began to capture this newfound vision. The camera shutter opened and closed, echoing her own widened eyes, her heart, the very pores of her skin. Every click was a testament to her shifted perspective, every photograph a shrine to the unjudged, the unbridled, the unfettered.

She moved through the world, intoxicated by this amplified perception. Her eyes traced the contours of faces, hands, bodies, looking for stories untold, souls yet unexplored. Each frame she captured was a window into another world, another heart, another soul. The camera had once again become an instrument of truth-telling, not an exploiter of vulnerabilities, but a revealer of the unseen, a chronicler of raw, unfiltered humanity.

Her perception was her superpower, her bisexuality a strength, her openness to polyamory her ticket to a world hitherto unseen. And bloody hell, she was ready to dive right in. The world was her canvas, and she was just getting started with her masterpiece.

Her camera became an extension of her self, a third eye that captured a world unseen, emotions unexpressed, and stories untold. Emma had once again picked up her trusty camera, but this time, it felt different. It was no longer just a device, a mere tool, but a conduit to another dimension. She was the bloody shaman of the modern era, using her camera as a spirit guide to navigate through the labyrinth of human complexity.

Her new work was unlike anything she had done before. There was no exploitation, no imposed narrative, no stereotype. Instead, she held a mirror to humanity, showcasing the beautiful, the ugly, the raw, the real. Each photograph was an open letter to the world, a bold declaration that screamed, "Look at us! This is who we are."

Her lens roved the streets of Melbourne, the urban arteries pulsating with life. She photographed a homeless bloke with his dog, his weather-beaten face etched with a thousand tales of hardship and hope. A queer couple, hand in hand, the vibrant colours of their love as loud and defiant as the pride flag they proudly donned. A single mum juggling her job and kids, her tired eyes reflecting a strength that could move mountains.

Through the viewfinder, she saw souls bared, raw emotions etched on faces, stories woven in the lines of time. Her photographs were a silent rebellion against the clichéd, the stereotypical. She shot in monochrome, colour, infrared; there were no limits to the world she captured. From the gutters to the skyscrapers, every inch of the city became her canvas, and every soul, her muse.

The photographs breathed life into forgotten narratives, shone light on marginalised voices, and celebrated the plurality of human existence. They were not just images, but visual symphonies that sang of the unsung, painted the unseen, and spoke the unspoken. Each frame was a testament to her empathetic lens, her raw, unfiltered view of the world.

Her work started to make ripples, conversations sparked, perspectives challenged. People began to look closer, delve deeper, beyond the facades, beyond the stereotypes. The power of her camera was slowly shifting narratives, influencing perceptions, stirring emotions. And Emma, she was just bloody getting started. In this uncharted territory of authenticity, she found her true calling. For the world was a kaleidoscope of stories, and she, the storyteller.

Time moved in strange, fluid patterns. Days melted into nights, as Emma found herself drawn more and more into the intricate dynamics of the couple's relationship. Their polyamorous connection was a far cry from the black and white narratives of love and attraction that she'd grown up with, the kind that were peddled in sappy romantic movies and fairy tales.

They were no Ken and Barbie in a shiny convertible, but real people, with real flaws and real stories. The bloke, Jake, was a larrikin with a heart of gold. He had the kind of laugh that could light up a room and a kindness that could make a heart melt. Maddie, the sheila, was a firebrand. She was fierce, smart, and she had a spark in her eyes that could ignite a thousand stars.

It was not just about sex, though that was a part of it, but also about the emotional connection, the shared intimacy, the give and take. The way they were together, it was more than just love; it was a dance, a delicate ballet of emotions and desires. They were free, free to love, free to explore, free to be. It was a bit like the tide, flowing and ebbing, yet always there, always constant.

Emma found herself inexorably drawn to both of them. Jake, with his infectious laughter and the way he wore his heart on his sleeve. And Maddie, with her fiery spirit and that piercing gaze that seemed to see right into her soul. She felt an attraction, a connection, something that had her heart pounding and her mind buzzing. The way they held each other, the way they held her, it was a revelation.

Polyamory wasn't a theoretical concept anymore; it was real, tangible. Emma found herself peeling off layers of mystery, understanding the complexities, the challenges, the joys. She was on the precipice of a new journey, a path less travelled. It was a bit scary, but there was also an exhilarating sense of liberation.

Her days were spent shooting photos that spoke volumes, her nights getting to know Jake and Maddie, discovering herself in the process. The world around her seemed to pulse with a new rhythm, a beat that was in sync with her heart. Life, it seemed, had turned a corner, steering her towards a path she never thought she'd tread. But here she was, standing on the threshold of something beautiful, something that felt bloody right.

The sun was always a bit brighter, the sky a touch bluer, and the stars a tad more glittering when Emma was with Jake and Maddie. An intense connection bubbled between them, washing over Emma like an ocean tide, soaking her in a concoction of attraction, intrigue, and something a touch like fear.

The sheila, Maddie, was like a mid-summer thunderstorm, wild and breathtaking, her laugh echoing like distant thunder, her gaze as electrifying as a lightning bolt. She was a force of nature, unapologetically authentic, her passionate aura pulling Emma towards her like a moth to a flame. The bloke, Jake, was a stark contrast yet a perfect complement. He was a cool drizzle on a hot arvo, soothing and calming, his words rolling over Emma like a comforting blanket, his gaze gentle and warm like the setting sun.

Attraction brewed between them, a potent brew that intensified with each passing day, each shared laugh, each whispered secret. The conventional narratives of love and desire that Emma had once held dear began to blur, replaced by a complex dance of emotions that transcended the age-old dichotomies.

The way Jake would run his fingers through his hair when he was deep in thought, or the way Maddie's eyes lit up when she spoke about something she was passionate about - Emma found herself drawn to these quirks, these intricacies. They weren't just attractive; they were magnetic, pulling her in with an irresistible force. She felt it in her bones, in her heartbeat, in the breath that caught in her throat when she was around them.

Attraction, they say, is the spark that starts the fire. And oh boy, was there a bloody inferno burning within Emma. She was drawn to them, not just physically, but emotionally, intellectually. She wanted to explore the universe they had created, delve into the depths of their shared dynamic. She wanted to understand their love, their bond, to decode the enigma that was polyamory.

It was an uncharted territory, far removed from her comfort zone, far removed from societal norms. Yet, she felt a compelling desire to venture into this untamed wilderness. Emma wanted to embrace the raw authenticity, the boundless freedom, the profound connection that Jake and Maddie had so generously offered her.

It was intense, it was overwhelming, but most of all, it was real. And for Emma, who had always sought truth, both through the lens of her camera and in her life, this was a tantalising prospect. An adventure she was more than ready to embark upon, an adventure she knew would irrevocably change her life.

The world is a big bloody circus, thought Emma, but right now, she was at the centre ring, juggling the chaos of her feelings like a seasoned performer, even as her heart pounded like a drum. Her feelings for Maddie and Jake weren't just skin deep. They seeped into her veins, pumped through her heart, seared her mind. More than just desire, it was connection — a connection as potent as a bottle of Bundy rum, intoxicating her with its allure.

With every conversation, every shared glance, every seemingly insignificant moment, Emma found herself more and more entwined in their lives. She was drawn to them like a roo to water in a scorching summer. The feeling was all-consuming, an emotion so profound it left her breathless, her heart pounding like a stampede in her chest.

Her understanding of love and attraction, once as clear as a cloudless outback sky, was now as murky as the Yarra after a heavy rain. This wasn't just physical, oh no, this was deeper, a fiery blaze that consumed her, licked at her insides and left her yearning for more. It was terrifying and exhilarating, like riding a ripper of a wave, never knowing when you might wipe out.

Her days were filled with snapshots of Maddie's laugh, vibrant and contagious, echoing in her mind like a favourite song. Her nights, with dreams of Jake's comforting gaze, his gentle strength a steady anchor in the tumultuous sea of her emotions. She longed for them, yearned for them, an insatiable hunger that seemed to grow with each passing day.

Yet, it wasn't just desire that fuelled her feelings. No, desire was a part of it, a significant part, but it was so much more. It was the way they made her feel seen, understood, loved. It was the way they challenged her, pushed her, made her want to be a better version of herself. It was the way they accepted her, with all her quirks, all her fears, all her dreams. It was the way they loved each other, a raw, unadulterated love that Emma found herself desperately craving to be a part of.

She was drawn to their world, a world where love wasn't confined by societal norms, where desire wasn't dictated by gender, where connection wasn't measured by conventionality. And as she looked into their eyes, Emma realised with startling clarity that this was where she belonged. With Maddie's fiery spirit and Jake's calming presence, in the chaos and beauty of their love, Emma found her home.

This realisation brought with it a sense of calm, like the quiet stillness of the bush after a raging storm. She knew this journey would be far from easy, but she also knew she had the courage to face whatever came her way. Because, in the end, it was all worth it — for the love, for the desire, for the connection. For Maddie. For Jake. For herself. And with that, Emma was ready to dive headfirst into this new chapter of her life, with the courage of a honey badger and the spirit of a dingo. For the first time in her life, Emma was ready to truly live.

Life, Emma figured, was much like her beloved Australian landscape — wild, untamed, and refusing to fit into anyone's neat little boxes. Much like her feelings for Maddie and Jake, a relentless river that refused to follow the well-trodden path and instead carved its own way, bending and twisting in unexpected directions, flooding her senses and challenging the very foundations of her understanding of love.

Society, with all its rules and regulations, its rigid binaries and closed doors, felt more like a cramped, stuffy pub on a hot summer's day. But what she felt for Maddie and Jake? That was like stepping out into the cool night air, head tilted back, eyes drinking in the vast expanse of the star-studded outback sky. It was liberating, a breath of fresh air that filled her lungs, set her heart racing, made her feel alive.

In their company, she found herself drawn towards a love that was as wide and varied as the Australian landscape itself. It wasn't confined to a single gender or number; it was as expansive as the outback, as multifaceted as a rough opal, and as unending as the coastal line. It was a spectrum, a kaleidoscope of emotions that encompassed the raw, powerful pull she felt towards both Maddie and Jake.

She'd once thought of love in terms of black and white, a binary where you chose one and stuck to it. But now, she was beginning to see the world in technicolour, recognising the shades of grey and the stunning hues that existed in between. And in this newfound understanding, Emma found herself redefining what love meant to her.

Instead of feeling lost or confused, Emma felt the liberating rush of a surfer riding a wave. The rigid guidelines society had shackled her with crumbled, replaced by a sense of freedom as wide as the Nullarbor Plain. She realised that love wasn't a cage; it was the endless sky above, a space to explore and roam freely.

The recognition was as startling as a bushfire, sudden and all-consuming. It was like coming up for air after being submerged in murky water. It was clarity and understanding, all wrapped up in a single, profound realisation — that love was love, in all its forms and manifestations.

But there was also an undercurrent of apprehension, the nagging voice in her head that echoed societal norms, reminding her of the dangers of swimming against the tide. Yet, Emma had always been a bloody good swimmer, and she knew she was strong enough to face the riptide.

Love, Emma realised, was more than just a singular entity shared between two people. It was a connection, a feeling, a choice. It was Maddie's infectious laughter and Jake's comforting silence. It was the way her heart skipped a beat every time she looked at them. And it was the decision to embrace this new understanding of love, despite the challenges she knew lay ahead. The road was uncharted, the destination unknown. But Emma was ready to start the journey, ready to explore the unseen spectrum of love.

In the midst of the human hustle, Emma had always felt a bit like a dingbat lost in the Never-Never. But Maddie and Jake, with their intertwined lives, offered her a compass, a beacon in the rough and tumble, a strange kind of home. It wasn't a typical white picket fence dream, but a picture that had room enough for three.

Emma watched them. The ebb and flow of their dynamic, the subtle shift of their bodies, the quiet understanding in their eyes. It was an intricate dance of give and take, a synchronised ballet danced by two individuals so in tune with each other, they moved as one. Emma found herself drawn to that dance, drawn to the music that guided their steps, and she yearned to join in.

That desire was a kangaroo loose in the top paddock, bounding and unstoppable. It welled up within her, a surging tide that pulled her towards Maddie and Jake. It was an urge as natural as the turn of the tides, as instinctive as a wallaby's leap. It felt right, resonated with her on a level she'd not known before. She wanted to be a part of their dynamic, a part of their dance.

Their relationship wasn't without its struggles. There were moments of discord, the occasional misstep that disrupted the harmony of their dance. But they faced those moments together, two individuals standing as one, working to maintain the balance of their relationship. And in their struggles, Emma saw the beauty of their bond — the honesty, the vulnerability, the strength. It was a raw, powerful display of love that fascinated Emma and made her yearn to experience it for herself.

Emotions tangled within her like the jungle vines of the Daintree Rainforest, fear, desire, apprehension, longing, all twisted together. Yet amid the tangle, one emotion stood out — the desire to belong. It was a desire as potent as the scent of the blooming wattle, a hunger that gnawed at her with the relentlessness of a Tasmanian devil. It was an intense, aching need to be a part of something, to find a place where she truly belonged.

Emma wanted to be a part of Maddie and Jake's world, to join their dance. She wanted to learn their steps, share in their laughter and tears, navigate the intricate landscape of their relationship. She didn't just want to observe from the sidelines; she wanted to plunge into the heart of the action, to be an active participant in the delicate balancing act that was their relationship.

The desire was daunting, yet exhilarating. It was a bold leap into the unknown, into uncharted waters that could be calm one moment and tempestuous the next. But Emma was ready for the challenge, ready to navigate the stormy seas and the calm waters alike.

For the first time in her life, Emma found herself standing on the edge of something extraordinary, teetering on the brink of a new adventure. A journey not into the vast, untamed landscapes she was used to capturing through her lens, but into the equally wild and mysterious landscape of love and relationships. The desire to belong, to be a part of Maddie and Jake's dynamic, was a call to adventure she couldn't resist. And as daunting as the journey ahead was, Emma was ready to take the leap.

It was late in the evening, the sky painted in shades of indigo and orange, a canvas showcasing the twilight's last gleaming. Emma sat alone in her flat, surrounded by the remains of a long day and the silence of the impending night. She cradled a glass of red in her hand, the dark liquid reflecting the dying embers of the day.

Her mind was as restless as a mob of roos on the run, bouncing from one thought to another. Maddie and Jake, their relationship, their shared dynamic – everything whirled around in her head, a cyclone of emotions and considerations. The conventions she'd known were crumbling like a sandcastle hit by an Aussie surf, replaced by a profound understanding she was yet to fully grasp.

Emma was no galah. She knew well enough what this was all about. Her attraction to Maddie and Jake was as real as the Sydney Harbour Bridge, as undeniable as the roar of a footy crowd at the MCG. It was physical, certainly, but there was more to it. The emotional connection she felt was like nothing she'd ever experienced, a bond that drew her to them with the force of a rip current.

Sipping her wine, Emma mulled over her feelings. It was an unusual situation, one that veered away from the beaten track she was familiar with. Yet, it felt so bloody right, like finding the last piece of a jigsaw puzzle or a cold tinny on a scorching summer's day.

She considered the potential pitfalls – the judgment from mates, the raised eyebrows, the whispered conversations behind hands. Yet, for all the potential blowflies in the ointment, Emma found herself drawn to the idea of a polyamorous relationship, to the prospect of joining the dance of Maddie and Jake's dynamic.

Emma was an explorer at heart, a trailblazer willing to blaze her own path. And this? This was uncharted territory, a wild landscape of love and relationships yet to be explored. It was a challenge, and Emma had never been one to shy away from a challenge.

As the night deepened, a sense of tranquillity settled over her. The thoughts quieted, the internal storm calmed, leaving in its wake a clear understanding. It was time for her to acknowledge the truth – her attraction to both Maddie and Jake, her desire to be a part of their dynamic, her yearning to explore the world of polyamory.

In the quiet of her flat, under the watchful eyes of the stars, Emma acknowledged her feelings. She accepted her desire, her curiosity, her need to explore the uncharted territory of polyamory. The admission was as exhilarating as a plunge into Bondi's waves, as liberating as an open highway stretching out before her.

Her decision didn't mean that she had all the answers, nor did it mean that the journey ahead would be easy. But Emma was ready.

Ready to navigate the twists and turns, ready to face the bumps and the potholes, ready to explore this new landscape of love and relationships.

With that acknowledgement, Emma felt a sense of peace, a sense of rightness. She was on the brink of a new journey, standing on the precipice of an adventure unlike any other. And with a final sip of her wine, Emma made a toast to herself, to Maddie and Jake, and to the unknown journey that lay ahead.

Here's to love, she thought, in all its forms and in all its complexity. Here's to exploration, to discovery, to diving headfirst into the unknown. And above all, here's to life and all its bloody beautiful chaos.

Stumble Through Shadows

Emma sat in her makeshift studio, the air heavy with the weight of anticipation. The world beyond the lens of her trusty camera had offered her stories, not in words, but in moments - stark, unfiltered snapshots of life. The roughened hands of a bushman, the cracked soil under the scorching outback sun, the unshed tears in a bloke's eyes, the raw power of a storm over the ocean - all captured in their unadorned truth.

The resilient spirit of her fellow Aussies was laid bare in each frame, their trials and tribulations echoing in the shadows and light. The camera, her faithful mate through the highs and lows, had been more than a tool; it was a conduit, a silent narrator of the human condition.

Yet, as she scanned through the monochromatic tapestry of her work, two faces stood out amongst the crowd - Jake and Maddie. Each click of the shutter had etched a deeper imprint of them in her heart. Jake, with his disarming smile that seemed to light up the darkest corners. Maddie, with her fiery gaze that bore an intensity rivalling the sun. The lens had captured more than just their smiles; it had captured a part of her soul, a desire as deep as the pacific.

As Emma delicately placed each photo into its frame, she realized these weren't just pictures; they were narratives, each a chapter in the tale of her journey. The rugged beauty of the outback, the unfettered joy of a roo bounding in the wild, the heartbreaking melancholy of loss, they all found a place in her gallery. But amidst them, Jake and Maddie's photos had a heartbeat of their own, resonating with the rhythm of her newfound emotions, a symphony of affection and longing.

In the hushed silence of the room, bathed in the pale glow of the setting sun, Emma found herself lost in thought. The exhibition wasn't just about sharing her work; it was about sharing a piece of her life. It was about unveiling the spectrum of her experiences, her growth, her discovery of new facets of love. And in that moment, she realized she was ready. Ready to share her journey, ready to bare her soul, ready to let the world in on her precious secret.

And as the final photo found its place, a candid shot of Jake and Maddie, their smiles as radiant as the Aussie sun, Emma knew it was more than just an exhibition. It was an exploration of her soul, a testament of her emotional odyssey, and above all, it was a tribute to the unlikeliest of loves that had blossomed in the most unexpected of places.

In the stillness of the evening, Emma finds herself dialling numbers on her worn-out phone, reaching out to each soul whose story she had committed to film. Each conversation, a unique dance of disclosure, of explanation, and of requests. The idea of the exhibition, a raw, visceral exploration of life, humanity, and all its attendant nuances through her lens, needed to be shared, needed to be told.

Each subject, each face, each pair of eyes that stared back at her from the prints, they held their breath as she explained her vision. Some wore an expression of surprise, the thought of their lives being put on display an unexpected twist in their everyday existence. Some were flattered, a blush creeping up their cheeks at the notion of being the centre of attention in an art gallery.

But the bulk of them felt an odd sense of appreciation, a pride in their existence that Emma's words and photos had instilled. For, in her pictures, they weren't just subjects; they were stories. Stories of resilience, of dreams, of loss, of joy, of the harsh bush and the gentle shore, of life in all its glorious complexity. Stories that bore testament to their struggles and triumphs, and stories that deserved to be told.

And then there were Jake and Maddie. A lump formed in Emma's throat as she approached their names in her contact list. Dialling their number, her fingers trembling ever so slightly, she tried to keep her voice steady. As she explained the concept of the exhibition to them, the thought of their reactions was like a stampeding roo in her mind.

Their lives together, their bond, their love had been a beacon for her, a guiding star in the vast wilderness of her emotions. The thought of sharing their moments, their story, their love with the world was daunting, and yet, she felt it was something that needed to be done. Their relationship, unconventional yet so profound, was a tale that the world needed to witness, to appreciate, to understand.

As she heard their voices over the line, the surprise, the flattery, the silent appreciation, Emma knew she'd made the right choice. Their consent, their faith in her, only strengthened her resolve to bring this project to life. Each of her photos was more than just a piece of art; it was a slice of her heart, a part of her soul, and she was ready to share it with the world.

In the heart of the hustle, amid the crackle of bubble wrap and the crisp scent of fresh prints, Emma found herself surrounded by a symphony of preparation. The upcoming show, a looming giant in her life, commanded her full attention, every detail demanding precision, every element yearning for perfection.

She sifted through her prints, each one a gateway to a moment, a memory, a world in which Jake and Maddie's love was the constant. The raw emotions, the unspoken stories, the candid humanity of the Aussie battlers – they all demanded to be seen, to be felt. The stark monochrome on the prints only accentuated their essence, their vibrant stories standing out in sharp relief against the greyscale backdrop.

Frames lined up, waiting to encase the stark narratives of joy and sorrow, triumph and loss. They were mere vessels, humbly aiming to enhance the powerful testament of life Emma had captured with her trusty camera.

Logistics, those beastly little details that had a habit of tangling themselves, clamoured for attention. Yet, in her capable hands, they were tamed, lined up, and set in order. Hosting a gallery event was like corralling a mob of roo's – unpredictable and daunting, but not impossible.

And then there was the gallery owner, a crusty old bloke who had seen more sunsets than he could count. With skin like weathered leather and eyes that sparkled with a thousand untold stories, he was a well-respected figure in the art scene, a veritable stalwart who had seen it all. A heart of gold pounded in his broad chest, often camouflaged by his gruff exterior, but not to Emma. She saw the passion in his gaze, the love for the craft in his every gesture. His advice, weathered with years of experience, was as valuable as the precious opals of Coober Pedy.

As the days slipped away like sand through fingers, Emma toiled on, powered by the thought of the exhibition and the chance to tell the world Jake and Maddie's story. Their love, their bond, their unconventional relationship, needed a platform, a stage. And Emma was more than ready to be the curator of that stage, to throw open the doors and let the world take a gander at a love that dared to defy norms, a love that was as real as the hot Aussie sun.

The whirlwind of preparation often led to moments of stillness, moments when Emma found herself entangled in a web of thoughts about Jake and Maddie. Amid the chaos of mounting prints and framing stories, the couple seemed to take on an ethereal presence in her mind, their laughter echoing in the quiet corners, their smiles illuminating the gloomy shadows.

There was affection, blooming like the resplendent Sturt's desert pea after a rare rain, spreading its vibrant tendrils through her heart. It wasn't just for the candid snapshots she'd taken of them, the shared glances caught in the frame, the intimate moments frozen in time. It was for Jake and Maddie themselves, for their raw, unapologetic love that had cast an indelible imprint on her heart.

Desire, that tantalising emotion that danced on the edge of her consciousness, made its presence known too. It wasn't simply a physical yearning, but an insatiable hunger to explore the uncharted territory of their love, to delve deeper into the enigmatic world they had so generously welcomed her into. It was as overwhelming as a dust storm sweeping across the outback, as intense as the searing heat of the midday sun.

And then there was anxiety, an uninvited guest at the feast of her emotions. It was the feeling of standing at the edge of a towering cliff, the ocean waves crashing relentlessly below, the wind whispering tales of the unknown. It was the fear of rejection, of not being enough, of disrupting the beautiful balance that Jake and Maddie shared. Yet, it was this very anxiety that added a thrilling edge to her feelings, a bit like taking a daring plunge into the cool waters of a billabong on a scorching day.

The swirl of emotions within her was a tempest, a wild whirlwind that stirred up her insides like the powerful cyclones of the northern coastline. It was confusing, terrifying even, but there was an undercurrent of exhilaration, an indescribable thrill that sent her heart pounding to a new rhythm. The chaos was a testament to the profound impact Jake and Maddie had on her, a testament to the real, tangible connection they shared.

And so, even amidst the tumult of the upcoming exhibition, Emma found herself carried away by thoughts of Jake and Maddie. Their faces appeared in the grainy prints, their laughter echoed in the empty frames, their love filled the air like the intoxicating scent of blooming wattle. They were in every detail, every plan, every dream - a constant in the flux of her life, a lighthouse in the stormy sea of her emotions.

Finally, the day of the exhibition was upon them. The sun rolled lazily in the sky, a warm, orange glow pouring through the gallery windows. The air inside buzzed with a kind of magic, like the hum of cicadas on a balmy Aussie night. It was the sound of anticipation, of energy crackling through the air.

Emma's heart was thumping like a roo on the run, nervous energy bubbling under her skin. Her hands fiddled with the camera strap, a subconscious reflex, as she surveyed the bustling crowd filtering into the room.

Her photos - snapshots of life caught in the raw, stark, brutal, and beautiful - adorned the gallery walls. Each image was a testament to the human spirit, a slice of life captured through her lens and rendered in monochrome. They were stories, unfiltered and unembellished, chronicling the highs and lows, the joys and sorrows, the triumphs and losses of life in the bush.

The crowd was an eclectic mix - the city slickers, dressed to the nines, chatting animatedly about artistic perspectives; the seasoned photogs, their eyes roving across the frames, a knowing smile playing on their lips; the curious passersby, drawn in by the buzz; and the brave subjects of her photos themselves, standing a little taller as they gazed at their likenesses captured so beautifully.

The room was filled with the clatter of lively chatter, punctuated by the clinking of wine glasses, the rustling of exhibition programmes, and the occasional burst of laughter. It was a symphony of sorts, an orchestra of sounds that filled the gallery, bouncing off the high ceilings and stark white walls.

As Emma navigated through the crowd, her gaze landed on Jake and Maddie. They were there, their presence felt like the glow of the sun on a winter day, warming her from the inside. Jake, with his easy laughter and open heart, was a beacon, his excitement palpable even from a distance. Maddie, with her fiery spirit and piercing gaze, was a tempest, a storm that pulled you in, thrilling and terrifying in equal measure. The two of them were a sight to behold, a juxtaposition as striking as the contrasting images on the gallery walls.

Despite the chaos around her, Emma found herself drawn to them, like a moth to a flame. Her heart fluttered as she saw Jake's eyes light up while talking to a group of enthusiasts, his hands animatedly describing the shape of a photo frame. Maddie was off to the side, a glass of wine in her hand, her eyes scanning the room, alighting on Emma every now and then, a soft smile gracing her lips.

Watching them interact with the crowd, supporting her silently with their presence, Emma felt a surge of affection, a wave of warmth that washed over her, anchoring her in the whirlwind of emotions. This was not just desire. It was more profound, more complex, a potent cocktail of feelings that stirred within her, confusing yet exhilarating.

A soft sigh escaped her lips as she raised her camera, her trusted confidante, and peered through the lens. In that split second, with the click of the shutter, she captured the moment - the essence of the evening, the raw energy of the crowd, the piercing joy of creating something beautiful, and most importantly, the unspoken love that danced between her, Maddie, and Jake.

As the echoes of the shutter faded into the buzz of the exhibition, Emma found herself grinning. This was her life, chaotic, unpredictable, and bursting with a wild kind of beauty, much like the untamed Australian landscape she so loved to capture. And in the midst of it all were Maddie and Jake, two souls who had somehow found a way into her heart, stirring up a storm of emotions she had never experienced before. As she surveyed the room, her eyes twinkling with unshed tears, Emma knew this was just the beginning of her journey, a journey that was bound to be as breathtaking and unpredictable as the photos adorning the gallery walls.

The day of the exhibition arrived, hitting like an old freight train, all wheels churning and steam billowing. Emma woke with a jolt, the day's anticipation buzzing in her veins like a wild swarm of bees. The sun had already begun to bake the outback landscape to a blistering golden brown.

At last, it was time to showcase her handiwork to the world, the faces of the Australian bush folk that she'd captured through her camera's unforgiving eye. Raw, unvarnished, bare, each photo a stark tale of human survival and resilience, a testament to the Aussie spirit that refused to buckle under the harshest of environments.

A motley crowd filled the gallery - cappuccino sippers from the urban heartlands, fellow lens-lovers, and intrigued stickybeaks, all lured by the buzz around the gallery's latest offering. Some of her photo subjects were also in the crowd, the real Aussie battlers themselves, each showing a mixture of pride and shy awkwardness as they eyed their faces displayed on the gallery walls.

The gallery hummed with a palpable energy, like the electricity that precedes a thunderstorm. Chit-chat bounced off the walls, punctuated by the clink of wine glasses, and the occasional ripple of laughter, much like the twanging notes of a well-played didgeridoo.

In the thrumming crowd, her gaze caught sight of Jake and Maddie. Jake, her kangaroo of a man, tall and bouncing with an irrepressible energy, eyes sparkling with a childlike wonder as he admired the photographs. Maddie, on the other hand, was a fiery emu, all flashing eyes and spirited heart. They were two halves of a story, a tale that she was only just beginning to uncover.

Jake was off, grinning like a shot fox as he hobnobbed with a gaggle of photo enthusiasts, hands flying in all directions as he passionately discussed composition and contrast. Maddie was near, nursing a glass of vino, her sharp gaze skimming the crowd, a corner of her mouth curling up every time she met Emma's eyes.

Emma could feel the beat of her heart syncopate with the rhythm of the room. There was a kind of madness in the air, a blend of nervous energy and elation. She could see Jake and Maddie, their presence grounding her, their smiles reassuring her.

With a shaky hand, she picked up her camera, the tool that had started this all. As she peered through the lens, the room suddenly crystallised into a perfect frame. And then, she captured it. The moment was frozen forever, a monochrome testament to her journey, to the spark in Jake's eyes, to Maddie's knowing smile, to her love for the Australian outback, to the journey that had led her here.

As the echo of the camera's click died down, she let out a breath she hadn't realised she was holding. Her heart was ablaze, a wildfire fuelled by an intoxicating mix of emotions. This was her life - a tumble through shadows and light, a journey with no maps or compass, a stumble through the raw, unforgiving, yet breathtakingly beautiful landscape that was Australia.

And through this wild tumble, she'd found Jake and Maddie, two souls as rugged and as beautiful as the Aussie outback itself. As she looked around the room, eyes bright, a small smile played on her lips. This was just the start, a single step into an uncharted territory. She knew not what the future held, but one thing was certain - she was ready for the wild ride.

Like a dingo in a bush fire, Emma was weaving through the crowd, the gallery filled to the rafters with chattering folks and echoing with a steady buzz that hammered against her skull. Through her camera's lens, she'd captured moments of raw humanity, her art bared for all to see, now held up for scrutiny under the gallery's harsh lights.

She caught snippets of conversation, the crackling fire of opinions and interpretations about her work. Some of the punters seemed to pick up what she'd been throwing down, their words striking chords deep within her. Others, they were lost in the bush, their interpretations veering as far off the track as a roo in a headlight.

There was an old bloke, hair white as the ghost gums that dotted the outback. He was standing before one of her favourite shots - an old farmer, face crinkled like a dry creek bed, eyes that bore the look of a man who'd seen many a harsh summer. The old bloke nodded slowly, "The bloke in the photo...he's seen some tough times, hasn't he?"

A group of young inner-city trendsetters, all skinny jeans and large glasses, were huddled in front of another. A picture of a woman, her face hardened by time and weather, but her eyes sparkled with a defiant light. "This woman, she's like the earth itself, resilient and unbowed. Don't you think?" one asked, her voice edged with wonder.

Then, there was Jake and Maddie. Emma watched as they moved around, lost in the world she'd created. Their faces lit up with fascination and excitement. It warmed her heart to see them so engrossed. Jake would point at something, saying something that made Maddie laugh. And Maddie, her laughter was like a dappled sunbeam piercing through a canopy of gum trees.

But then, there were those who saw different narratives, ones she hadn't intended or seen herself. Like a man who saw a tale of isolation and despair in a photo that, to her, represented the indomitable spirit of outback Australia. And a woman who saw rebirth and hope where Emma had seen sorrow and loss.

It was a strange feeling, having her work picked apart and stitched back together in new ways. But wasn't that the beauty of art? Its interpretation as varied as the folks looking at it. It was a mirror that reflected not just what was shown, but also the mind that was viewing.

As Emma listened to the chorus of thoughts and opinions, a sense of satisfaction settled over her. She'd accomplished what she'd set out to do - she'd started a dialogue, created a ripple in the pond. She held her camera a bit tighter, a small smile playing on her lips.

The voices around her continued, a symphony of perspectives that blended into the hum of the evening. Each comment, each laugh, each sigh, each gasp added to the tapestry of the night, creating a symphony of human experience as varied and as beautiful as the photos on the walls.

A whirlwind of faces, voices and clinking glasses, the exhibition was in full swing. Like a river in flood, the crowd flowed around Emma, swallowing her up in its current. Amidst the sea of strangers, a familiar pair of faces bobbed into view - Jake and Maddie. Their presence felt like a dingo's howl slicing through the midnight silence, triggering a storm inside her.

Her heart did a dance as jittery as a kangaroo on hot coals. Seeing them there, amidst the artsy crowd, their eyes trained on her snapshots of life, filled her with a strange mix of pride and unease. The sheer realness of them, right there, amid her slices of reality, it was all a bit of a mind bender. It was as if two worlds were colliding - the stark monochrome world in her photos and the vibrant, full-colour world of Jake and Maddie.

Their eyes roamed over her work, sparkling with an interest that made her belly flip. They were seeing the world through her eyes, witnessing the same raw emotions, the resilience, the triumphs and losses she'd seen. But it wasn't just her art they were looking at. They were looking into her soul, the bits and pieces she'd poured into each shot. And that was a scarier proposition than any critique of her work.

Her heart thudded like a kangaroo thumping the ground, a drumbeat of trepidation in her chest. Tonight, she wasn't just laying bare her art; she was revealing the tangled web of feelings she held for Jake and Maddie. The camera had been her shield, a barrier between her emotions and the world. Now, the veil was being lifted, the spotlight trained on her.

She watched as Jake leaned in close to Maddie, pointing something out in a photo. The sight of them together, their heads touching as they shared a private moment, stirred a longing deep within her. A yearning for connection, for shared moments, for being part of something that went beyond art.

As they moved from photo to photo, their laughter echoed around the room, mingling with the hum of conversations and the clinking of glasses. It was a sound that brought warmth to the cold sterility of the gallery, colour to the monochrome of her photographs. It made her want to freeze the moment, capture it in her camera's viewfinder, make it as everlasting as the images on the walls.

Yet, amidst the wave of emotions, Emma felt a curious sense of calm. Despite the trepidation, there was a sort of satisfaction in being seen, truly seen by someone. By Jake and Maddie. And as she looked at them, their smiles reflecting the light of the gallery, she couldn't help but feel a certain rightness in this chaotic tumble of emotions. It was terrifying, yes, but it was also exhilarating.

The night was still young. The exhibition was far from over. Emma held her camera tighter, her fingers brushing over the cool surface, a reminder of the journey she had taken to be here. And now, a new journey was beginning, one that was as terrifying and exciting as the raw emotions captured in her art. She took a deep breath, ready to embrace the whirl of emotions, ready to stumble through the shadows and light of her own story.

Their response was a pause, one that stretched out long enough to knit a jumper. Surprise flared in Jake's eyes and Maddie's mouth fell open a smidgen, both caught off guard by Emma's confession. The gallery noise faded into the background, the lively chatter and clinking glasses were reduced to distant murmurs against this new, overwhelming revelation.

Jake was the first to find his words, letting out a soft whistle. "Blimey, Em... That's a fair dinkum surprise, isn't it, Maddie?"

Maddie gave a silent nod, her gaze shifting between Jake and Emma, studying their faces as if they were pieces of an intriguing puzzle. Emma held her breath, her eyes pleading for understanding. This wasn't a whimsical fancy, it was a confession carved from the depths of her heart, raw and real as the images gracing the gallery walls.

"We... we need time, Emma," Jake finally broke the silence, his voice surprisingly gentle. "This... It's a lot to process."

Emma nodded, feeling a wave of relief wash over her. There was no immediate dismissal, no rejection, just a need for time. Time she was more than willing to give them. She had exposed her heart, laid bare her desires. If they needed a bit of a breather, well, she wouldn't begrudge them that.

"Of course," she agreed, her voice barely above a whisper, her relief mingling with a faint taste of uncertainty. "Take all the time you need."

The conversation ended on that note, leaving an unspoken agreement hanging in the air. Emma turned, leaving Jake and Maddie amidst her monochrome portraits, their faces reflecting a mix of emotions. A blend of surprise, confusion, and perhaps, a hint of curiosity.

The gallery had transformed from a public exhibition to a private confession booth, each photograph a silent witness to Emma's courageous revelation. She could feel a sense of accomplishment coursing through her veins, a satisfaction that came from the release of pent-up feelings, the freedom of honesty. It was a stumble through shadows and light, but it was her stumble. Her story, raw and real, was now part of the exhibition, lingering in the air even as the evening wound down.

With the end of the exhibition drawing near, Emma found herself swallowed up by a sea of emotions. The gallery, now winding down, buzzed with the remnants of the evening. The laughter and whispers had dimmed, the wine glasses were fewer, and the crowd had dwindled. The shadows were growing longer, merging with the soft glow of the gallery lights, casting a surreal ambiance over the room.

She'd kicked the tin alright. Tossed her feelings at Jake and Maddie like a handful of dice, not knowing where they'd land. Her photos had painted stories of raw humanity, but this, her confession, was perhaps the rawest tale of all. A confession bared from her soul, streaked with vulnerability and longing.

The night had been a bumpy road, a bloody rollercoaster of emotions - excitement, fear, relief, and now, a curious sort of tranquillity. It was as if a storm had passed, leaving behind an odd calm. The cat was out of the bag, her feelings thrown into the open, raw and naked for Jake and Maddie to see.

Emma walked through the gallery, the eyes in her photographs following her, their gazes imbued with newfound meaning. They were her confidants, silent witnesses to her feelings for Jake and Maddie. She felt an intimate connection to them now, bound by the shared exposure of truth. Her truth.

Her journey, the one she'd captured through her camera, had taken a turn she hadn't anticipated. It had veered off the beaten track, led her down an uncharted path. And yet, Emma felt a sense of peace amidst the tumult. The nerves that had been twisting her gut were gone, replaced with a quiet acceptance. She'd said her piece, let the chips fall where they may.

Emma was ready to face whatever came next, whether it was rejection or acceptance, awkwardness or understanding. There was no turning back, no retreating into the comfort of silence. Her feelings, once confined to the boundaries of her heart, were now part of the universe, an echo in the vast expanse of emotions.

As the last of the guests trickled out, Emma was left alone amidst the gallery's silence, her mind buzzing with reflections. She looked around at the monochrome stories adorning the walls one last time, her gaze lingering on each one, each a chapter of her journey.

And thus, the exhibition drew to a close. A stumble through the shadows and light, a journey of the heart captured in the grainy black and white of her photos. And at the end of it all, Emma stood stronger, her feelings laid bare, ready to face the dawning of a new day, ready for the aftermath of her confession. Whatever it was, she was ready.

Exposure In Contrast

The day had finally arrived when Emma's works were to be unmasked to the hungry gaze of the art-lovers. The gallery, an old converted warehouse, was a pandemonium of chattering intellectuals, rubber-necking bystanders, and the odd flash of a camera. There was an electric hum in the air, an intoxicating mix of anticipation, admiration, and raw emotion. Emma's photos, harsh black-and-white snapshots of life and struggle, hung like secrets revealed on the barren walls.

The room was brimming with a sea of faces, some familiar, some new, all drawn in by Emma's raw display of human spirit. Her works were each a story captured in a flash, a moment of truth snatched from the daily grind. As Emma stood amidst the crowd, her heart pounding like a rabbit in a dingo's mouth, she felt an overwhelming sense of accomplishment. The very marrow of her soul was exposed on these walls for all to see.

Just then, the room's clamour seemed to drop, replaced by a slow throb of silence. Emma turned to see Jake and Maddie sauntering in through the gallery door. Her heart hitched at the sight. The couple, with their air of untamed ease, were an incongruity in the room. Yet, there they were, strolling through the door as if they owned the place, their presence making her heart flutter like a trapped bird.

As Jake and Maddie weaved their way through the crowd, their eyes took in the framed stories hanging on the walls. There was a hint of awe in Maddie's eyes as she glanced at a photo of a bushman battling the unforgiving Aussie weather. Jake, on the other hand, seemed deep in thought, his gaze lingering on a picture of an old bloke, his wrinkled face etched with resilience and time.

A wave of excitement surged through Emma as they neared her. She could feel the sweat prickling her palms, her pulse racing as if she was out in the bush, chasing that perfect shot with her trusty camera.

She'd captured the soul of the outback, the spirit of its people, but tonight, she was aiming to capture something much more personal - the heart of the couple who'd unwittingly become the protagonists of her story. She took a deep breath, steadying herself. This was it - her own moment of truth, waiting to be captured.

Having caught her breath, Emma cast a gaze over her captive audience. She clasped the microphone, the din of the crowd dropping into a hushed silence. Then she began. She started narrating the stories hidden behind her monochromatic stills, each tale painting a vivid picture of struggle and triumph, joy and despair. The room hung onto her every word, the atmosphere charged with rapt attention.

Each photograph was an open window into a life lived, an unfiltered glimpse into the heart of the bush and its people. Emma narrated the tale of a seasoned stockman, his face a roadmap of time and adversity, captured against the backdrop of an unforgiving dust storm. She revealed the story of a young sheila, her eyes reflecting a maturity beyond her years, cradling her newborn against the harsh realities of life. Each narrative painted a vivid picture, the raw emotions making the crowd draw in collective breaths.

As she unwound the threads of her narratives, Emma could see varied reactions etched on the faces of her onlookers. Some looked on with widened eyes, aghast at the unforgiving realities she'd captured. Others nodded in solemn understanding, perhaps reminded of their own battles. She even noticed a few teary eyes, her stories resonating with their own lives. But none of this phased Emma. She welcomed it, understanding that her work, once revealed, was now a public artifact, open to scrutiny and interpretation.

Jake and Maddie stood amidst the crowd, their eyes never leaving Emma. They listened as she bared her soul, her voice steady and her words stirring. It was a side of Emma they hadn't seen before - the storyteller, the artist who saw beauty in adversity, hope in despair. This revelation added another layer to the complex woman they had come to know.

Throughout the evening, Emma found herself engaged in conversations, the guests eager to share their interpretations of her work. Each opinion was a revelation in itself - some saw defiance where she had captured resignation, others found beauty in the raw, stark reality she had portrayed. These varied perspectives only affirmed Emma's belief in the subjectivity of art. What she had captured with her camera, these people were recreating through their own lenses, their own experiences, reshaping the meaning she had originally imbued in her work.

Through it all, Emma remained graceful, absorbing the praise, the criticism, the interpretations with an open mind. For art was an ever-evolving entity, its true beauty in its ability to evoke a myriad of emotions, as varied as the audience itself. And tonight, she had witnessed the transformative power of her art.

The steady thrum of conversation and the clinking of glasses formed a soothing white noise in the background. Emma, however, was oblivious to it all. Her world had narrowed down to two faces in the crowd - Jake, with his rugged charm, and Maddie, the epitome of grace. She'd spent the day exposing her art to the world, but now she was about to lay bare something even more personal - her heart.

She watched them from a distance, their smiles lighting up the room, their eyes reflecting a shared secret world she longed to be part of. Her heart hammered a frantic rhythm against her rib cage. She had faced down wild beasts, trekked through harsh terrains, confronted hostile locals - all to get the perfect shot. But this? This was terrifying on a whole new level.

Yet, there was an adrenaline rush to it, akin to the thrill of capturing an elusive moment on camera. Emma knew the risk she was about to take; the possible reward, however, made her stomach flutter with anticipation. She breathed in deep, rolled her shoulders back, and approached Jake and Maddie, each step heavy as if she were wading through quicksand.

She found herself standing in front of them, her heart pounding like a jackhammer. Her palms were damp, and she wiped them surreptitiously against the fabric of her dress. Her throat was dry, and words seemed stuck somewhere between her racing heart and her fear-clenched throat. Looking into their eyes, she saw warmth, curiosity - they had no inkling of the emotional bombshell she was about to drop.

But there was no turning back now. She was on the precipice, the words teetering on the edge of her lips. With a final deep breath, she closed her eyes for a moment, gathering her strength, then opened them, looking directly into the eyes of the couple standing in front of her. And then, she started to speak.

Framed under the bright gallery lights, Emma's words echoed in the silent space between her and the couple, raw and profound. The atmosphere buzzed with a quiet intensity as she confessed her feelings for both Jake and Maddie, her words stumbling over each other in their haste to escape, laying her heart bare in the most public of settings.

"I... I fancy you both," she admitted, the words tasting foreign yet true on her tongue. "Not just individually, but the... the unity, the bond that you share. I don't just want to intrude, I... I want to add, to be part of that dynamic."

Her heart pounded so loudly in her ears that she half-expected Jake and Maddie to hear it. Her words hung heavily in the air, a jumble of emotions and hopes out there, open and vulnerable.

The couple looked at her, their expressions unreadable. Surprise, confusion, perhaps a hint of something else flickered in their eyes. The gallery noise seemed to fade into a hum as Emma held her breath, waiting for their response.

After what felt like an eternity, Jake finally broke the silence. "Emma, that's... that's a fair dinkum shock. We need time, love. We need time to chew over this."

Emma felt a knot of anxiety loosen slightly in her chest. They hadn't rejected her, not outright, and that was enough for now. She nodded, mustering a smile that was more a grimace. "Of course, take all the time you need."

As she walked away, leaving them in a bubble of whispered conversation, she felt a strange mix of relief and uncertainty. She had done it. She had let the cat out of the bag. Now, all that was left was to wait and see where the pieces would fall.

With the last of the patrons trickling out into the brisk night, the gallery gradually emptied, leaving Emma alone amidst the remnants of the exhibition. The day had been a ripper of a rollercoaster, a whirlwind of emotions that had left her feeling spent yet exhilarated.

The images on the walls now bore an added weight, each one a testament to her journey, both as a photographer and a woman caught in the throes of complex feelings. But it was the picture of Jake and Maddie that held her gaze now, their shared gaze within the frame mirroring the intensity of the reality outside it.

As she began the task of cleaning up, the hush of the now-empty gallery wrapped around her like a comforting shroud. The adrenaline had faded, replaced with a quiet satisfaction and an undercurrent of anxious anticipation.

Every swept floor, every re-aligned frame, felt like she was restoring order to her life, a life that had been tipped off balance by the revelation of her feelings. But as she packed away the last of her equipment, Emma felt a sense of peace settle within her.

She had done it. She had shown her work, bared her soul to an audience of strangers, and most importantly, she had spoken her truth to Jake and Maddie. Regardless of what their response would be, she had put her heart out in the open, and that was an achievement in itself.

Alone in the silent gallery, Emma allowed herself a small smile. Tonight, she had not just exhibited her photographs but had also displayed a part of her hidden self. As she switched off the lights and locked up, the uncertainty of what lay ahead was eclipsed by the fact that she had taken the first step. She was ready for whatever came next.

Embracing Turbulence

N avigating uncharted waters, that's how this felt. Emma, Maddie, and Jake, three souls tangled in an intricate ballet. A dance of laughter, tears, but above all, of learning. They'd been mates, cobbers in the truest sense, and now they were venturing into an unfamiliar realm, tiptoeing around the perimeters of romance.

Maddie, the bold firecracker, her passion as vivid as a summer storm; Jake, a steady rock against the erratic currents of their lives, his soft-spoken ways belying the strength underneath. And then there was Emma, the observer, the capturer of moments, now caught up in one of her own. Their dynamic was as diverse as the landscape of this sunburnt country, as intense as a hot tin roof under the midday sun.

Each had their quirks, their habits that had to be unlearned, relearned, and sometimes merely accepted. Morning grumpiness, the absurdity of nocturnal creative bouts, a penchant for Vegemite on toast with a bizarre combination of peanut butter - they were an eclectic jigsaw, each piece oddly shaped, but fitting snug as a bug together.

Their conversations, once filled with light-hearted banter, had deepened. It was as if they'd plunged into the heart of the Great Barrier Reef, navigating the vibrant coral of their emotions, the shadowy depths of their fears, and the radiant school of their dreams. There were misunderstandings, alright - squabbles that seemed as pointless as a kangaroo in Antarctica, but necessary, bloody necessary. For with every spat, every tender make-up, they discovered a little more about themselves and each other.

Growth, it's a sticky wicket. It meant pushing against the grain, enduring the heartache of disagreement, the sting of words uttered in heat. But it also meant standing up after a nasty stack, dusting off the dirt, and moving forward. And they did, with all the tenacity of a riled-up 'roo.

Every sunrise brought with it a new challenge, a new perspective. But as they say, you can't make a rainbow without a little rain. And so, they learned to dance in the downpour, brolly be damned. This was their journey, their tale unfolding, a raw testament to the resilience of the human heart. And they wouldn't have it any other way.

There's an old saying, "Aussies love an underdog", and it seemed Emma fit that bill. Her exhibition had left a mark on the city's Artscape, a rough-hewn etch on a clean slate, resonating with the public like a didgeridoo's haunting drone.

Art critics, the public, journos alike, they were all sniffing around like bloodhounds on a trail. Her style, raw and poignant, stripped of any highfalutin veneer, struck a chord. Her pictures spoke volumes, every snapshot a peek into the soul of her subjects, every portrait brimming with narratives of struggle and triumph. It was as if she'd bared the underbelly of life, unvarnished, for all to see. And people dug it, they dug it like a wombat digs his burrow.

The exposure was blinding. One day she's just Emma, toiling away behind her camera, the next, she's Emma the artist, the name on everyone's lips, the force behind the captivating black-and-whites. The phone was ringing off the hook, invitations to radio interviews, artsy shindigs, requests for collaborations; her life had become a whirlwind. But she took it in her stride, like a true-blue Aussie battler.

If anything, the attention bolstered her drive. Here was a chance to shine a light on the unseen, to give voice to the silent tales of ordinary folks. It was a bit like holding a mirror up to society, a distorted, but truthful reflection. She wasn't just a woman with a camera now. She was a storyteller, an observer, a revealer of truths. And with Maddie and Jake by her side, she was ready to tackle this new adventure head-on, come hell or high water.

Aussies are a tough lot, and the art world, mate, it's like a mob of roo's in a drought – unpredictable and feral. With her newfound fame, Emma found herself smack bang in the middle of a proverbial dust-up. The critics, as they do, had their two bob's worth.

There were those who saw beauty and truth in her work, who felt a connection with the lives etched on paper in stark monochrome. They lauded her, poured praise like sweet honey, affirming her talent. The stories she shared, the lives she'd brought into light – they mattered, resonated with the everyday bloke and sheila.

Then there were the naysayers, the tall poppy cutters, those who saw her work and screamed exploitation. They labelled her an opportunist, accused her of sensationalism, using the underprivileged for her gain. Every click of her camera, in their eyes, an act of intrusion, of disrespect.

But Emma, she was no pushover, not a drongo by any stretch. She took the brickbats with the bouquets, as any artist worth their salt would. She listened to the criticism, reflected, used it as a yardstick to measure her work. Not all of it was fair, she knew, but there were kernels of truth she could learn from.

Then there were moments of vindication, a sudden hush in the raging storm. A heartfelt letter from a fan, an unexpected endorsement from a respected figure in the art world, a heartfelt thank-you from one of her subjects - they served as potent reminders of why she picked up her camera in the first place.

Through it all, Emma remained true to her convictions. She was the same woman who had shed blood, sweat and tears, trudging through city streets, chasing stories, humanising the forgotten with her camera. She had Maddie and Jake by her side, their support her rock in this raging sea of public opinion. And that, to her, was worth more than any praise or critique.

Despite the stormy seas, a beacon started to shine through. It wasn't a flashy lighthouse, but a humble glowworm, illuminating the darkness. Emma's genuineness, her raw talent, and the heart she put into each click of her camera began to resonate. The critics, they had their say, but it was the everyday punter that she reached out to, that she touched with her stories, and they responded in kind.

They saw the woman behind the camera, the one who ventured into forgotten alleyways, who lent an ear to the unheard, who painted their stories in shades of black and white. They respected her, not for the fame or the attention, but for the kindness she'd shown to the underdogs, the battlers.

For Emma, this recognition was more than a pat on the back. It was an affirmation, a validation of her mission. Each positive response, each message of gratitude, they served as reminders of why she'd embarked on this journey in the first place.

And the impact on her subjects? Now that was a real corker. These were the folks who'd lived in the shadows, their tales untold. Emma's camera gave them a voice, brought their stories into the limelight. Public awareness grew, people started to pay attention, to help. It was a ripple effect, each photo a stone cast into a lake, creating waves of change.

There was a woman she'd photographed, living rough on the streets, her life story etched into the lines of her face. Emma's photograph sparked a public funding campaign, and the lady, she now had a place to call home, thanks to Emma's exposure.

Then there were Maddie and Jake, the couple she loved, standing beside her through it all. Their relationship had seen a fair share of bingles, but they were navigating it together, growing stronger each day. And as Emma basked in the glow of acceptance, she knew she had more than just her camera and her art – she had a family.

It was the turbulence that shaped them, the ups and downs that brought them closer. They'd embraced it, held on tight, and as the dust settled, they found themselves standing strong, ready for whatever came their way. Because in the end, they weren't just partners in love – they were mates, true blue. And in the rough and tumble of life, that was what truly mattered.

Love, like a resilient gum tree, finds a way to grow amidst chaos. Emma, Maddie, and Jake were no different. Theirs was a bond being forged in the fires of change, an unconventional love story in the making.

Their days were filled with quiet moments, brief respites from the chaos. Times when the world outside seemed to cease, when it was just the three of them, each understanding the other's silences, the hidden smiles, the unspoken words.

A simple glance from Maddie was enough to brighten Emma's day, while Jake's hearty laughter was a tonic they didn't know they needed. There were tender moments too, gentle touches, soft whispers shared in the dead of night, moments that made their hearts flutter and souls dance. These were the ties that bound them, subtle yet strong, invisible yet palpable.

Amidst the commotion of a world that was constantly changing, amidst Emma's rising fame and the scrutiny it brought, they found solace in each other. It was their haven, their little corner of the world where love reigned supreme.

They held each other up, a steady rock in the swirling tempest. When Emma was fraught with doubt, it was Maddie's comforting words that eased her mind. When Jake felt overwhelmed, it was Emma's quiet strength that grounded him. And when Maddie felt lost, it was Jake and Emma's unwavering support that guided her home.

They were a trio, a unit. Their love was not the conventional sort, but it was theirs, unique and profound. And in the throes of a world that was as turbulent as a roo with a hangover, their bond only deepened, becoming a beacon of hope, an anchor amidst the chaos. It was this bond, this love, that gave them the courage to face any ruckus that came their way. After all, they were mates, through and through.

The evening was drawing to a close, and as Emma sat down, her camera by her side, she couldn't help but reflect on her journey. It had been a wild ride, like trying to saddle a bucking bronco. There were highs and lows, cheers and jeers, joy and sorrow. But that's life, she mused. A bloody rollercoaster that only goes up when it feels like it.

As she looked at Maddie and Jake, her heart filled with warmth. They were her mates, her companions on this wild ride. Their relationship was far from perfect, but it was real, it was raw. It was theirs.

She picked up her camera, feeling its familiar weight in her hands. This device, her silent partner in crime, had seen it all, captured the essence of her world. It was through its lens that she told her stories, that she unveiled the human soul. And it was through its lens that she found herself.

She was more than just a photographer. She was an artist, a storyteller, a friend. She was a voice for the voiceless, a spotlight for the hidden. She was Emma, in all her glory and flaws.

Looking at Maddie and Jake, she knew she had made the right choice. She had opened up her heart, laid bare her feelings. She had taken the plunge into the unknown, and though the waters were rough, she wasn't drowning. She was swimming.

Emma smiled, feeling a sense of peace wash over her. The journey had been rough, and there would be more bumps along the road. But she was ready. Ready to embrace the turbulence, ready to ride the waves. She had her camera, she had Maddie, she had Jake. She had herself.

And as she looked into the future, she knew she wouldn't have it any other way. The future was uncertain, as murky as a billabong, but she was willing to dive in. After all, it was all part of the journey, part of her story. And Emma, she was just getting started.

Future Through The Lens

It was a quiet, bewitching hour, the remnants of the exhibition whispering stories in the dim light. Emma, stuck between yesterday's shadows and the promise of a new dawn, found herself drowned in an ocean of her own captured reality. She shuffled through her impactful photos, each a testament to the lives she'd stumbled upon, a raw reflection of existence itself.

Her fingers danced over each photograph, touch bringing memories alive. There was the grizzled old bloke from Sydney, with life etched onto his face like an unedited manuscript. The wide-eyed bush kid, with dreams bigger than the Outback sky. Each click of the camera had peeled back a layer, exposing a world unseen, a story untold.

A wistful sigh escaped her, mingling with the stagnant gallery air. Far out! She was no longer just Emma with a camera; she was Emma, the teller of tales, the revealer of truths, the bleeding heart behind the lens.

In the silent solace, Emma realised how far she'd come. From an onlooker peering into life's window, she had become a participant, drenched in emotions, entangled in the lives that unfolded in front of her camera. The journey had roughed her up, the abrasive sands of experience refining her into a pearl within the oyster of life.

She'd hit pay dirt and hit rock bottom, ridden waves of jubilation and been sucked into whirlpools of despair. But it was worth every bloody bit. Because it was her journey, her fight, her victory. The stark reality that stared back from the walls of the gallery was her doing. And bugger me if it didn't make her feel like she could conquer anything that came her way.

The room was ripe with silent confessions of love, echoing within the confines of their shared space. Emma sat with Maddie and Jake, their bodies close, radiating an energy that danced in the dimmed lights. In the quiet, they were an unspoken poem of belonging. Their relationship wasn't just a fluttering of heartbeats anymore, it was the steady rhythm of understanding, a tune they had composed together.

Their bodies were strewn over an old sofa, tangled and touching in places. A foot over a leg here, a hand gently resting on a hip there. A landscape of shared warmth and affection, the map of their love etched in these gentle imprints.

Theirs was an unconventional love, one that didn't fit within the usual lines. Yet, it was perfect in its imperfection. It was their love, like a glass of good Aussie shiraz - complex, deep, a little wild, yet oh so divine.

Emma found her head resting on Maddie's lap, Jake's arm slung casually over her shoulder. The comfort they shared was palpable, the air humming with their shared connection. This was their world, their cocoon of love, woven from countless moments of understanding, trials and triumphs.

The decision to continue their relationship hadn't been a grand declaration, no ceremonial grandstanding. It had come to them as naturally as the ebbing tide, a quiet understanding in the spaces between their words, a look that conveyed more than any verbal contract could.

The journey ahead was unknown, like the wild Australian outback, filled with challenges and surprises. But Emma, Maddie, and Jake, they were ready. Their love was their compass, and their commitment, their driving force. Their bond had grown strong, like a River Red Gum standing tall amidst the harsh Aussie climate, deep-rooted and thriving.

As the night yawned into the early morning, they held on to each other, cocooned in their shared warmth. The silence of the room was punctuated only by soft breaths and the rhythmic beating of three hearts in sync. It was a promise of a shared tomorrow, a silent commitment to love, to understand, to be there, as they navigated the complex tapestry of their shared lives.

A feeling stirred within Emma, potent and profound. It wasn't just love, it was something deeper, something sturdier. It was a commitment, as unwavering as the Australian sun beating down on the outback. She looked at Maddie and Jake, her eyes heavy with unspoken sentiments.

Maddie was her harbour, a sanctuary in the rough seas. Her gentleness was a balm to Emma's wounded soul, her laughter, a symphony that livened her heart. Maddie had a way of making every moment feel like a cherished memory, each shared glance was a secret, every touch a promise.

Then there was Jake, a bloke who wore his heart on his sleeve. His rough edges were a testament to the battles he'd fought, the pain he'd embraced. His strength was a silent assurance, a rock amidst the roaring waves. With him, every moment was an adventure, a journey of discovery.

Love had a funny way of turning the world on its head. It made the most mundane moments magical, the brief silences intimate. It made you want to promise tomorrow even when today was all you had. For Emma, her love for Maddie and Jake was the lens through which she saw the world, a viewfinder that captured moments of raw intimacy and pure affection.

It wasn't just about words of love whispered in the dim light, or promises made in the hush of the night. It was about making breakfast together in a kitchen filled with laughter, it was about holding each other after a long day, it was about fighting and making up, about knowing that they were there for each other, no matter what.

Emma, Maddie, and Jake didn't need grand gestures or vows written in the stars. Their love was etched in the shared moments, the shared smiles, the shared lives. Their commitment was as palpable as the air they breathed, as comforting as a warm blanket on a cold winter night. And as Emma basked in the feeling of completeness, she knew that this love, their love, was here to stay, embedded in their hearts, a fixture as permanent as the ancient Aussie rock formations dotting the landscape.

Emma's eyes sparkled, mirroring the same light that seeped through the curtains, illuminating the room. The dawn's glow found a reflection in her, not only illuminating her face but also the hope nestled in her heart. She was no longer just Emma, the girl with a camera. She was Emma, the artist, the story-weaver, the chronicler of souls.

Every click of her camera was a story, every developed image a saga of humanity. She was eager, more than ever, to keep telling those stories. Emma knew the path was strewn with challenges, but the thought didn't faze her; it only fuelled her determination.

She looked at her camera, the simple device that had become an extension of herself. It had witnessed her highs and lows, it was the silent observer that helped her capture the world, one frame at a time. It was her ticket to exploring the labyrinth that was the human soul. And as she held it, her heart pounded with a renewed sense of purpose.

"Here's to more souls, more stories," she muttered to herself, a quiet promise echoing in the silent room.

She could already see it: more people, more lives, more shadows and light caught in her lens. Emma wasn't just ready for it; she was yearning for it. The thought of more experiences, more human connections, and the prospect of growing further as an artist ignited a fire in her.

And then there was her personal life, her own colourful canvas. Maddie, Jake, their bond, their love – they were her anchors, her safe havens. Her relationship with them was not just about love anymore;

it was about growing together, evolving together, facing whatever life threw at them, together.

As the early morning light filled the room, Emma felt a surge of anticipation, a whirlwind of hope. The future was a blank canvas, and she was ready to fill it with her colours. The artist in her was raring to explore, to dive into the depths of human emotions, while the woman in her was excited to see what lay ahead for her, Maddie, and Jake.

Her journey was far from over; it was merely a new chapter beginning. The roads ahead were untraveled, the stories untold. And as she stood there, looking at the break of a new day, Emma knew one thing for certain – she was ready to embrace it all, camera in hand, love in heart. And with that thought, she welcomed the future, a future filled with potential, promise, and endless possibilities Emma found herself standing amidst the quiet remnants of her exhibition, each photo a poignant reminder of the journey she had undertaken. Like silent guardians, they stood as testament to her growth, her evolution as an artist, as a lover, as a woman. It was a humbling realisation, and Emma couldn't help but be grateful.

The exhibition had been a mirror into her soul, a bold declaration of who she was, unmasked and unabridged. She had stripped her heart open and offered her truth to the world, and it had been nothing short of liberating. It was a turning point, an awakening, a testament to her courage.

Emma, Maddie, and Jake - their lives intertwined, their spirits tethered. Their love was unconventional, maybe even frowned upon by some, but it was their truth, their reality. It was as raw and as real as the photos Emma captured. It was as intense as the look in Jake's eyes when he smiled at her, as warm as Maddie's touch when she held Emma close. It was a commitment, a promise - unspoken but palpable. A promise of tomorrow, a promise of 'us'.

Through her lens, Emma had not only captured the world but also the myriad emotions that stitched their lives together. Her camera had been her ally, an extension of her that was as much a part of the story as she was. Through it, she had witnessed life in all its shades - the good, the bad, and everything in between.

As she looked around at the photographs, each a time capsule of a precious moment, Emma felt a surge of hope. She was not done yet. There were still countless stories out there waiting for her, countless moments to be immortalised, countless emotions to be captured.

In the silent company of her photographs and the echoing whispers of her triumphs and tribulations, Emma found a sense of peace. Her heart was heavy, but it was a beautiful weight, the kind that only fulfillment could bestow. It was the weight of love, of understanding, of a journey well-travelled.

Her future was a canvas waiting to be painted. With Maddie and Jake by her side and her trusty camera in her hand, Emma was ready. Ready to capture more stories, ready to continue her exploration, ready to love and to be loved. The future was uncertain, yes, but Emma knew one thing for certain: she was ready to seize it, to make it her own.

As the final echo of the evening settled, and the first ray of tomorrow peeked from the horizon, Emma, Maddie, and Jake stood on the brink of a promising future. And with the dawn came a newfound determination, a resolve that promised to make every moment count.

Their story was far from over; it was only just beginning. And with that, Emma welcomed the dawn of a new day, a day filled with promise and a future full of potential. It was the end of an extraordinary chapter, but the book was far from closed. The future was hers to write, and she couldn't wait to pen the next chapter.

Emma's journey continues...

Epilogue

Two years had passed since Emma's transformative journey of self-discovery and acceptance. She is now living in Brisbane, in a small but cozy apartment adorned with her own photographs, an exhibition of the world seen through her lens, through her perspective. It was a far cry from her old flat in Melbourne, from the woman she used to be, but this new space felt more like home than anywhere else she'd been.

Her work had taken off. Her photographs, raw and compelling, graced the walls of local cafes and were showcased in the pages of popular magazines. But for Emma, it was about more than just commercial success. Each snap was a cathartic process, a way to capture and externalize the internal struggle and triumph she'd experienced, a silent testament to her journey of self-acceptance.

And love? Well, that was another journey in itself. Emma found herself in a relationship that was as beautiful as it was complicated, with a woman who was as understanding as she was intriguing. Like Emma, she was a free spirit, unafraid to tread uncharted paths. Together, they explored the wilderness of love and desire, each moment captured not just in Emma's memory, but through her lens. A visual diary of their lives together.

Every once in a while, she'd look back at those old self-portraits, the raw depictions of a woman wrestling with her identity. They served as a powerful reminder of her evolution, of the tumultuous journey that led to her ultimate self-discovery. Emma wasn't just a photographer; she was a story, a narrative of resilience and acceptance, beautifully unfolding one frame at a time.

And as she'd sit on her balcony, looking out at the city that was now her home, Emma would smile. She was finally comfortable in her own skin, finally at peace with her desires. She was Emma, the photographer, the lover, the woman who dared to accept herself for who she truly was.

Her camera – the loyal companion in her journey – lay beside her, ever ready to capture the next chapter of her life. Life was a myriad of colours, a constant interplay of light and shadow, and Emma was ready to capture it all through her lens. This was just the beginning, she thought. The adventure was far from over.

About the Author:

N ow at 47, my life's journey has taken me through a mosaic of Australian landscapes, from my childhood home in the small town of Muswellbrook to the bustling cities of Brisbane and the Gold Coast. Along the way, I've made homes in Scone, Tamworth, and Armidale, each place leaving its unique imprint on my life's narrative.

Tragedy struck early in my life with the loss of my mother in a heartbreaking accident, an experience that taught me resilience and strength in the face of life's most profound challenges. In the face of another tragedy, I found the strength to draw upon these lessons once again. When my youngest son, at just 21, attempted to take his own life, our world was thrown into turmoil. But out of that darkness emerged a new light. My son, having survived the darkest time in his life, now proudly identifies as my daughter. The pride I feel for her bravery and honesty is beyond words.

These experiences, coupled with the joy and love I've discovered through my two gorgeous children, have shaped the person I am today.

"The Photographer's Lens" is my personal testament of self-discovery and acceptance. It is my coming-out story, a celebration of my identity as a bisexual male. Through this book, I wish to communicate a powerful message: Be proud of who you are, embrace your true self, and know that our individual experiences and identities are what make us uniquely beautiful.

This story reflects my journey, my acceptance, and my pride in being who I truly am. I hope it serves to inspire and uplift everyone who has ever wrestled with their identity, reminding them they are not alone. To my beautiful daughter, I want you to know, no matter how tough life gets, I'm just a phone call away. Always.

Don't miss out!

Visit the website below and you can sign up to receive emails whenever Bryce Sterling publishes a new book. There's no charge and no obligation.

https://books2read.com/r/B-A-JDTZ-NNHMC

BOOKS 2 READ

Connecting independent readers to independent writers.